LEGAL FLAMES

LEGAL FLAMES

DRAKETHORN LEGAL™
BOOK FIVE

ISABEL CAMPBELL
MICHAEL ANDERLE

DISRUPTIVE IMAGINATION®

Copyright © 2024 LMBPN Publishing
Cover by Mihaela Voicu http://www.mihaelavoicu.com/
Cover copyright © LMBPN Publishing
A Michael Anderle Production

LMBPN® Publishing
2375 E. Tropicana Avenue, Suite 8-305
Las Vegas, Nevada 89119 USA

Version 1.00, September 2024
ebook ISBN: 979-8-89354-272-1
Print ISBN: 979-8-89354-273-8

THE LEGAL FLAMES TEAM

Thanks to the JIT Readers

If I've missed anyone, please let me know!

Veronica Stephan-Miller
Daryl McDaniel
Dorothy Lloyd
Diane L. Smith
Jeff Goode
Peter Manis
Christopher Gilliard
Zacc Pelter
Sean Kesterson
Jan Hunnicutt

Editor
The SkyFyre Editing Team

CHAPTER ONE

"Since when have we had fucking cable?" Stacy Drakethorn asked as she plopped onto the sofa in the estate living room, remote in hand, while the TV blared. It was the only place in the whole house that looked like something out of *The Gilmore Girls*, not an ornate living space for the wealthy heiress of the Drakethorn estate. Over the past several weeks, Stacy and Amy had made the room their own, much to Rowan's chagrin and their delight.

"We've always had cable," the dryad remarked from the hallway where he was rifling through a pile of mail. One thing Stacy was glad not to do was check the mail. It was Rowan's job to filter what was important for her to see and what wasn't.

"Do we need to pay for it?" she asked. "I mean, I've been here about two months and only now realized we had it. No one else watches TV."

Rowan poked his head into the room, frowning.

"Except you?" Stacy added.

"I watch the news."

She threw her hands up. "There's a lot of ways to watch the news without paying two hundred dollars a month for a bunch of channels we won't use!"

"It isn't two hundred dollars—" Rowan stopped himself. "I'll cancel it if you'd like."

"We're in the streaming age," Stacy reminded him. "Do we have a DVD player and some movies, at least?"

Rowan chuckled. "I'm surprised at you. You throw a fit over cable, and now you want me to drag a DVD player out of the attic?"

Stacy glowered. The TV behind her, which she had turned on a minute ago, was playing a movie, but she didn't pay attention to what it was until Amy ambled into the room with a giant bowl of popcorn and an obscene amount of chocolate. "Ooo, *Bride Wars!* I love this movie!"

Stacy eyed the TV. The movie had just started.

Rowan's eyes glittered. "See?" He turned to Amy and frowned.

"What?" she demanded around a mouthful of a chocolate bar.

"What are you wearing, and what is on your face?" He asked the second question with far more alarm than the first.

Amy was dressed head to foot in pink silk pajamas with feathery fringe at the ankles and wrists. She had a facemask applied to her skin. Apparently, Rowan had never seen one before. "This is my girls' night uniform. You wouldn't under-stand," she replied.

Rowan muttered something about not wanting to understand and turned to leave the room. "You girls enjoy yourselves. I'll be in my study if you need anything."

Amy giggled as she plopped onto the sofa beside Stacy. "I think tormenting Rowan with the ways of womanhood is my new favorite hobby."

"I don't get it," Stacy chimed in as she used the remote to adjust the volume. Anne Hathaway's voice on screen joined hers. "Rowan knows everything about how a woman's menstrual cycle works, but he can't fathom why we would want to wear hydrating face masks and eat chocolate on a Friday night."

They laughed and settled deeper into the sofa, throwing a

blanket over themselves. They dug into their snacks, and Amy claimed she'd seen this movie about a hundred times but never got tired of it. "Anne Hathaway is a timeless beauty!" she declared. "I swear that woman never ages. We're watching *The Princess Diaries* and *The Devil Wears Prada* next time."

Stacy wished she had grown up on such movies, but with a father like Khan, she'd seen only war documentaries, dramas based on real life, and the occasional BBC production of a Shakespeare play. The closest thing to a cartoon she'd watched before the age of sixteen had been *The Muppets*, and only because Torin had shown it to her.

Stacy didn't care what she and Amy watched as long as they were doing something fun. She'd been swamped with legal practice paperwork all week in addition to her Monday and Thursday magic lessons with Ethan. She needed this downtime.

It was a quiet night at the estate. Rowan was in his study, probably googling why women needed to talk through every movie they watched. Kiera had gone out for some "nighttime errands," which was code for kicking ass and taking names. Miles was somewhere in the garden, "communing with nature." At least, that was what he told Amy. She was convinced that meant he was smoking a joint.

They'd watched the scene where Chris Pratt's character proposes to Anne Hathaway's. Personally, Stacy was more of a Kate Hudson fan, but she didn't tell Amy that. "I can't wait for someone to propose to me!" Amy sighed.

Stacy eyed her. "You're not dating. And no, swiping on apps doesn't count if you don't message anyone or go on any real dates. Window shopping isn't dating."

"So? I've been fantasizing about being proposed to since I was, like...eleven! I don't think about weddings much, though. Is that weird?"

Stacy laughed. "I think fantasizing about being proposed to is weird. Do you like surprises or something?"

"Oh, I don't think a man could ever surprise me. I'm too observant." That was true. Amy was a talented and reputable investigative journalist for a reason. "I like the romance of it all." She sat on the sofa with her back against the arm, facing Stacy. "The sunset, the roses, the way my heart flutters when he gets down on one knee."

"Do you imagine a particular man?" Stacy asked.

"When I was a kid, it was Dimitri from the animated *Anastasia* movie. Now, it switches between Viggo Mortensen as Aragorn and Hayden Christensen as Anakin. *Revenge of the Sith* Anakin, to be specific. I love a man with long, wavy hair."

Stacy laughed. "How nerdy."

"*Lord of the Rings* and *Star Wars* are both pretty mainstream."

Amy nudged Stacy with a toe covered in fuzzy pink sock. "Can we expect you to be engaged anytime soon?"

Stacy nearly choked on the sip of wine she'd taken. "We kissed *once*. Technically, I kissed him, and he didn't have time to kiss me back." Stacy barely remembered the details of that moment despite having played it over in her mind several times.

The thought alone of what happened between her and Ethan tinged her cheeks pink and made her stomach feel full of something warm and sugary. Little had happened between them since.

A week had passed with nothing more than professional spell casting in person and mild flirting over text. Neither had brought the kiss up, and Stacy was beginning to wonder if Ethan wished it hadn't happened. *Or did I make the damn thing up?* she thought.

At this moment, Kate Hudson and Steve Howey engaged in a passionate on-screen kiss.

"Have you guys slept together yet?" Amy asked.

"Amy! I just told you we kissed, and that was it."

"What about sex dreams?"

Stacy threw popcorn at her friend.

Amy giggled. "Well, when you do get into bed with him, I want to know how big his—"

"Amy!"

"Kidding!"

Stacy was about to dump the rest of the bowl of popcorn over Amy's head when a sprite flitted through the room and jumped onto the remote with enough force to change the channel.

Amy groaned. "Damn sprites!"

They'd switched from *Bride Wars* to a local news station. The sprite zipped off as if it had done nothing. Amy reached for the remote to turn it back, but Stacy stopped her with a hand on her arm. Images on the TV had caught her attention.

"What is it?" Amy asked.

Stacy pointed. "Listen."

The anchorman was reporting on a series of missing persons cases in the city. Stacy felt drawn in despite the fact that this sort of shit happened all the time. He described nine cases of people ranging in gender, age, and background vanishing. The disappearances happened a few days apart.

The police force was working night and day to solve the cases, the anchorman promised, but had yielded little evidence about where the victims had gone or who was behind the abductions.

"Even children," Amy murmured. "How sad."

Stacy was on the edge of the sofa. A year ago, she would have been concerned about the cases but deemed herself unimportant to solving them. That was when she was Stacy Drake, attorney at law and little else. Now, she was a self-proclaimed Drakethorn who had marked the underworld as hers to infiltrate and change. If the slimy rulers of the underworld were responsible for this, she felt a duty to root them out and ensure they met justice.

Stacy was inclined to believe this was the case since the disappearances were expertly planned. Though many had vanished in the night, several had gone missing during the day. According to the anchorman, the disappearances seemed to center around one place—a cemetery outside the city. This clue led detectives and police to believe the disappearances were linked.

That and a strange symbol left behind each time it happened. The symbol was of two horn-like images curving toward one another. They'd been etched in stone or written with charcoal on gravestones. One was blood smeared on a stone wall. Whoever was responsible for this was sick-minded.

I'm no detective, but maybe there's something I can do about this, Stacy thought. Amy could help too, since her investigative journalism skills might yield some helpful insight. "I know this was supposed to be a movie night with no mention of work," she started, turning toward her friend. She didn't get to finish because Rowan walked into the room.

He had the office phone pressed to his ear. "She's right here. I'll ask her now." Who could be calling at nine p.m. on a Friday? Everyone knew her work hours ended at six.

"Mr. Gray is on the other end, Stacy," Rowan related. "He would like to speak to you about an urgent matter." He glanced at the TV and grew grim-faced, noticing what the report concerned.

"I'll clean up our mess," Amy murmured, clearly bemoaning the end of their girl's night. Stacy cast her an apologetic look as she took the phone from Rowan and walked out of the room.

"Hello, Mr. Gray. How are you this evening?" He wouldn't be calling unless it was important.

"I am well, Miss Drakethorn. I hope the same is true of you."

"And how fares the pack?"

"Well, Miss Drakethorn, but I'm calling you about an urgent matter."

Stacy entered Rowan's study and closed the door, hearing low murmuring between Amy and Rowan down the hall. "I'm listening."

The emissary of the Graytail wolf pack, with whom Stacy had become recent allies thanks to her victory in court on their behalf, began his explanation in a low tone. "As you know, we have some pack members acting as spies within the city. It's a protective measure, you see. We previously had a wolf member who belonged to the Circle. That is, the underground regime. Once, the underground wasn't run by greedy money-makers eager to take land and resources from others."

This was news to Stacy.

"It was originally for members of paranormal types to meet. This was back when we were hunted as terrorists. Though many of our kind, including shifters, are still hunted as such, the Circle once provided a safe haven for us. We met with other kinds, shared resources, and became allies in times of need."

"How did it change?" Stacy asked, wondering why she'd never heard this before.

"Men with magic *and* money gained power, and before we knew it, many of us were kicked out. The alpha of our pack before our current leader was one such member. I say all this to give you context. We still send pack members to spy on the Circle in case any of them move to strip our rights from us again."

As Victor Corbinelli had done by stealing their land, Stacy recalled.

"And you've discovered something?" she prodded.

"Yes, and it's not good. There seems to be a sudden emergence of vampires in the city. A small group, but capable of heinous deeds. I'm sure by now you've heard of the missing persons' cases?"

"Yes," Stacy answered. "You think these vampires are behind it?"

"We are fairly certain," Mr. Gray replied. He described a series of instances that led his pack to believe this was the case. In one instance, a wolf spy had seen a pale-faced being dragging a body through a cemetery, only to stop before reaching its destination to drink blood from its victim. Stacy shuddered.

"You have seen the symbol they leave behind?" Mr. Gray asked.

"Yes. They look like horns."

"Not horns. They represent fangs. The symbol was used frequently back in the day when our former alpha was a member of the underworld circle. Vampires were members then, too, but have since been banished, the same as shifters."

"Do you think these vampires are working on their own, then?" Stacy questioned.

"Possibly, but it's also possible they have once again found a way to infiltrate the Circle or been hired by someone in the underworld. For what purposes, we cannot yet determine."

"I don't need to know that. People being abducted is enough reason to drag their asses out into the light," Stacy replied coldly.

"I thought you might feel that way," Mr. Gray replied. "It is why I called you. We will continue our spying efforts, but we thought you should know what we've learned."

"Thank you, Mr. Gray. Please keep me updated on any developments."

Mr. Gray promised to do so, then said goodbye. After their phone call ended, Stacy sat in the study in contemplative silence. There'd been no word of vampires in New York City for several years, except for the existence of one.

Only a week had passed since Stacy's encounter with the vampire assassin who'd gone by Isadora Voss. Stacy wasn't eager to encounter more vampires anytime soon. Or ever. *This isn't Dracula or Twilight,* she thought. *These are vicious predators with evil intentions.*

A new sense of unease stirred within her. Whether these vampires were working for someone in the underworld or not, they could drive conflict among the supernatural factions in addition to the havoc they wreaked in the lives of non-magic humans.

How many more people would go missing before she found them and learned what they were up to? Had the vampires always been around and kept themselves hidden, or were they new arrivals to the underworld?

Stacy only had one way to find out. She needed to ask someone who had once been part of the underworld before he decided the whole thing was beneath him. With Mr. Gray's revelations, Stacy had many new questions.

She only hoped her father, Constantine Drakethorn, would be willing to answer them.

CHAPTER TWO

The mid-morning sunlight cast the road leading from Stacy's home to the place where she grew up in a golden glow. She drove with the windows down, appreciating the balmy September air. It was warmer today than it had been all week, and she could think of few things more appealing than brunch at the Drakethorn estate on a Saturday morning.

She navigated her car through wreaths of mist stained with sunlight under a canopy of trees preparing to turn color for the impending autumn. Though Rowan normally drove her to her father's estate and everywhere else, Stacy insisted she go alone this morning. Nothing could happen to her during a four-mile drive, right?

She'd told Rowan she wanted time to think alone, so he had finally relented. Kiera's temptation of pastries had also helped. Stacy left them both in the kitchen.

She'd chosen to collect her auburn hair into one braid today and wore a simple pair of blue jeans and a black blouse. Brunch attire, she called it when Amy asked where she was going.

Stacy parsed through mixed emotions on the brief journey to her father's estate. She anticipated the conversation with her father and the insight it might yield her, but she was also apprehensive about her father holding back or going daddy-ballistic on her, wanting to protect her from the vampire threat.

She rehearsed some of what she would say and reviewed the information Mr. Gray had passed her last night. Soon, she reached the estate gates, and they opened for her. The wards recognized her as someone with Drakethorn blood and allowed her in. The grounds sprawled out, manicured to perfection. The house rose in the distance, never failing to appear prestigious and centuries old.

Stacy waved to the groundskeeper, Torin, who was trimming hedges along the driveway. She exited the car, approached the house, and climbed the porch steps. The estate butler, Reginald Blackguard, who had been like a kindly uncle to Stacy growing up, opened the door.

"Good morning, Regi," she greeted.

"What a surprise this is!" he exclaimed as he ushered her into the house. Normally, Stacy called before coming, but she figured showing up unannounced would be nice for the staff. Reginald asked how she had been, and Stacy engaged in normal pleasantries. Reginald revealed that all was well with her father's estate. "I can take you to him now." He offered his arm.

The butler led her not to Khan's grand library as she expected but through the wide back doors to the gardens. Her father was pacing along the cobblestone path, speaking to someone on the phone. Khan spotted her, smiled, and put up a finger as if to say, "Hold on."

Reginald disappeared into the house, and Stacy wandered through the garden. It was the same as it had always been since her first memories of the place. The narrow path wove among hedges and rosebushes, around pear and apple trees, and to stone fountains and small alcoves carved into the shrubbery where one could rest on a bench.

As a child, she'd spent much of her time hiding from lessons or chores. Sure, she had grown up in a grand house with staff, but her father had insisted she learn hard work from an early age. She often played hide and seek in this garden with Torin, who knew every spot as well as she did.

From somewhere in the garden, Stacy heard her father's smooth tenor and commanding tone, both signs he was conducting business with whoever was on the other end. Their conversation ended, and he called out, "Stacy?"

"Over here!"

Khan met her near a small stone fountain a moment later. "My apologies. That was Greenfield on the phone. They were informing me of your latest suggestions for change." He chuckled. "They're not happy with you."

Stacy shrugged. "Oh, well. They'll have to get used to it."

"That's what I told them. I said I didn't always agree with your more…progressive methods but had entrusted the assets to you for a reason."

It was a classic Khan response, Stacy thought. Her father found a way to show her how proud he was while also suggesting her way of going about things was questionable. Stacy wasn't sure how to feel, so she brushed it off.

Khan hugged her, then asked, "What luck has been bestowed upon me that my daughter should deign to visit me this fine morning?"

Stacy arched a brow. "Why are you talking like that? All…fancy."

"We used to talk like this! I am quite old, remember."

It was a difficult thing to forget. Stacy laughed. "I don't know who 'we' is, Dad, but we're in the twenty-first century now. No one talks like that except actors in Shakespeare plays."

"Have you come to discuss werewolves today?" Khan quipped, his green eyes glittering. The last time Stacy came here was to talk about the Graytails' case.

"Vampires, actually," Stacy replied. She recalled her father's reaction to what happened with Isadora Voss. Stacy might have downplayed some details, like that the assassin had wounded her arm and nearly killed Rowan. She also might have waited several days after the fact to share it with him.

Khan had not been happy to hear her estate had been infiltrated again and suggested she might need someone from *his* estate to implement new security measures.

Security measures had not been an issue, though, Stacy had told him. She'd lured Voss onto her estate on purpose, and it worked. The vampire was dead, swallowed by the ground, with any remaining trace of her blood swept away by the trees.

"Ah, vampires," Khan replied with a stoic expression. "Not my favorite topic of conversation, but tell me what you must." He offered his arm. "Walk with me."

As they strolled through a small corridor of apple and pear trees, Stacy told him about her conversation with Mr. Gray and what he'd shared regarding the missing persons cases and the emerging sect of vampires.

"More like a cult," Khan murmured. "All of them are."

However, he did not fly into over-protective mode, which surprised Stacy. She pointed this out.

Khan arched a brow and eyed her sideways. "You're not exactly being fair. Do you want to take charge of your future and be pissed off that I'm doing what you want, or do you want me to dote?"

Stacy saw his point. Sometimes, she couldn't figure the man out. It was as if he had two sides inside him, battling for dominance. One was his dragon nature. What was the other? *The dad side,* Stacy surmised. *I think he's still trying to figure it out.*

She sighed. "You're right. Either way, I want your advice and whatever knowledge you have about vampires." Khan had once been a member of the Circle and must know something. At this point, she figured anything would help.

Khan patted her hand, which she'd placed in the crook of his arm. "Let's discuss this over brunch, shall we? I'm famished."

"You're a dragon, Dad. You're always famished."

His eyes twinkled. "Don't act like you aren't either."

Stacy's stomach grumbled in response. All she'd had before leaving home was a pastry Kiera had made. Inside, they went into a sunroom where Esme, the cook, had laid out an elaborate meal complete with every breakfast food Stacy could ever want.

This was common for a Saturday at the Drakethorn estate. Stacy had grown up with such brunches every weekend. Kiera was an excellent cook, but nothing quite beat the way Esme made blueberry waffles.

After they were seated and had piled their plates high with sausages, fruit, and more carbs than Stacy could eat, Khan delved into a long, steeped lore regarding vampires. Or "those blood-sucking mongrels," as he called them.

Stacy preferred to keep to technical terms and not develop any unnecessary prejudices. Once, she'd thought all werewolves were awful creatures. Now, she had a whole pack as neighbors and allies. Could the same be true of vampires? One day, maybe. But for now, she had to deal with the bad sort.

"The account of your Mr. Gray is correct. The underworld was once a place where the members of the paranormal world could ally with one another for protection. By the time I joined the Circle, it was already in decline. When your mother came along, the likes of Victor Corbinelli were in power."

Catherine had sought to change that, Stacy remembered.

"I'll admit that I wouldn't mind seeing a day when the Circle returned to its original state," Khan stated. "We could begin educating the world on paranormal species, not only witches, who are about all regular humans are aware of."

"I'm surprised to hear you say that, Dad. I thought you wanted nothing to do with the Circle or changing the state of the underworld."

Khan lifted a teacup to his lips and frowned. "Maybe I'm turning a new leaf, Stacy."

"Dragons as old as you don't do that," she pointed out with a laugh.

"I stand against the Circle and discourage you from attempting to change the underworld because I'm being realistic. Accomplishing such a thing would take years."

Well, she was his daughter, wasn't she? She would live for a long-ass time. Much longer than non-magic humans anyway. Stacy hadn't considered the concept much, mostly because it was difficult to wrap her mind around. It slightly terrified her, too.

She wondered at his comment that change would take years in another light. Perhaps the change had begun not with her but with Catherine Thorn. Maybe she was simply carrying on what her mother had started.

Stacy wondered if it wouldn't be a bad idea to bring more non-magic humans into her circle. She could turn her private practice into a firm and hire up-and-coming lawyers dedicated to helping minorities, both magic and non-magic. They could gain a gradual sense of awareness of the paranormal world and the part she played in it. So far, Amy was the only non-magic human who knew Stacy's true nature.

Khan's deep voice broke through Stacy's thoughts, drawing her back to the topic at hand. "Most vampires have been unpleasant at best and cruel, vicious killers at worst, even at the beginning of the Circle's formation. They were the first ones kicked out because they sought power they shouldn't have. A good thing it happened, too. Imagine someone like Victor Corbinelli but as a blood-sucking parasite instead of a manufactured werewolf."

Stacy nearly shuddered at the thought.

It quickly became apparent that Khan had a complicated and strained history with vampire-kind. "I fought them when I was in

Europe centuries ago. Beastly jerks. They loved the wars in Rome and always came in at the worst times."

Stacy arched a brow. To hear her father talk about being in Rome—the empire, not the city—baffled her. He was really fucking old. "The vampires my age know not to screw with me now, of course," Khan went on. "I suspect these new vampires abducting people in the city are younger."

Stacy snorted. "But still probably centuries old?"

"Oh, yes."

Such things made Stacy feel like a tiny minnow swimming in a great ocean. Instead of sharks, she faced vampires and billionaires who hired assassins to come after her. She'd come to accept this was the nature of her life. Always in danger, yet privileged in many ways. The resources and wealth helped her protect not only herself and her home but her friends and neighbors.

It was time to expand her network. Supernatural factions existed throughout the city. Many were not connected to the underworld, and she had an opportunity to meet them and create more allies.

Stacy placed the thought at the back of her mind, intent on asking Rowan about it when she returned home.

"Vampires are like werewolves in one way," Khan continued, drawing Stacy's attention. "They are territorial and protect their own above all else. One family will stick together for millennia and often become involved with each other's vendettas. You must be careful of this. They are cunning types. Though ambitious, they are not blind, bumbling idiots like the money-hungry millionaires you've dealt with before."

Stacy had to admit that Victor Corbinelli and Gregory Hines hadn't been the best at planning her demise. Would this cult, as her father called it, of vampires be better? Were they aware of her presence in the city and the changes she sought to make?

Isadora Voss had been one hell of a killer. Had she been part of this cult or separate? She had worked alone, as far as Stacy could tell. She half wished she'd kept the assassin alive for questioning, but that night had been a fight for her life.

They finished brunch not long after, and Khan warned Stacy once again about the dangerous web she was stepping into.

"I'll be careful, Dad. I promise." After a shared hug, Stacy departed from the estate.

The drive home left her with a torrent of thoughts. Her father had formidable power, which resulted in an intricate balance he had to maintain among the various supernatural entities that coexisted in their world. She wondered how much was true of herself.

I'll speak to Rowan about meeting with other groups, Stacy decided. More werewolves, witches, or other paranormal types she hadn't come across. She didn't care. If they were going to battle vampires, she would need all the allies she could get.

CHAPTER THREE

Stacy drew a deep breath. *I can do this.*

She glanced again at the open journal on the kitchen counter beside her. Catherine's instructions for the incantation were scrawled on yellowed paper. Stacy traced them with her finger as if doing so would pass her mother's skill into her body. She'd been at this for about twenty minutes with little luck.

The golden afternoon sun flooded the kitchen, and several sprites sat along the rim of the sink, watching her. Or making fun of her with their tiny, pointed fingers.

Stacy had used complex spells before, but this one was proving challenging. Probably because it wasn't a common spell, but one her mother had created. Usually, Stacy practiced with Ethan around, but they had lessons only two days a week, so she had to practice alone the other days.

Rowan was busy interviewing potential new hires and couldn't see Stacy yet. He would have dropped everything to help her if she had asked, but she had left him to his duties instead. Now she was in the kitchen, trying to figure out this damn spell.

The goal was to untangle a complex web of wards over the table that Miles had woven at her request. She was glad he wasn't here to watch her fail at removing it. Frustration simmered inside her, and a low snarl slipped past her lips. The innate dragon nature inside her awoke to the feeling of her frustration.

The next she knew, an heirloom doily on the table caught fire.

"Shit!" she exclaimed.

Rowan would light her ass up if he saw this.

Stacy yelped and ran for the sink, grabbing the first thing that could hold water. She was filling a vase up, hoping the whole table wouldn't catch fire next, when someone ambled into the room. Stacy had no time to hide.

Kiera chuckled. With a simple wave of her fingers and a murmured incantation, she undid the wards. Stacy threw water onto the doily. Too late. The lace was burned, and a patch of the table had turned black.

Stacy groaned. "Rowan's going to kill me."

"You burned his favorite doily," Kiera remarked. "Kidding. He doesn't have a favorite. I'll help get rid of the evidence, though. I don't need his pissy attitude today, especially over something as small as this."

It might have seemed small to Kiera, but the sensation of failure burned in Stacy's chest.

"Thank you," Stacy replied fervently. "You won't tell him, will you?"

Kiera chuckled again. "Do I look like a tattletale?" She went into the pantry to find something to help remove the stain. When she returned, Stacy noted that Kiera looked tired. She'd seemed less energized the past few days, thanks to Rowan sending her out on nighttime missions.

"How did you do that?" Stacy asked, pointing at the table. "The spell was only supposed to work if you used the instructions from my mother's journal."

"I learned the spell from Rowan when I came here. He knows it well. Your mother must have taught him and anyone else in charge of the wards."

Stacy marveled at the sidhe fae woman. Not only had she known the incantation, she'd unraveled the wards as easily as opening and closing a window.

Kiera raised a brow at Stacy, who held the loose scraps of the burned doily. "Are you sure those lessons you're having with Ethan are helping?"

Her tone was teasing, but Stacy couldn't help but wonder if something was missing. That or it was as simple as her dragon nature getting in the way. She said as much to Kiera, then grumbled, "Sometimes, I wish I could put the dragon in timeout."

"At least the dragon doesn't come out in full form whenever the hell it wants to," Kiera reminded her. "You have more control of your power than you think."

"Better that than to leave it unchecked, right?"

Kiera gave a half-smile. "Right."

Stacy wanted better control, though. The better she was, the more capable she would be at leading her coven. So far, it was only her and Ethan as co-visionaries. Last week, after an initiation ceremony, Stacy had decided a young woman belonging to the Graytail pack would make an excellent addition.

Ethan had agreed, but they decided to wait until the young woman had adjusted to her position in the pack. No need to offer her a part-time job when she'd recently received a promotion at her full-time one.

"Kiera, are you in here?" Rowan called from the hallway.

"Hurry!" Stacy whisper-yelped.

Kiera jumped in front of the table. She hadn't done away with the burn mark on the surface yet. Stacy stuffed the burned doily into a trash can and whirled around when Rowan walked into the kitchen.

"Ah, there you are," he greeted Kiera, then noticed Stacy.

Kiera was skillful enough not to let anything show on her face, but Stacy's expression made it obvious they were up to something. Rowan arched a brow. "What are you two doing?"

"Rowan, exactly the person I wanted to see!" Stacy announced. "Can we talk in my office?"

"I, uh... Yes, but—" Whatever the dryad was going to say, he didn't finish. Stacy steered him out of the kitchen with both hands pressed against his back. Kiera's lips twisted into a smile as they went.

In her office, Stacy told Rowan about her conversation with her father that morning. "I don't think it's a bad idea to begin reaching out to other supernatural factions within the city and feel out who might be potential allies," she told him. "If this vampire problem grows any bigger, working together will be in everyone's best interests. We already have the Graytails on our side, but it wouldn't hurt to have allies inside the city, too."

"But not from the Circle, correct?" Rowan asked.

"Correct. There are other groups of paranormal types, right? You have a lot of connections. I figured you were the best to ask."

"I may be," Rowan replied. "But what about your father? He's lived in this area and done business for far longer than I have."

"That's the problem. Most of the people he used to be friends with are dead now. They lived a long time, but not as long as a dragon."

Rowan nodded curtly. "I'll see what I can do. Would you like me to set up meetings with anyone interested?"

Stacy had been pacing in front of her desk. Now, she rounded it and plopped into her seat. "Yes, though I'm not certain anyone will want to meet with me. These factions have remained hidden for years for a reason."

"Perhaps." Rowan smiled slightly. "However, they would have heard of Anastasia Drakethorn by now. They'll be curious, if nothing else."

Stacy returned his smile. "I can work with that."

"I will help you press upon them the gravity of the situation we're working with," Rowan promised. "My own history with vampires is bloody. I hadn't encountered one in New

York until Voss, but I fought many of them before coming here. None of those experiences is one I would like to repeat."

Khan had shared a similar sentiment. Stacy wondered if any vampires could be reasoned with.

"How long between the last vampire you dealt with and Voss?" Stacy asked.

Rowan thought about it. "About five hundred years?"

Stacy whistled. "Damn, you are old."

Rowan winked. "In dryad years, I'm almost middle-aged."

He promised to reach out to his contacts and get back to her. After he was gone, Stacy murmured, "In the meantime, I need to figure out a way to replace that doily before he discovers it's missing."

Rowan was in the middle of making calls on Stacy's behalf when Kiera appeared in the doorway of his study, leaning against the doorframe with casual, otherworldly grace. Her arms were folded, and her eyes were a soft violet today. That was a good sign. No scheming, only plain old Kiera.

"You wanted to speak to me earlier?" Kiera stated after he'd hung up the phone and scribbled a note on a pad of paper. The name of a contact who'd agreed to meet with him and Stacy tomorrow evening.

Rowan stood, realizing how long he'd been cooped up in his study today. "I wanted to ask you for a favor."

"Are you sure you're asking me for a favor, or are you giving me another task?"

"Both, I suppose."

"You're my boss, so it doesn't *have* to be a favor. You tell me what to do, and I'll do it. Within reason, of course."

Rowan raised a brow at this. "What happened to the Kiera

Swiftshadow I know? I remember a version of you that resisted all form of command."

Her eyes twinkled. "I've changed, okay?"

Rowan rounded his desk and leaned against it, adopting her nonchalance. He wasn't as good at it and ended up looking more awkward than casual. "I may be your boss, but I'm also your friend, I hope. And this job is a bit different than some of your recent ones. You can say no if you want."

"Tell me what it is," Kiera responded lightly.

"You've heard of the vampire threat."

Stacy had brought her up to speed that morning before racing out the door to visit her father. Kiera smiled. "I'll kill as many vampires as you want. I dislike them almost as much as I dislike the fae."

Rowan's lips twitched, but he managed to maintain a stoic expression. "I'm not asking you to hunt and kill vampires, Kiera. Not yet, anyway. You didn't let me finish."

"Well, that's disappointing."

"The time for that will come. I need you to find out what you can about their movements through your usual spying."

"I thought you said this job would be different."

Rowan fixed her with a look.

"Right. I didn't let you finish," she murmured.

"There's an underground library in the city that is difficult to get into. It's run by a magical who permits no one inside. I've been trying to find a way to get in for months."

"Why?" Kiera asked.

"Ever since a vampire threat arrived in the form of Isadora Voss, I've wanted to find out more about them. Catherine's library doesn't have a lot on vampires, and neither does Ethan's bookstore, but this place might. It's full of ancient, sacred texts that could help us glean helpful information. Many were once outlawed or banned, even among magical types."

"I'm sure if you ask the librarian nicely, they'll let you in."

Rowan sighed and dragged a hand through his long white hair. "I wish it was that easy. I've tried asking nicely before. The librarian looked like he wanted to spit in my face."

Kiera studied her long, sharp nails as if considering a plan. "What would you have me do to get in?"

"Ask nicely," Rowan replied.

"But you said—"

"The librarian is sidhe. I was hoping your heritage could gain you favor and access."

"I might be half-sidhe, but I look fae. If anything, I'll only piss the librarian off more."

"Please, Kiera. It's the only thing I can think of."

The earnestness in his eyes made her heart ache. She considered his proposal and figured it didn't hurt to go there and try. She pushed off the doorframe, strolling toward him, her boots silent on the wooden floorboards. "And if the sidhe lets me in, what should I look for?"

"Anything on vampires," Rowan told her. "Also, ask the librarian what rumors they've heard. He collects rumors and gossip like a dragon hoards gold."

Kiera grinned and halted two feet from him. Rowan tracked every movement as she asked, "Why haven't you brought him gossip before, then? I'm sure he would have let you in if you gave him something juicy."

"I don't participate in that sort of talk."

Kiera rolled her eyes. "Try it sometime, Rowan. It's fun."

"It creates enemies."

"Miles and I talk shit about each other all the time, and we're not enemies."

"Sometimes, I wonder if you are," Rowan returned, a half-grin pulling at his mouth.

Kiera realized many things were weighing on him, so she withdrew her teasing. "For Stacy, I'll do it." She turned to go, then thought of something else. "She and I were talking earlier, and she said something that made me admire her. She's a humble person, and she doesn't want power. Not for the wrong reasons, anyway."

Rowan showed a hint of a smile. "She is much like her mother."

"Yet that dragon side comes out sometimes."

"So far, it has come out at the right times."

Kiera thought of Stacy's accident in the kitchen. "Yeah. Sure."

Rowan raised a brow in question.

Kiera waved a hand. "It's nothing. When do you want me to try getting into this library?"

"Tomorrow night, if you can. I won't require anything of you tonight. You need the rest."

Kiera nodded. "I'm all for these night missions you have me going on, but it's a lot when I'm housekeeping all day and playing your dark angel all night. Maybe you could look into hiring a few people to help with the daytime work?"

"I'll get right on it." Rowan pushed off the desk and strode to her, laying a hand on her arm so she turned fully toward him. He skated his hands up her arms and rested them on her shoulders. She nearly shivered at his touch. "Thank you for everything you do."

"Are you giving me managerial encouragement so I'll continue doing well at my job?" she asked with a smirk.

Rowan chuckled. "I'm telling my friend that I appreciate all she does."

Kiera never blushed, but she almost did when hearing those words. She cleared her throat. "I'd better get started on dinner."

Rowan nodded and released his hold on her. She felt him watching her every step out of the room. It wasn't until she was down the hall, out of his sight, that she picked up her pace, a smile broadening her lips.

CHAPTER FOUR

Rowan didn't tell Stacy much about who they were meeting or where, only that the contact was a woman of elven heritage who had been curious about the growth of Stacy's influence in the city over the past few weeks.

"I'm loosely acquainted with her," he told Stacy. "We met a few centuries ago while fighting for land north of here. We weren't fighting one another, you see. We were driving out a strange, dark pestilence from the land. I left not long after and heard word of her in these parts after coming to work for your mother."

Rowan said "a few centuries ago" the same way Stacy would have said "a few years ago."

Stacy hadn't heard of any elves in the city, so it surprised her that one as hidden as this woman would bother meeting with them at all. "I wonder why they came to the city," she mused. "Aren't they like you? Can't be away from trees for too long?"

Rowan glowered. "You think you're being funny, but you're also right. These elves came to the city a long time ago for a particular reason. I don't know why, though. They've kept that secret close to their chests." A pause followed, then Rowan added,

"We're meeting at a neutral location. That is, we're not meeting in any place where the elves normally meet or live."

More secrecy. They were already holding this conversation in the car.

The sun was going down on a Sunday evening, and Rowan drove Stacy's sleek, black Bentayga away from the Thorn estate toward the city. They lapsed into silence the rest of the drive, with Rowan focused on the road and Stacy considering what she would say to the elven leader. Rowan had warned Stacy against making grand, altruistic speeches. The leader of the elves was past talking.

"She wants to meet you to gauge who you are in person, but she's far more concerned about action than words," Rowan had told her earlier.

"Sounds like someone I would like," Stacy had replied.

Rowan's response had been a frown. "Don't get your hopes up about liking her." A pause. "Or her liking you."

Rowan drove them into the heart of the concrete jungle and stopped at a large parking garage between a theater building and a bank headquarters. He parked on the lowest level, then beckoned for Stacy to follow him. They descended a staircase that smelled strongly of urine, and Stacy wrinkled her nose. "Please tell me you're not taking us into the sewers."

Rowan flashed a smile. "No, but we are going underground."

They reached the bottom of the stairs, and Rowan used magic to unlock a utility door. The room beyond was small and gray, with another doorway leading out. Rowan opened this one, revealing another set of stairs leading down into darkness. "After you," he invited.

Stacy gave him a look, then sighed. "I'm trusting you, Rowan."

The place was damp and musty. Stacy descended twelve stone steps before she reached a flat floor and a dimly lit room. Here, a wooden table sat in the center of the room surrounded by wooden chairs. Though the corners of the room were dusty and full of cobwebs, the table appeared clean.

Several empty crates were stacked against the wall, as if someone had brought supplies down here and transferred them to someone else. The table and chairs indicated this was a common meeting place, but Stacy couldn't figure out why anyone would want to meet here.

"There's no one here," she pointed out at the sight of the empty room.

Rowan frowned, then opened his mouth to respond. Whatever he might have said died on his tongue. The next moment, a figure materialized out of thin air.

Stacy jumped. "What the hell?"

The figure standing before her was a tall woman. Over six feet, if Stacy had to guess. She was lithe and willowy, with brown skin and braids tumbling down her back. She wore a simple white tunic and dark green, billowy pants. The cloak around her shoulders was black like her boots. If not for the outfit's simplicity, Stacy would have thought she'd left a Ren Faire and hadn't stopped at home to change before coming here.

The woman wore a sleek, curved sword at her side. Gradually, other features became obvious. The woman's face lengthened, and her ears became pointed. Her glamour was shedding.

Stacy realized the woman hadn't appeared out of thin air. She had been glamoured to camouflage with the room. That explained the outfit. She could wear typical elven garb and blend in by simply becoming part of her surroundings. Neither Stacy nor Rowan had noticed her when they walked in.

The elf scanned Stacy, then produced a slow smile. "Anastasia Drakethorn. It's good to see you in the flesh. Your reputation precedes you."

Stacy wished she could say the same about this woman, but she barely knew anything about her. She stuck out her hand. "It's nice to meet you, Miss…"

"Elentya is fine, with no 'Miss.'" Elentya shook her hand, then turned to nod a greeting at Rowan. "How do you do, dryad?"

"I am well, *Rigan*," he curtly replied.

The elven word for queen, Stacy remembered. This woman wasn't merely a leader but considered royalty. It took her aback at first. Then, Stacy considered the alpha of the Graytails pack. That woman was queenly, too.

The elf motioned toward the chairs. "Shall we sit to discuss this?"

Stacy agreed, and they took chairs across from one another. Rowan did not sit but stood behind the chair next to Stacy instead.

Elentya leaned back, crossing her arms and appraising Stacy with sharp eyes. Stacy could have sworn the elf's eyes were somewhere between emerald and silver. "I'll admit I've heard of your reputation, Miss Drakethorn. I've grown curious. So, when your estate keeper contacted me about meeting, saying you would like to discuss the vampire problem in our city, I agreed. Mind you, I didn't agree to *help*. I came here to see what you were made of."

Stacy had expected as much, thanks to Rowan's warning. The dragon part of her nature stirred, allowing warm magic to flow through her. Was it because that part of her saw the elf as a threat or something else?

The elf continued before Stacy had a chance to respond. "I'll also admit I don't care much for werewolves, but what you did for that pack in court against Corbinelli's pool of vermin was admirable. Then, there was that weasel Hines, who disappeared. I'm sure you had something to do with that."

"She didn't," Rowan cut in. This was technically true. Rowan had dispatched Kiera after Hines without telling Stacy. It had irked her that he'd done it without asking her permission, but it ended up being for the best.

Elentya fixed Rowan with her sharp eyes, and a slow smile curved her lips. "Okay, sure."

"I'm not overly concerned about the Circle at this point," Stacy spoke up. "Unless they're involved with this vampire issue. I'm sure you've heard about the disappearances."

The elf nodded.

"I plan to investigate what they're doing, but I've been warned by those close to me that if I do, I should prepare for quite a conflict. I've been meaning to make your acquaintance and others, should I need…"

"Reinforcements?" Elentya guessed. She had a youthful face, but the wisdom in her eyes spoke of many years.

"Allies," Stacy corrected.

Elentya leaned forward and rested her folded hands on the table. "Look, I admire the work you're doing, Miss Drakethorn. I'd rather see someone like you take Victor Corbinelli's vacant throne in the underworld over anyone else. But we elves have remained hidden in this city for years with good reason. I will not risk the safety we've built by making unnecessary alliances."

Stacy had anticipated this might happen. Time to switch tactics. "I don't blame you for not wanting to risk your safety. I only wonder what threats you might face if these vampires aren't dealt with. They'll keep hunting down as many people as they can get away with, and we can all assume they will come after us magical people in time."

Elentya's eyes narrowed a fraction. "I am not blind to the threat they pose, only to what degree they might choose to come against us. If they can. We're well hidden, you see. No one but our kind knows where we live and work. We're among the best members of the magical community at hiding in plain sight."

"Are you part of this community?" Stacy challenged. "If you're hidden all the time and only look after yourselves, can you call it that?"

She expected an unpleasant response from the elf, but Elentya merely smiled. She glanced at Rowan. "I like this one. She has her mother's spirit."

Stacy jolted. "You knew my mother?"

"Barely. Catherine and I ran in different circles. Witches and elves don't often cross paths if they can avoid it. I dislike most witches, but your mother was among those I admired. I was sad to hear about her coven when they succumbed to the tragedy. For her sake, I will consider allyship with you, Miss Drakethorn."

The locket around Stacy's neck warmed against her skin as if in response.

The elf continued. "If you can prove you intend to root out the vampires for a good purpose and not for your personal gain or fame, I will help you. Investigate them and tell me what you find. We will go from there."

"Thank you," Stacy replied, rising. "I am confident that an alliance between us will favor our respective groups down the line."

Elentya raised a brow. "Groups? Have you joined a coven, Miss Drakethorn?"

Stacy hesitated to give the elf information. In the end, she decided that showing a card or two would help her earn trust. She smiled. "Not technically. I've formed my own, but we're only two members now. My inner circle includes magicals of many kinds. I don't discriminate."

The elf produced a cold smile. "Except against vampires."

Stacy shrugged. "Maybe there are some good ones."

Elentya laughed darkly. "If there are, I've never met one. Those with insatiable appetites such as theirs never learn to be happy with what they have. They are miserable beings who can't bear the thought of anyone else being happier than them."

"Sad way to live," Rowan murmured.

The elf stood, nodding. "Indeed." She turned her green-silver eyes on Stacy. "We'll be in touch, Miss Drakethorn."

"That didn't go so badly," Rowan remarked when they returned to the car.

Stacy sat in silence until he nudged her and added, "I expected a flat-out no from Elentya, but at least she's considering helping us."

Stacy turned toward him. "Sometimes, I don't see why I'm the only one willing to lay my life on the line for others. I know you are, too, Rowan. Don't take it the wrong way. All my closest friends are. I think I've found true community, then I try to expand that, and everyone else wants to stay hidden. What are they so afraid of?"

Rowan's features were solemn. "You weren't alive when our kind started being noticed by the world governments. Witches were one thing, but when they realized there were far more of us than they ever imagined, things got dicey. A lot of people were hunted down and killed, elves among them. Elentya and her people have found safety, and they want to keep it that way. I say this to help you understand. I think they should help if they want to remain safe."

Rowan pulled the car out of the garage, still considering her words. "You've created a name for yourself, Stacy, but that doesn't mean everyone will automatically like you. The Drakethorn name carries weight, but not everyone has appreciated your father's wealth and power. I think Elentya and the elves need to see that money and power isn't your goal."

"It isn't," Stacy insisted.

"And they will realize that in time."

Stacy was quiet for a heartbeat before she grumbled, "This isn't a fun lesson to learn."

Rowan chuckled. "It never is." It wasn't until they were out of the city, headed back toward the estate along country roads, that Rowan asked who she wanted to meet next.

"I think it's a good idea to hit up a contact of my own," Stacy replied.

"Hit up?"

"Reach out."

"Ah. And who might this contact be?"

"I had a case at the beginning of the summer before I met you," she explained. "It involved members of the Shinnecock nation having their land compromised. Victor was behind it, of course. I was put on the case. In the process, I discovered the chief once knew my mother. My first exposure to magic came from meeting him. It would be nice to reach out, see how they are doing, and make them aware of the vampire threat, if they don't already know."

Rowan's eyes lit up at the mention of the tribe. "I would very much like to meet them. They knew Catherine before I came along." A wistful smile crossed his lips. "It will be like gaining part of her back."

Stacy's heart ached at those words. "We can go together in the morning."

CHAPTER FIVE

Kiera Swiftshadow didn't mind dark places, but it would help if she could fucking see.

It was pitch-black here in the tunnel. In the city under the night sky, she'd been able to navigate without problem. She'd come to the secret door in the side of a brick building in the alley and used the incantation Rowan had told her while pressing a hand over the wall. Magic had rippled out, forming glowing blue symbols. The door had appeared and opened, leading down into pitch darkness.

Ever the graceful assassin, Kiera didn't like that she was stumbling around in pure darkness. She pulled on her magic to give herself light, but nothing would come. She cursed. The damn sidhe librarian had cast enchantments through the tunnel, muting the magic of anyone who passed this way. A defensive measure. She would have done the same thing, but she sure as fuck hated having it used against her.

Time to do this the modern way, she decided, taking out her phone and turning on the flashlight function. The tunnel was narrow, with a ceiling only inches from her head. Kiera imagined Rowan coming through this tunnel, hunching his back so he wouldn't bang his head. The image was almost amusing enough to make her forget her irritation.

The tunnel walls were covered in a latticework of spells, interconnecting and sprawling across the stone surface. The whorls were old enough to tell Kiera the librarian had been here for a long time. Longer than the building she'd found the wall in. Once, another entrance was used to come here.

A faint bluish glow appeared along the wall, a sign she'd tripped the alarm. *Probably when I opened the door,* she thought.

Kiera switched off her flashlight. The spell's glow was enough to see by. The tunnel curved around, continuing downward. It was cold. She followed it, her steps silent and certain despite not knowing where this would lead.

Finally, she spied another door at the end of the tunnel. At first, it looked like a dead end. A stone wall leading nowhere. Kiera knew better, though. It was another secret door.

She laid her hand over it as she had done with the first and spoke the incantation. Instead of magic rippling out to open the door, sparks shot at her.

Kiera yelped and snatched her hand away as a stinging sensation spread from her palm through her fingers. "Fuck you," she whispered to the librarian she hadn't met yet. Would banging on the door and demanding entrance help? Kiera didn't think so, but she was tempted.

Then, to her surprise, a section of the wall simply vanished, and an opening yawned before her. Kiera raised a brow. The librarian had some strange ideas about security.

She stepped through the opening to find herself in a wider space. The ceiling was higher here, and the walls farther apart. Another opening arched before her, but this one was protected by wards. It was a complicated set, though nothing she couldn't handle under normal circumstances. When her magic would fucking work!

Kiera simmered with frustration, unsure what to do next.

ISABEL CAMPBELL & MICHAEL ANDERLE

She wished she could simply blow the wards wide open and march into the library. Beyond the wards was a wide, circular room. It contained nothing but a pillar of blue light shooting toward a tall ceiling. A magic elevator, she realized. One could stand in that blue light on the floor and be shot up to another level.

A figure was floating down through the light.

Finally.

Kiera observed the figure from behind the wards.

He was tall and willowy, with wisps of midnight-black hair floating around his head. His face was young, though she knew he was quite old. Thin, interconnecting lines marked his ivory skin. Not scars, as she first thought, but intentional lines etched into his face. Magic of a sort. Kiera wasn't sure what the marks were for.

His eyes were completely light blue. No whites, no pupils. It was one feature of the sidhe Kiera was glad she had not inherited. The two of them shared the same pointed ears and elongated features.

The sidhe moved with an elegance the fae also possessed. However, where the fae were often trained killers, the sidhe possessed a reserved gentleness. They moved as if they had all the time in the world and little reflex for survival. It was all an illusion, though. They were not prone to violence, but they were smart and cunning. They had their own set of tricks.

Such as putting up spells that take away someone's magic, Kiera thought as the figure glided toward the wards. She remembered the sparks in the doorway and flexed her hand. It still stung, and she couldn't call up healing magic to take the sensation away.

I might not have magic, but I still have my knives, she thought. However, looking like a threat right now wouldn't do her any favors. Not with the wards between her and the sidhe, and no way through them except persuasive speech. Kiera was used to getting her way by putting a knife against someone's neck. Not by *talking*. Maybe Miles should have come along for this job. He made friends every damn place he went. Kiera? Not so much.

The sidhe wore simple black robes with an elaborate shawl of black feathers draped around his shoulders and across his neck. When he reached the wards, he scrutinized her. "What do you want, fae?" He spoke the ancient fae tongue with ease, emphasizing the last word to tell Kiera he wasn't happy about her being here. Kiera knew the fae language well, though she hadn't spoken it in five hundred years.

"I want in to your library," she replied in the same language. Knowing this statement, though true, wouldn't be enough, she added, "And I'm not *only* fae." She stated this in the sidhe tongue. She didn't know it well, so the words sounded stilted, but she had learned pieces of it when she was a small child from a sidhe nurse who'd known her mother.

The sidhe male lifted a brow, then laughed deeply. "The fae do not bother mating with my kind." He paused. "Yet I sense something familiar on you. I also know when people are lying. You are not."

"My mother is what you sense," Kiera replied, switching to plain English. "She was a sidhe servant in a fae court. My father took advantage of her." She relayed this as if it happened every day. Well, it did.

The sidhe male clicked his tongue, also switching to English. "All rapists and bastards."

Kiera sighed. She wasn't interested in a debate on prejudices and long-held hatred between any magical groups, even if she belonged to one or more of them. She didn't have time for it, either. "Look, I know you live underground and never make it to the surface, but there's a problem up there, and I need access to your library to fix it. So, please, take down these damn wards."

The sidhe male eyed her. "I have no interest in helping anyone on the surface."

Selfish bastard.

Kiera dug something from her pocket and held it up to him. "I thought you would say that, so I brought a bartering piece."

The male's eyes widened at the sight of a golden circular object hanging from a chain. The symbols on its surface glowed blue, like all the magic in this place did. Sidhe magic.

"Where did you get that?" he hissed.

"I told you, my mother was sidhe. She left this to me when she died." Kiera grinned. "An heirloom of the royal sidhe of Anvaris." The ancient world of sidhe had not existed in any livable condition for centuries, thanks to the fae invading it long ago and taking their people as slaves. People like Kiera's mother.

This relic had come from that world into the fae realm. Then, when Kiera was banished to the human world, she'd brought it with her. She'd taken it because it had once belonged to her mother, but also because she'd wanted to raise one last middle finger at her fae family. Parting with it would break her heart, but...

Stacy needs my help. Her work for the city is counting on me succeeding here. Now that Kiera had met the difficult librarian, she was determined to succeed out of pure spite. To prove she could.

"I will let you have it in exchange for one thing," Kiera went on. "You allow me to come here whenever I need to and read whatever I want. I will never take anything from your library, but I will have access to it. I will never tell a soul about this place except Rowan, who already knows it exists."

"You are a friend of Rowan's?" the sidhe asked. "That makes sense. How else would you have found this place?" He studied the relic. "How do I know it isn't a trick? You could have brought any piece of jewelry here and glamoured it to look like a sidhe artifact."

"I thought you said you could tell if I was lying." Kiera shrugged. "You'll have to let down the wards so I can come in and give it to you. Then, you can test it."

The sidhe's slim black brows drew together. Finally, the wards vanished. "Don't touch a thing while you're in here," he hissed.

Kiera smiled as she strode toward him. He extended his hand, and she dropped the necklace into his palm. He turned to the pillar of blue light and stepped in, motioning for her to follow. They floated up about fifty feet to a stone platform, and Kiera gasped at the sight before her.

The vaulted ceiling appeared made of glass, displaying a night sky. It wasn't the true night sky, but it looked real enough. The stars were numerous, and a great, full amber moon shone through arched glass windows.

Spirals of books were stacked throughout the library, forming weaving pathways throughout. There were no shelves, only those spirals. They were not fastened to the floor but floated a few feet in the air. Golden lights bobbed around the space. That was when Kiera realized the sidhe librarian was not the only living creature here. Sprites inhabited this space, too.

Pages fluttered from the floor into the air, spinning above the stacks of books. The floor and walls glowed with blue sigils. This place was not only sacred but incredibly special. A small piece of the old sidhe world preserved in the human one. Kiera had never been to Anvaris, but she'd heard about it from her nurse. This was the sort of thing she'd described. Kiera doubted the librarian had been to Anvaris, either. He wasn't *that* old.

Kiera wasn't one for reading, but she suddenly felt she could spend forever in here. She didn't blame the librarian for not leaving.

"This way," the sidhe murmured, walking off the platform toward a wide, dark wooden desk. He rounded it and set the artifact on its surface before jerking open a drawer and rifling through its contents for testing materials. The drawer was full of miscellaneous tools and objects, none of which Kiera recognized.

"What is your name?" she asked.

"Adrian," he replied curtly.

She arched a brow. "That's a human name."

"You also have a human name."

"I've lived in the human world for a long time. I don't expect people in this world to adjust well to a name like Adrilonziglia."

Adrian's head jerked up, his gaze meeting hers. "That is a sidhe name."

She shrugged. "My mother named me. I think it was her last stroke of defiance before my father killed her. The fae weren't fans of it, either, but it was too late. I switched to Kiera when I came here." A plain human name, yet she felt it suited her. Swift-shadow was the name she had adopted from her time in the assassins' guild. Several of her old comrades had nicknamed her that, and she'd stuck with it.

Kiera gestured at the relic. "How long is that going to take, Adrian?"

"Some time," he replied stiffly. His gaze darted about as if a dozen thoughts raced through his mind at once. He opened more drawers and tossed out various items. They landed with clinks and thuds on the floor.

What an odd fellow, Kiera thought.

Her hand itched to reach for her knife. She could threaten him and get this over with much faster. However, when she did reach for it, she found it was gone. *What the hell!* Kiera patted other parts of her body and checked her boots. All her knives were gone.

"Where did you put them?" she snarled.

For the first time since they met, Adrian smiled. "I confiscated them as soon as you stepped past the warded wall. They will be returned to you when you leave."

Another damn sidhe trick.

Oh well. She could use her bare hands.

As if reading her mind, Adrian fluttered a hand, and a wall of thin, shimmering magic went up between them.

Kiera balled her hands into fists. "I'm going to look around, then."

His head snapped up. "No, you're not."

"I'm not going to stand here forever and watch you," she hissed.

He considered this, then nodded. "Don't touch anything."

How was that supposed to work if she needed to read the damn books? "I'm looking for books on vampires. Can you at least point me in the right direction?"

Adrian eyed her. "Why in hell would you want to read about vampires?" The disdain in his voice was obvious. At least they had that in common.

Kiera leaned on his desk and folded her arms. Adrian inched away as if irritated by her proximity despite the magic between them. He was in the process of weaving threads of a sidhe searching spell over the relic, prodding and poking at its substance to ensure its authenticity.

"I told you before, there's an issue on the surface." Kiera explained the problem briefly. "I'm employed by someone who intends to do something about the vampires, but we have few sources on the surface about their origin and history. I'm here to find what materials you have."

"Nasty things, vampires," Adrian muttered. "Why should I care, though? They won't bother me down here."

"You don't know that," Kiera returned coldly. "Besides, it doesn't matter. That wasn't the deal." She pointed at the sidhe relic.

He sighed. "Over there. Third stack from the window. The books are locked into place with magic, but the sprites can undo the enchantment."

"The sprites work here?"

Adrian nodded without looking up from the relic. "There's one sprite for each stack."

Sprites at the Thorn estate did little other than splash in the fountain and steal small objects from inside the house. Here, they had a purpose. Jobs. There had to be hundreds, if not thousands, of sprites bobbing about the library. "How far does this library go?" Kiera asked.

"Far."

Kiera was close to vaulting over the desk and sucker-punching him. *This is how they act when they've been alone for... however long he's been here,* she thought. Sprites weren't talkative company. Not in any tongue that a being other than a sprite could understand, anyway.

"Who is this person who has employed you?" Adrian asked.

"Why do you care?"

He looked at her. "I'm merely curious."

"I can tell *you* are lying." Kiera figured it didn't hurt to tell him, though. He wouldn't leave this place, and no one else had come here for decades. Who was he going to tell?

"Her name is Stacy. She's a competent witch and shifter."

Adrian raised a brow at this. "Rare that someone would be of two kinds, especially two that oppose one another."

Witches and shifters. Fae and sidhe. Kiera understood Stacy well in that regard. "It happens," she murmured.

"So rare, in fact, that prophecies have been written about such people," Adrian murmured. The magic vanished from the relic, and his eyes widened. "Interesting. It's real."

"It's all yours," Kiera replied, biting her tongue to keep from adding, *I told you so.*

Adrian considered her. "You want to help your friend, don't you?"

"Yes, I do." A hint of a smile came to Kiera's lips. "I believe Anastasia Drakethorn is going to do a lot of good for the city."

Adrian's face was pale by nature, but it paled further as Kiera spoke Stacy's name. "What did you say?" he demanded breathlessly.

Kiera frowned. "I said my friend could do a lot of good for the city."

"No, her name!"

"Stacy?"

"You said Drakethorn. Is she the one who is half witch and half shifter?"

"Yes. But why—"

"Dragon?" His voice trembled.

Kiera hesitated. "What does it matter?"

"The prophecy. It...it can't be," Adrian murmured, his eyes wide with shock. He held the sides of his head as if struck by a sudden pain.

"What—

Before she could finish the question, the sidhe male fainted on the floor.

CHAPTER SIX

It was early morning the following day when Stacy and Rowan arrived at the Shinnecock Nation reservation, having driven south of the Thorn estate to reach it. It felt good to be surrounded by nature during her search. Better than scrounging around underground places in the city for allies. Getting the Shinnecock people to help her might take some convincing, but she was more confident about this meeting than the one she'd had with the elf.

"Are you ready?" Rowan asked as they climbed from the car.

She nodded.

To their surprise, the elder she'd met at the beginning of summer stood at the front of the reservation, his face unreadable. Stacy had called him the day before, asking if she could speak with him today. He had answered that the daughter of Catherine and Khan Drakethorn was always welcome at their home.

She dipped her head in greeting. "Thank you for having us today. It's been too long since my last visit, and I have news for you and your people." She gestured at Rowan. "The guardian of my estate and a former dear friend of my mother's." Stacy added the last part knowing the elder would appreciate meeting anyone who'd known Catherine.

The elder nodded to Rowan. "I sense you are like Anastasia. The way of trees is in you."

"It is," Rowan replied, matching the elder's stoicism.

"I sense wisdom in you, tree man," the elder added. "I can see why Anastasia's mother favored your work as guardian of her home." The elder returned his attention to Stacy. "I welcome you to our land once again, but you will have to excuse my demeanor today. We've been struck with deep sorrow. Our people have suffered a great tragedy."

"What happened?" Stacy asked, softening her voice.

The wrinkles in the elder's face deepened. "Two nights ago, one of our members went missing from her bed. Signs of great violence were left behind."

Heart hammering, Stacy asked if he could take her to where the signs were left. "I'm beginning to wonder if this woman's disappearance is connected with the reason I've come to you today."

Deep concern showed in the elder's face, but he agreed. "This way."

He led them through a row of houses. Children played basketball on a small court, but no one else was visible. The elder halted at the end of a row of houses and knocked on a door. A woman's voice answered, and the elder asked if they could come in. The woman opened the door. Her eyes were bloodshot and puffy from crying.

The elder and the woman conversed in the Shinnecock language for a minute before the woman allowed them in. She showed them to a bedroom at the back of the house. "It happened in here. I was asleep and didn't hear it. I awoke to a scream, then she was...g-gone." The woman broke into fresh tears.

"Much of it was cleaned up," the elder explained. "Blood, hair, and such. However, this remains." He pointed to an image drawn in charcoal on one of the walls. The vampire fangs.

Stacy felt like a stone had lodged in her throat, preventing her from pushing sympathies off her tongue. A kindled rage mixed with fresh sorrow. She saw it on Rowan's face, too. The vampires had gone outside the city to take someone. Stacy's heart thundered, and she felt like she would be sick. How far did their operation reach? Had the city been an end goal or the beginning?

She turned to the elder, cleared her throat, and told him everything she knew and her purpose for coming here. "I wonder if the vampires have done this on purpose. It's almost as though they *want* to be tracked."

Had a trap been laid? If so, for whom?

The sorrow in the elder's face was unmistakable. He was unfamiliar with vampires, aside from the fact that they were dangerous. "You must be cautious, Anastasia. These blood creatures are wicked things."

"Something must be done about them," she replied with conviction. The woman's soft crying in the background was further motivation. *No one should lose a child this way,* Stacy thought.

"If our people can assist you in any way, we will," the elder replied, his voice deep and resonating.

"I will do all I can to find the woman who went missing," Stacy promised.

The elder's eyes shone with tears. "Catherine would have done this, too. You are much like her." He folded his hands around hers. "I saw it as a sign when you asked to come here."

Ethan poured two cups of tea while Stacy sat on his sofa in the back of the bookshop where he lived and worked. He'd been making tea for the past ten minutes while she updated him on her conversations with the leader of the city's elves and the elder of the Shinnecock nation.

Rowan had dropped her off an hour ago, then left to meet a contact elsewhere in the city with the promise to return when Stacy was ready to leave. She didn't see herself wanting to leave anytime soon despite it already being 10:00 p.m.

She and Ethan hadn't had a true moment alone since the night she'd kissed him. He'd come to her estate several times, but people were always around. As a result, they hadn't discussed what happened between them. Stacy had been trying to find a way to broach the subject for about twenty minutes now.

Ethan walked to the sofa with the tea in hand, giving one to Stacy. "You've been busy," he remarked as she finished her story.

Stacy accepted the cup with a grateful smile.

Ethan sat beside her. "Between all your friends, the Graytails, the Shinnecock, and the elves, you will have plenty of allies. There's your father, too, of course."

Stacy sipped her tea before answering. "One, I hope not to have to rope my father into all this. He wants nothing to do with vampires, including the process of getting rid of them. I need to do this apart from him as much as possible. We don't exactly see eye to eye on the whole matter. The elves are a question mark for now. I need to 'prove' to Elentya that I'm doing this for the right reasons. Problem is, I don't know how to do that."

"Keep working the way you have been," Ethan replied. "It'll be obvious before long."

"In all this talk about allies, I've wondered about someone else," Stacy remarked after a moment of silence. "What would you think of paying a visit to your old friend Vi?"

Ethan's brows shot up in surprise and alarm. "Stacy, be serious."

She set her teacup on the coffee table. "I am being serious, Ethan. Think about it. Vi hears shit all over the city, and she could be a valuable asset in getting rid of the vampire threat."

"First of all, she's not my friend. I'd barely call her an acquaintance," Ethan cut in. "Second, she's a literal snake. Vi isn't short for 'Violet.' It's short for 'Viper.'"

"Okay, great! We're both shifters! We'll have a lot in common. Snake and dragon."

Ethan sighed. "You and Vi are nothing alike. For one, you're... you know, *normal*. She's a centuries-old seductress in the body of a twenty-five-year-old who tries to get into the pants of every man who walks through her door. Plus, she's an expert thief. I've never seen someone hoard more odd objects than her. You should see her teeth collection!"

Stacy grinned. "The more you describe her, the more I like the idea of pitting her against vampires."

"That would mean having to work with her," Ethan grumbled.

"I think I can handle her." As Stacy spoke, an inkling of doubt entered her mind. Her first encounter with the snake shifter hadn't gone badly per se, but she wasn't itching to repeat it anytime soon.

Ethan slumped further into the couch and dragged his hands down his face. "Fine. I'll talk to her. No promises, though. She'll probably have weird conditions about her involvement, and I refuse to sleep with her."

Stacy laughed. "I would hope you wouldn't sleep with her." She hadn't thought the words through, and she blushed as soon as they left her mouth.

Slowly, Ethan removed his hands from his face, his cheeks as red as hers. He cleared his throat. "One weird thing comes up, and I'm out."

Stacy gave him a thumbs-up. With the conversation about gathering allies over, she gathered her courage. Time to rip off this damn Band-Aid. "Maybe we should talk about...other things."

"Other things?"

"Us."

"Us. Right." Ethan met her gaze. "About the kiss, right?"

Stacy smiled. "I was beginning to think I'd imagined the whole thing. I'm sorry if that was weird for you. I wasn't thinking, but I guess I've been trying to figure out how to tell you that I like you and—"

Ethan closed the short distance between them before Stacy could get out the full sentence. She registered his hands cupping her face, then drawing her to him. Their lips met. The press of his mouth against hers was firm but soon turned tentative and soft, as if he was feeling out her reaction. Stacy made a small sound of surprise, then melted into him.

Ethan soon pulled back, his breathing ragged. "It wasn't weird for me except for the part where it didn't last longer."

A smile broke across Stacy's face. "Does this mean you—"

He kissed her again, more hungrily this time. She opened her mouth, and his tongue slipped in. Her body warmed all over. Their lips separated, and with his forehead against hers, he breathed into her, "Yes, it means I like you. I've been trying to think of a way to ask you out without making it weird."

"We should go on a real date, right?" Stacy asked. "Take a break from all the spells and sleuthing?"

"Yes, we should—"

Stacy cut him off this time. She didn't feel close enough to him. The next thing she knew, he was hauling her ass off the sofa and onto his lap. Their kissing turned feverish. She slipped her fingers into his hair. *I've wanted to do this for weeks.*

She didn't realize she'd said it out loud until his chuckle brushed her ear. "Me too, Stacy. Me too." The scruff on his face scraped her cheek as he moved to place his lips beneath her ear. However, they jolted apart at the sound of the front door opening and a voice calling to them.

"Stacy, are you in here?"

Rowan.

"Shit!" Stacy moved off Ethan's lap, straightening her shirt. In the process, she accidentally knocked over her teacup on the table. She groaned and reached to pick it up.

"Don't worry," Ethan told her. "I'll clean it up." Cheeks flaming, he fled into the kitchen.

Rowan appeared, arms folded and brows drawn together in a frown. He eyed the spilled tea and Stacy's rumpled appearance. "What's going on back here?"

Stacy felt like a teenager caught making out with a boy in her room. Instead of explaining anything or making up an excuse, she glared at Rowan as if to say, *You ruined a great moment.* Out loud, she replied, "I thought you weren't coming back until I said I was ready to go home." Now, she sounded like a teenager, too.

"My meeting ended early, and I came to see what you were up to. I thought it would be magic lessons, not…other lessons."

Stacy didn't think she could blush harder, but she did. She hoped Ethan hadn't heard that.

Ethan returned from the kitchen with a towel and mopped up the tea on his table. "Hello, Rowan." Stacy could have sworn his voice squeaked.

Rowan smiled knowingly. "Hello, Ethan. Forget to comb your hair today?"

Stacy glared at the dryad again. "Your meeting must have gone well if you're done this *early*."

Rowan's glinting green eyes slid to hers. "It did. As soon as it wrapped up, Kiera called. I sent her on a mission last night, and she didn't return to the estate until an hour ago. Apparently, she has important news regarding the vampires and something else. She didn't say what it was, but I figured we should head back."

Stacy was instantly curious, and it was nearly enough to banish her annoyance at having her moment with Ethan interrupted. She didn't care that she sounded like a pouting teenager when she replied, "Okay, we can go home now."

CHAPTER SEVEN

Kiera strode into the dim confines of the library, and Stacy, Rowan, and Ethan turned toward her.

Stacy stood with her back to the fire, wondering what news the fae assassin might have for them. Ethan sat on one of the long couches, face drawn. After hearing what Rowan had to say, he'd asked to tag along. Stacy had agreed, knowing whatever Kiera's news, she would pass it along to Ethan eventually.

Since leaving his shop, they could barely glance at one another without blushing, so they'd stopped looking. They wanted to keep a certain decorum around Rowan.

The dryad paced in front of the table where they often placed stacks of books. Stacy thought of Miles and Amy, who had gone to bed before anyone else arrived home. Rowan would fill them in tomorrow.

Stacy glanced at the grandfather clock in the corner. A minute before midnight. They would be up for another hour or so, depending on what Kiera had to tell them.

When Kiera entered the library, Rowan stopped pacing and placed his hands on her arms in a gesture Stacy found affectionate and endearing. "Are you all right?" he asked.

Kiera nodded. "Nothing bad happened, but I've had one hell of a time since I left here last night." She leaned against the table, and Rowan moved closer to Stacy. "Your sidhe friend is quite the character," she began, glancing at the dryad.

Rowan's brows furrowed. "He's not my friend, exactly. I don't know his name."

"His name is Adrian. That's his human name, anyway. I never learned his sidhe name."

Rowan's white brows arched. "So, you got into the library?"

"I gave up the only family heirloom I had left to do it, but yes."

"Hold on," Stacy spoke up. "Can we back up and explain what this library is, who Adrian might be, and why you had to give up an heirloom?"

"You didn't tell her about my mission?" Kiera asked Rowan.

The dryad glanced from Kiera to Stacy. "No. I didn't want to get anyone's hopes up in case it didn't work."

Stacy bristled but said nothing. She was more interested in hearing Kiera's story.

Kiera slid into an armchair and sighed. "I went to an underground secret library in the city to ask an elusive, oddball sidhe librarian to help me find ancient, rare texts on vampires. You know, the usual."

"I know what you're talking about," Ethan inserted excitedly. "That library is closed to everyone, and the librarian is known as an asshole. To the people who believe it exists, anyway. Most think it's made up."

"Made up, no. Asshole, yes, but he ended up being helpful," Kiera replied. "He's sidhe, so we had that in common." Kiera described what she had done to gain entrance to the library and the conversation she'd had with Adrian. Until he fainted, anyway. "I couldn't use my magic to bring him back to consciousness," she explained. "The sprites seemed to know what to do, though. I'm not sure if the fainting is normal or if it was simply a reaction to the realization he'd come to."

"Yeah, I want to know about this prophecy he mentioned," Ethan commented.

"And why he was so bothered when he heard my name," Stacy added.

Rowan remained silent and contemplative.

Kiera continued. "When he came to and remembered who I was and why I had come there, he told me about an old prophecy regarding someone who is half-witch, half-shifter. He took me deep into the library to an ancient scroll protected by an obscene number of wards and enchantments.

"It took him nearly an hour to undo the damn things. I couldn't take the scroll with me, and he forbade me from rewriting the words. Said it would do 'great damage to the future' if I did. I memorized it, though."

Her audience looked at her expectantly. Kiera recited the prophecy.

Dark pestilence abounds
Of strife, war, and blood it sounds
On wings of gold comes our vindication,
Born of witch and serpent both.
Magic and might as condemnation
Shall strike with sword and breath of flame
That which stands with death in hand
Through a powerful, inherited name.

Rowan arched a brow. Ethan shifted.

Stacy frowned. "I don't like riddles."

"This one sounds pretty straightforward to me," Ethan remarked.

Stacy eyed him. "What do you mean?"

"Witch and serpent both. That's someone born of a witch and a shifter dragon. I only know one of those."

"Powerful, inherited name," Rowan inserted. "Strike with sword and breath of flame. Stacy, that's you."

She laughed. "There are no prophecies about me."

"It literally talks about using a sword made of fire *and* breathing it," Ethan returned. "You can do both."

"How old is the prophecy?" Rowan asked Kiera.

"It came before dragons," she answered.

So, pretty fucking old, Stacy thought as she plopped into a chair by the fire. "I'm not going to defeat a great darkness. First of all, how can we know the prophecy is true? If it is, someone else could fit the bill, right?"

"You're a rare person, Stacy," Ethan insisted. "You might not be the first to be born of a shifter and a witch in the last few centuries, but you sure as hell are the first to be born of a *dragon* and a witch. Maybe the first ever."

"I agree with Ethan," Rowan announced. "Also, Adrian isn't the only one who has heard of the prophecy."

All eyes turned to him. "What do you mean?" Stacy asked.

Rowan looked solemn. "I heard parts of it from your mother, and the elf queen had heard of it, too. It was why she was so interested in meeting you. I'm sorry for not telling you before we went to meet her. I don't quite believe the prophecy myself, and I didn't want to bring anything unnecessary up. I've never been one to have much faith in prophecies."

"I'm with Rowan," Kiera spoke up. "As far as I know, most prophecies are bullshit made up by sects with agendas. Maybe this one is true, but why does it matter? You'll keep doing you whether that fulfills a prophecy or not."

Stacy wasn't sure if Kiera's words comforted her or added to the burden of the Drakethorn legacy she already felt. Her mind was still stuck on what Rowan said about her mother. Her heart thudded faster. She glanced at Ethan for his opinion, but he remained silent.

"I don't know if Catherine believed it, either," Rowan supplied. "But she may have set things up for your life in a certain way in case it was."

"It might not be a bad idea to ask your father about it," Kiera suggested. "If your mother did believe in the prophecy, she might have said something to him."

Cold realization settled over Stacy. Maybe her mother had, and Khan's efforts through the years to keep her magic from her and protect her had been about more than simply keeping her safe and alive.

Her first inclination was to march over there and ask him immediately, but it wouldn't work that way. Khan might not be willing to expose the whole truth. "Not yet," she told Kiera. "I want to unravel more of this before I go to him. Besides, we have the vampires to deal with."

"They might be connected," Kiera replied. "If not for that, I wouldn't have bothered bringing up the prophecy." She stood and began pacing, her arms folded over one another so her hands held her elbows. "Adrian helped me find books on vampires, too. He had more on the topic than I dreamed I would find there.

"That's why I didn't come back until tonight. In one of the books, I found sources that discuss where vampires come from. Like fae, elves, sidhe, and most shifters, they come from another world. Only witches, sorcerers, and the like have always lived here, morphing from humans or coming from a line where a human and a magical mated. I knew that already, but what I found next was new and alarming."

She paused, turning to meet Stacy's eye. "Records throughout history show that shifters and other kinds began showing up in this world as early as the Roman empire, but it seems vampires came long before that. They may be among the first magicals to ever set foot in this world.

"They come from a world called Malabbra, which in the language of dark magic simply means 'darkness.' Dark magic itself is sometimes referred to as 'malabbra,' presumably because that world is full of it. I wonder if this is linked to the prophecy."

Did the darkness spoken of in the prophecy reference the world vampires came from?

Stacy's mind raced with new thoughts. "I wonder if vampires were the ones who came to my mother's land and killed her coven."

"I don't think it was vampires," Rowan stated. "The darkness your mother faced was more abstract than that, and if it was vampires, your father would have said so. No, what they dealt with was otherworldly in a non-solidified way. It was more like battling a force than a living creature."

"But maybe that darkness came from the same world as the vampires," Kiera prompted.

The room fell silent except for the crackling of flames. Ethan broke the spell. "You mean to say the world of the vampires isn't home to only them?"

Kiera shrugged. "Could be. The fae have legends in their world about a source of darkness in a far-off place that spawned several different creatures. Vampires, what humans call demons, and more. Maybe vampires came from whatever that world was and are the first signs of evil leaking into the human world."

Stacy felt like her mind had been blown wide open. She didn't give a fuck about the prophecy, but she suddenly sensed her world had grown much larger. The issue with the vampires wasn't merely about finding missing people and bringing the perpetrators to justice. She swallowed, then held Kiera's gaze. "Then we must get rid of them as soon as we can."

Kiera nodded. "I knew you would say that, so as part of my research, I tried to figure out what to do next. Adrian mentioned a contact of his who might be able to give you more information on why the vampires came here specifically and what they might be doing. Adrian seems to think his contact hears and sees things that might be of value."

"I don't see how the librarian has any contacts if he's been underground for centuries," Ethan murmured.

Rowan smiled faintly. "Very old friends, I presume."

"Who is this contact?" Stacy asked.

"A Scottish gnome by the name of Father Angus McFadden," Kiera answered. "Yes, he's a priest, and his church is in the city. Adrian gave me the address and a strange tidbit. Father McFadden doesn't like to be visited about anything unrelated to the church unless it's nighttime."

"Weird," Stacy replied.

"You can go there tomorrow night," Rowan suggested as Kiera fished a piece of paper from her pocket and handed it to Stacy. The handwriting was not Kiera's, so Stacy assumed it was Adrian's. She'd never seen such elegant writing, not even her mother's.

"I will," Stacy agreed.

"He gave me another warning about the priest," Kiera continued. "Apparently, the gnome has a penchant for hard drinking. He isn't always the best conversationalist."

"Says an underground recluse," Ethan retorted, earning chuckles from Stacy and Rowan. "How do we know Adrian's contact is still there?"

"Only one way to find out." Stacy stood at last. "Do you want to come with me?" she asked Ethan, who nodded.

"Of course I do. How could I pass up a nighttime encounter with an alcoholic gnome?"

Kiera snorted. "I hope you know Scottish accents well. If he's drunk and hasn't adopted an American speech pattern, he'll be impossible to understand."

"I'll be your driver tomorrow night," Rowan stated. Stacy was unsure if this was an offer or a command.

"I'll come along, too," Kiera offered.

Rowan gave her a look. "You should take a night off, Kiera. You've done enough."

"He's right," Stacy agreed. "You've done a lot for me. I won't forget you giving up a family heirloom to get into that library. It was more than you should have done."

Kiera shrugged. "Adrian will appreciate it more than I ever did."

Stacy caught a hint of regret in Kiera's voice, but she didn't push the subject. "You've been up a long time, Kiera. Please go and rest if you want."

Kiera gave her a grateful smile. "I'll admit I've been thinking about rolling into bed since I came in here." She bade them all goodnight, then left the library.

Stacy turned to Ethan and Rowan. "We should head up, too. We'll plan our nighttime adventure in the morning?"

The men agreed, and Stacy left the room with dozens of questions and thoughts swirling around her mind. The vampires. The gnome. That damn prophecy. Her mother's secrets. She didn't want to think about anything right now.

When she slid into bed, she was happy to fall into slumber.

CHAPTER EIGHT

"Can't say I've ever been to church in the middle of the night," Ethan remarked. "A bit creepy, isn't it?"

He and Stacy stood at the gate of St. Pious Cathedral. Rowan was parked across the street, waiting for them and keeping watch. The night wind blew fallen leaves down the sidewalk and gathered them around Stacy's boots.

"I think it's because the building is so old," Stacy replied.

The stone cathedral was one of the oldest buildings in this part of the city, if not the oldest. Arched, stained-glass windows told the story of Saint Pious, and the closed wooden doors looked like something out of Medieval times. A wrought iron fence ran the perimeter of the small yard where aged statues adorned with moss were scattered.

Something about the place seemed to demand silence, and not in a reverent fashion. Stacy wasn't inclined to go inside the church and kneel before an altar with organ music playing, even during the day. Was it the age or something else?

She shivered. The place was probably full of ghosts. They didn't scare her, but the thought of something watching her that she couldn't see unnerved her.

"You think the priest is old?" Ethan asked. "Gnomes live a long time."

"Probably. We won't be going into the church, though." Stacy pointed toward a smaller building outside the gate and to the right. The part of the parish where the priest presumably lived was a tiny stone house that looked like it was built around the same time as the cathedral itself.

Stacy and Ethan took a cobblestone path off the sidewalk leading to the house and halted at the front door. Stacy knocked, hoping they would meet with a pleasant old gnome and not a grump they'd awakened from a deep sleep. Since the librarian insisted Father Angus McFadden would only meet about matters unrelated to the church in the dead of night, this was the only time to come.

I hope Adrian wasn't pulling a practical joke, Stacy thought. A long silence passed, so she knocked again. Finally, a grumbling man's voice reached them from the other side of the door.

"What in the turd-blowin', muck-stirrin', toad-toe-wartin' is that?" At least, Stacy thought she heard that. He muttered without pausing between words as if the string of pseudo-profanities were one sentence. The door jerked open, and a male gnome stood behind it, barely four feet tall. His bright red nose made Stacy wonder if he'd drunk sacramental wine from a cup too large for his face.

He glared up at them. "What in storming fuck do ya want? Can't a man be left to his bed in the middle of the damn night?"

Stacy winced, fearing the whole nearby neighborhood would wake at his bellowing. The gnome was holding a liquor bottle, though, so she doubted he'd been asleep. She noted his ruddy complexion, dark robes, and a black beard laced with gray.

"Hello, Mr. McFadden. I'm sorry to disturb you," Stacy replied as his gray eyes narrowed on her shrewdly. She felt as though she couldn't get the words out fast enough. "You are the priest, right?"

"*I sure hope I am!*" the gnome bellowed. "*What do you want?*"

Stacy was beginning to think this had been a mistake, but they'd already come this far. "Adrian sent us."

The gnome's eyes widened until she thought they might bulge from his head. "That damn librarian! Haven't heard from him in over fifty years. 'Course he'd send somebody else and not come here himself! Is the bastard still alive?"

"He is," Stacy confirmed.

The gnome seemed uninterested in knowing how Stacy had come across the elusive sidhe. "Well, whatever ol' Adrian sent ya here for, it musta been important, though I can't promise I can help ya." The priest moved aside and ushered them in.

The house's interior was dark except for a low burning candle on the kitchen table and a small fire in the living room hearth. It was small and cramped but homey and cozy. Or it would have been if not for the abundance of *things* piled everywhere. Stacy wasn't sure she'd seen anywhere more cluttered.

It wasn't like a hoarder's nest or a particularly disorganized person's space. Everything was neatly stacked on shelves, inside an abundance of old trunks, or placed in rows along the wall. Rugs dotted the wooden floors, and several old paintings and photographs adorned the walls over faded floral wallpaper. Scraps of paper with various writing were scattered around the room, and Stacy stopped counting how many bibles he had after she reached seven.

She was so busy registering her surroundings that she didn't notice the gnome was asking her a question until Ethan nudged her with his elbow. "Mr. McFadden would like to know if you want something to drink, Stacy."

She turned to see her only options were tap water from a rusty sink or a swig of something off the liquor shelf. "No, thank you, Mr. McFadden."

The gnome's inside voice wasn't much different than his

outside voice, though now his volume was cheerful instead of angry. "Oh please, call me Angus! All my friends call me Angus."

That was easy, Stacy thought. They were already friends.

"What're yer names?" the gnome demanded as he swigged from his bottle.

"Stacy." She stepped forward and offered her hand. The gnome shook it firmly. "This is Ethan." She wasn't sure if she was supposed to introduce him as a friend, colleague, or something more, so she added nothing.

Ethan smiled, also shaking the gnome's hand. "Pleased to meet you, Angus."

"Come in, come in!" Angus insisted, gesturing for them to follow into his quaint living room. Two large armchairs sat on either side of the fire, overflowing with pillows and blankets. Several cushions littered the floor. "Now, what did ol' Adrian send you two kids here fer?" Angus asked after taking a swig from a dark brown bottle.

Stacy explained the situation involving the vampires but left out the details about the strange prophecy Adrian had shared with Kiera. Until they found a definite connection, she didn't plan to give it much consideration. When she finished, Angus chuckled. "Me and dem vampires have a shared love of blood. Though my love is fer my savior, nothin' more."

Stacy wondered how true this could be since he was a priest and believed the sacramental wine was Jesus' actual blood. She didn't ask. Angus didn't give room for questions, anyway.

He seemed to quickly forget everything she'd said about vampires and launched into a monologue about how he'd grown up in Scotland and found a love for the clergy when he was young. "I ended up o'er here not long ago. 'Bout three hundred years I've been here, but only fifty as the priest."

Stacy smothered her amusement about what certain magicals considered a "long time." She and Ethan shared a glance, trying not to smile.

"Adrian was my first friend in the city," Angus continued. "But he kicked me out of his library for bringin' my flask around." He held up his bottle for emphasis, then realized it wasn't his flask. He began rooting around in the armchairs, flinging cushions over his shoulder. Ethan dodged one, and Stacy slapped a hand to her mouth to keep from laughing.

"Where'd the damn thing go?" Angus muttered, then found a flash of silver between cushions. "Aha! This is the one!" He held it up before continuing. "Anyway, Adrian said if I was gonna drink every time I came 'round, I might as well not come 'round. That was 'bout fifty years ago, and I haven't seen 'im since."

Stacy's impression from Kiera's story was that Adrian was a bit too uptight, but she didn't blame the sidhe for not wanting a drunk, overly jovial gnome around his precious tomes. "Adrian seems to think you can tell us something he doesn't know about the vampires. Such as how long they have been in this city and why they might be here," Stacy explained as Angus unscrewed his flask.

He tipped it to his mouth, found it empty, and cursed, throwing it back in the chair. He snatched his bottle from where he'd set it on a stool and took another swig. Finally, he replied, "Vampires have always lived in this city. At least as long as I've been here. In groups, though they keep mostly to themselves. You'd never know they were here."

"We knew of one, though," Ethan spoke up. "Have you heard of a vampire assassin called Isadora Voss?"

"Of course I have! Everyone has."

Stacy and Ethan shared another look before Angus barreled on.

"Damn toad-wartin', troll-turd-suckin' assassin, she was. Never met her, and damn glad for it! She mighta been a vampire, but them blood-suckin' motherfuckers banished her for one reason or another. Can't say why. Never cared to learn." Another swig.

ISABEL CAMPBELL & MICHAEL ANDERLE

They couldn't ask her now, Stacy thought. Voss was dead.

"'Fraid I can't tell ya anythin' else. These disappearances you told me about haven't reached my ears until tonight."

Stacy frowned. The TV mounted to the wall was on, and the news was playing. Had he not paid attention to it? Perhaps he was drinking enough not to remember what he was watching. Though she felt slight disappointment, Stacy knew they'd made a new ally.

"I'll tell ya if I hear of anythin' else," Angus added. "Somethin' might come to me."

Stacy smiled. "We would appreciate that." She drew a card from her pocket. "This has my phone number on it. Feel free to call if you would like."

Angus squinted at her name and the number. Then, with a gasp that sounded half like a belch, he exclaimed, "Drakethorn!" His gaze snapped to hers. "That's you?"

Stacy nodded, still smiling. "Anastasia Drakethorn."

Angus slapped a palm against his forehead, dropping the card on the floor. "If I'd known I'd was invitin' a dragon into my home, I woulda prepared better than this!" He laughed, waving a dismissive hand. "No matter. Long as you don't burn the place down."

Stacy shared his amusement. "I'll try my best not to, Angus." He was a strange fellow, and she was tempted to take his half-empty bottle and smash it against the wall, but he was endearing in a way. Stacy felt like she had known him all her life. He was like the weird uncle at family holiday gatherings. A year without him seemed too quiet, but everyone was glad when he'd gone home.

"We should be going now," she told their host. "Thank you for everything."

"I'll see you again, Drakethorn!" he called after them as they walked toward the front door. They opened it and left with the gnome still muttering behind them about where in all the troll-turd caves his flask had gone.

When they were on the sidewalk away from the parish, Stacy laughed hard enough to hold her stomach. A similar sound sputtered from Ethan. "I don't know what I was expecting, but that was not it," he commented. "Did you notice he finished the bottle in the twenty minutes we were there?"

Stacy was close to tears from laughing so hard. "It felt much longer than twenty minutes. I won't forget him anytime soon. Good thing Rowan didn't go in with us."

Her amusement vanished the second she glanced across the street to where Rowan had parked and realized the car was not there. She pulled her phone from her pocket to see if he had called or texted about a change in plans but saw nothing. She called him. The phone rang and rang, but no one answered.

"Shit, something happened to Rowan." Stacy had no sooner gotten the words out than Ethan cried out as someone slammed into him from behind.

She whirled to see a darkly clad figure barreling toward her. She spun out of the way, not thinking as she summoned a magic shield around her. She struck out with grappling techniques, getting her attacker to back off, but it only worked for so long. The figure launched at her again, brandishing a blade. Stacy kicked up, hitting the attacker's arm hard enough to send the knife flying. The attacker snarled.

She didn't have time to see what had become of Ethan and his assailant. She was too busy fending off the second one. Growling, she sent flashes of light at her opponent. The lithe figure ducked and spun with a grace Stacy had seen before. *From Voss!*

Grunting beside her signaled Ethan was still conscious, at least. She battered her assailant with magical blow after blow until, finally, the creature turned and fled. She spun back to Ethan, breathing hard. "You fucker," she hissed at the other

ISABEL CAMPBELL & MICHAEL ANDERLE

attacker. He realized his companion had fled and turned to do the same.

Stacy struck out with her magic, but the figure evaded it with ease, then vanished into the darkness behind the parish. She had half a mind to chase them, but she was more concerned about Ethan.

"Are you okay?" she asked as she turned. Ethan was on his feet, grim-faced and wincing. "You're bleeding!" Stacy exclaimed at the sight of red blooming across the back of his arm.

"Nothing serious," he gritted out. "That fucker's nails were like knives. Healing magic and some herbs from Kiera will do the trick, though." His gaze met hers. "You think those were vampires?"

"They fought like Voss did," Stacy replied. "I wouldn't be surprised if they were. Do you think they were trying to kill or kidnap us?"

"They might have simply wanted to provoke us into a fight," Ethan suggested.

Stacy didn't see why their attackers would want to do any of the above. They had to get out of here. *Hard to do when our car and driver are missing,* she thought. She was distracted by Ethan bending to pick up a fallen piece of paper. He held it up to a dim streetlight so they could read the crudely scrawled words on it.

Last warning, Drakethorn. We're coming. Stay out of our way.

Stacy's blood boiled. She was convinced the attackers had been vampires, but why make themselves so obvious to her? She shook her head. "I don't understand—"

"Look, there's Rowan!" Ethan interrupted.

Stacy spied her car coming around the corner with Rowan at the wheel. He squealed to a stop and rolled the window down. "What the hell, Rowan!" Stacy called as she marched toward the car.

"I know, I know. Something happened. Better get in the car. We're not safe here. I'll explain on the way." Rowan's voice was firm and urgent enough for Stacy not to ask questions until they were in the car and pulling away.

"I was sitting there, parked as normal," he explained. "Then, out of nowhere, a driver in another car attacked me. He rammed against me, then sped off. The car will need body repairs, but nothing too serious."

"I don't care about that right now. I'm glad you're safe."

"I saw someone else coming and figured I'd better circle the block, hopefully shake them, and come back," Rowan added. "Apparently, they saw that as an opportunity to get you two. I'm sorry."

"Don't be," Stacy told him. "You did what you thought was best. We handled it anyway." She showed him the card the thugs had left, then shared what they learned from the priest.

Rowan clenched the steering wheel, his knuckles turning white. "I don't like this one bit, Stacy. I want to find out the truth as much as you do, but the further we get into this mystery, the worse it seems."

"We have to find those vampires," she insisted. "Tomorrow, I'm taking a closer look at those missing persons cases and seeing if I can spot any patterns the police missed."

"You think you can?" Rowan asked. "The police have combed over those files many times."

"I have to," Stacy stated. "They're coming to this city for a reason, and I intend to find out." She didn't care that they'd told her to stay out of their way. She planned on getting in their way as much as possible. *There's no room in this city for a vampire cult and a dragon,* she thought. *One of us has got to go.*

CHAPTER NINE

Birds outside Stacy's office window chirped, and the sprites along the window sill played a game of tag. Sunlight flooded the old shed she'd converted into a workspace, but Stacy's mind wasn't on the pleasantness of the morning.

She sifted through several files, all from public records on the missing persons cases. Ethan stood beside her, rifling through the papers with the same intention—to find patterns and clues why the vampires had taken these people specifically.

It might be random, she admitted inwardly, but the vampires' work so far had been intentional and clever. The police were no closer to answers, and Stacy was beginning to feel she wouldn't find any either. Not this way. The missing people ranged from children to adults with different backgrounds and ethnicities.

"There has to be a connection here!" she declared at last, fists perched on her hips. "Unfortunately, it's not an obvious one."

Ethan sank into a chair, raking a hand through his hair. "I agree. I can't see one either, and my brain feels like mush." They'd been at this for almost two hours with nothing but a disorganized mess of papers to show for it. Stacy had several open tabs on her laptop with social media pages belonging to the victims.

Many of them displayed posts from their families with photos of the missing person and something about them. The comments were flooded with sympathy.

Stacy's attention lingered the longest on a photo of a young Shinnecock woman. She was only twenty years old. She sighed and sank into her chair. "We might need another set of eyes on this. Someone who knows what they're doing better than we do. It's time to call Amy."

When Amy answered the phone, Stacy asked where she was.

"About to take my lunch break at the dojo," Amy replied. "What's up?"

"We're onto something big, but the answer is out of reach. I need another set of eyes on this." Stacy remained vague with her comments. Rowan had updated Amy and Miles on everything that happened so far, and Stacy didn't want to say anything specific over the phone. "I can send everything over to you soon. The 'why' right now isn't so much the issue but 'who.' And Amy, this goes nowhere, okay?"

Amy's voice sounded with enthusiastic readiness. "I'm on it, Stace. Discretion is my middle name."

"Thanks a mil, Amy. You're the best," Stacy replied, then hung up.

"You know, I could go for some lunch, too," Ethan drawled, tugging Stacy toward him by the back of her thigh. They'd been getting more affectionate when they were alone. Though Stacy wished they could go back to making out on his couch, she had settled for occasional small touches for the time being. His fingers gripping the back of her leg sent a jolt of pleasant warmth up one side of her body. "You think Kiera has those sandwiches ready?" he asked.

Stacy smiled and bent to brush her lips across his cheek. "Only one way to find out." As they walked from her office, she wondered how a conversation about BLTs could feel so seductive. *Get ahold of yourself,* Stacy commanded inwardly. *You've got work to do.* Her stomach rumbled with sharp demand. *But first, eat.*

Stacy and Ethan weren't the only ones looking forward to Kiera's BLTs, egg salad sandwiches, and salad topped with roasted almonds and olive oil. Rowan was already in the kitchen when they appeared, carrying a plate of six stacked sandwiches. A seventh was stuffed halfway into his mouth.

"Any luck?" the dryad asked when his mouth was no longer full.

"Unfortunately, no," Stacy replied with a sigh. "But I'm having Amy look over everything in case there's something we missed."

"Actually, there is one other thing," Ethan mentioned.

Stacy turned to him with a questioning eye.

"I got a text from Vi. I called her yesterday to see if she could be of any help. She was difficult, of course, but said she'd pass along anything she thought might help."

"And?" Stacy prodded.

Ethan reread a text, then slipped the phone back into his pocket. "I don't know why I didn't think of it myself, but Vi suggested we visit the Midnight Market."

Rowan nearly choked on his sandwich.

"What's the Midnight Market?" Stacy asked. "And why does mention of it make me think one of us will have to give Rowan CPR?" The dryad started coughing and ran for a glass of water.

"It's only open at night and run by paranormal overseers. The whole operation is highly illegal," Ethan explained. "Any sort of black-market magical drug you could want will be there."

"Along with lethal weapons and a wide variety of special poisons," Rowan added. "Kiera goes for that reason."

"Does Miles go for the drugs?" Stacy asked, half-joking.

"Mead, actually," Rowan replied lightly.

"Do *you* go?"

"There's been an occasion or two."

She glanced at Ethan. "And you?"

Ethan simply grinned and shrugged. "All of us end up there at one time or another. When we're young and stupid and looking for a good time."

Stacy rolled her eyes. "You mean to say while I was smoking weed in some computer geek's basement in college on a Saturday night, you were marching around a magical nighttime market?"

Ethan cringed. "I'd rather not revisit those memories, but yes."

"It's a dangerous place if you don't watch yourself," Rowan told her. "I'm surprised you haven't heard of it by now."

Stacy couldn't help a nervous chuckle. "Why, dear Rowan, would a nice girl like me know about a dangerous, illegal market that's only open at night?"

Rowan didn't miss a beat as he shared a knowing smile. "Because even *nice girls* must venture into the shadows to bring light to the truth." His smile faded. "The market has strange, complex rules of trade. To become a vendor there, you need a certain type of…reputation."

Stacy snorted. "Not one I have, I take it?"

Rowan's half-smile was answer enough.

She glanced at Ethan. "What's this have to do with Vi?"

Ethan pushed off the counter where he'd been eating a sandwich and placed his empty plate in the sink. "Viper frequents the market and is one of their oldest vendors. That's how I met her. She used to own a club named after her. The Viper's Den. The coven I belonged to went there nearly every Friday. Can't say I'd like to share the stories about what went on there. Weird shit. She closed the place down after racking up more debt than she could pay off. She has a lot of friends."

"And enemies, it sounds like," Stacy inserted.

Ethan nodded. "Anyway, there's an old fae vendor who's had multiple run-ins with vampires. She thinks if anyone could tell you something, it's him."

First Adrian, then Father McFadden. Now, a pointy-eared guy

at an illegal nighttime market. Would they ever find someone who could tell them everything they needed to know?

Stacy sighed. They wouldn't. That was how shit like this worked. She'd have to find puzzle pieces in every corner of the city before she put the whole picture together. She hoped it wouldn't be too late for the victims who'd been taken before she finished it and hunted the blood-drinking bastards down.

"It won't be easy," Rowan stated. He leaned against the kitchen counter and folded his arms. "Everything in the Midnight Market comes at a price."

"Even information?" Stacy asked.

"Especially information," the dryad replied. "If it's a faerie you're going to, you might be asked to hand over something of deep, personal value. Something enigmatic." He gestured into the hallway. "Like your mother's wooden keepsake box or special water from one of the estate's trees."

Stacy touched the gold chain around her neck. "As long as I don't have to give this up."

"Of course not," Rowan agreed. "Maybe don't wear that or keep it out of sight. If you're going to the Market, you'll need to conceal your true identity, too. The folks there don't take kindly to power plays and the proud and wealthy walking around like they're above everyone else."

"I don't act like that," Stacy protested. She paused. "Do I?"

"You don't, but that's not the point," Ethan told her. "The Drakethorn name is enough for the vendors to make assumptions. The Market has no shortage of spies. Best you go as Stacy and leave the last name out of it."

"Your face isn't recognizable enough yet," Rowan added. "If you're worried about it, though, Kiera can glamour some of your features."

Stacy considered the plan. It didn't sound ideal, but it was something. *I can't keep running into dead ends,* she thought.

Miles called from the garden for Rowan, and the dryad left.

"What are you thinking?" Ethan prodded when they were alone.

She sighed. "That I was hoping our next night on the town would be our first date, not a visit to the Midnight Market in search of vampire abductors."

He brushed her arm. "We'll have our date, I promise."

"First, vampires." Stacy hoped Viper's contact would give them something. *Anything.*

They could go tonight and hope that by the morning, Amy would find a connection between the missing people.

Stacy headed out of the kitchen. "I guess I'd better go find a deeply personal possession to give away. What will I choose?"

CHAPTER TEN

It was a rare occasion when Stacy drove her own car, especially going into New York City. Rowan was not going with them despite being her official driver and bodyguard. "I had one or two...incidents in the Midnight Market many years ago that the superiors there will not soon forget," he'd said. "I would only be impeding your mission by tagging along."

The revelation had surprised Stacy. It was difficult to wrap her mind around a version of Rowan who was irresponsible or faced consequences from an authority figure. She supposed someone could change when they'd been alive for five hundred years. The Rowan she knew now was not the same who'd frequented their destination.

Ethan sat in the passenger seat, giving Stacy directions from a map of aged parchment that was more cryptic clues than actual direction. "I know of one way to get into the market," Ethan explained as Stacy drove through the countryside toward the city. "But it only opens on the full moon, and since there is no full moon tonight, we'll have to find another way."

Rowan had supplied the map. He'd said he hadn't used it in a long time, but the market seldom changed its rules, so he thought it would still help. Stacy hoped so.

Before long, they reached a wealthy neighborhood of white houses arranged in neat rows, with manicured hedges and shrubbery flanking small iron gates leading to pristine porches. To Stacy, it looked like something out of a movie set. Ethan directed her to park at the end of one street so they could walk to the other end, where the map seemed to indicate an opening.

"What kind of opening?" Stacy asked as she put the car into park. "Will a portal open up and suck us into another dimension? The Midnight Market dimension?" She chuckled. "These houses and talk of a hidden magical place remind me of *The Twilight Zone.*"

"Let's hope we aren't in *The Twilight Zone*. That theme music always gave me the creeps as a kid," Ethan replied.

Stacy hummed the theme, earning a scowl from Ethan, who added, "No portal. We're looking for an invisible doorway, and this map has several spells we can try to open it." He tapped the paper. "The trick will be figuring out which spell goes to this opening."

"How many openings are there?" Stacy asked.

"Over a dozen throughout the city. Probably more elsewhere, if we looked."

"We only need one," Stacy pointed out.

They exited the car, and Stacy stole another glance at Ethan. Every time she looked at him, she noticed the slight cosmetic reworking Kiera had done to his face with illusion magic. His eyes were blue instead of brown, and his face was thinner.

She'd made more adjustments to Stacy's appearance. Dark brown hair instead of her usual auburn, a longer nose, erasure of her freckles, and a lift of her eyebrows. Though small, the changes were enough to ensure anyone who knew Stacy Drakethorn's face wouldn't recognize her. Not without looking closely, anyway.

"This way." Ethan pointed down the street.

It was quiet with the residents inside their homes for the night. Anyone who peered out their window would have seen what appeared to be a couple out for a walk. The pair approached a small park with an ivy-wrapped iron archway entrance. They stopped short, and Ethan peered at the parchment under the glow of a lone streetlamp. "This should be it. Now, which spell should I use?"

Stacy wasn't sure how she felt about the stillness surrounding them. A slight breeze blew into her hair, tickling her neck, but there was hardly any other sound. At least until snickers sounded behind her. She turned to find three young men coming up the street, laughing with one another in low voices. Stacy sensed they were paranormal like her and Ethan, though she didn't know what kind.

Please, I don't want to deal with fucking werewolves tonight, she thought.

"Well, well, what do we have here?" one of the young men inquired as they sauntered to the archway where Stacy and Ethan lingered. "Goin' on a midnight stroll?"

"I could ask the same of you," Stacy replied evenly.

"We're on our way to a party." A tall blond man in the group jerked his head toward the archway. "Seems like you are, too."

"No party," she told him.

"What is someone pretty as you doin' with this nerd?" another young man asked, jerking a thumb at Ethan.

Ethan glanced up from his parchment, frowning. His round glasses and sweater rolled up to the elbows didn't look nerdy to Stacy. "You know, using 'nerd' as an insult makes you sound like a middle-schooler," Ethan drawled.

She folded her arms. "Look, we're busy. Go find someone else to bother."

The first young man laughed. "But this is much more fun than anything else we've done tonight. Come on, go to the party with us. It's in this club that—"

The third man jabbed the first with an elbow. "She don't need to know where we're goin'. She may not be able to, anyway. How do we know she's a—"

"She is. So is the guy," the first man stated.

Stacy caught a flash of silver as the second man drew a knife. He was going to fucking mug them! Gold flashed in her eyes as she snarled, "I said back *off*."

Slight fear flickered in the blond man's eyes. He put up his hands. "All right, lady. Chill. We'll go."

The men muttered to one another, and Stacy caught more than one "bitch" under their breaths. They went away, though. She was half-tempted to chase after them and show them exactly what screwing with her meant. She turned to Ethan and sighed. "I hope the people we have to deal with inside the market aren't like that."

"Depends," Ethan told her. "Some might be worse. Most people won't bother talking to us, though. Not unless we're trying to buy something." He tapped the paper again. "I think I figured out which spell to use."

Ethan cleared his throat and spoke an incantation. Stacy waited, breath held. The air rippled around them, and she gasped as a barely visible shimmering substance appeared in the archway. Ethan smiled. "Well, that was easier than I thought. Now, it's as simple as stepping through."

Stacy arched a brow, half-expecting the wall of magic to zap them instead. Ethan took her hand and brushed a thumb along the back of her palm for comfort. "Ready?" he asked.

She nodded.

Stepping through the archway felt no different than if it had been clear air instead of magic. The neighborhood melted away, and rather than a wide green park, a whole new sight met her eyes. Stacy could hardly believe what she was seeing.

The Midnight Market formed gradually. Rather than springing to life before her eyes, Stacy slowly became aware of every aspect. The road was a smooth, glossy black substance reflecting the warm lights bobbing above it.

Tightly-packed buildings flanked both sides of the road. Some were made of stone, others brick. Several looked like old wooden taverns. Cloth-covered and wood-framed canvas market booths stood between the buildings. The vendors were raucous with their haggling and declaration of their goods. The streets were as packed with people as Times Square.

The main difference was that people here didn't bother disguising who they truly were. Stacy gaped at werewolves in full animal form, ambling past her. A witch wearing a pointed hat and carrying a broom strode by on her left. Stacy couldn't believe it. She didn't know witches like that existed. *I guess stereotypes are a thing for a reason,* she thought.

Stacy laughed inwardly at the thought of soaring through here in dragon form but remembered Rowan's and Ethan's comments about being a Drakethorn in a place like this. Tonight, she needed to be Stacy Drake.

A smile crept across her lips. "This is amazing."

Ethan chuckled, still holding her hand. "You haven't seen anything yet. This is where all the shitty stuff is sold. Greasy food, cheap jewelry, and all that. Let's head up the street so you can see the river."

"The *what*?"

Ethan simply smiled and tugged her along. They wove through the crowd with relative ease. The other paranormals frequenting the market paid little attention to the passing witches. It wasn't long before the street widened and ascended to a square where a large stone fountain rose in the center, spouting blue and purple glowing water. In front of the fountain, two flute players held a small audience in rapt interest.

Stacy would have liked to hear the tune, but Ethan directed

her down a steep pathway to a strip of cobblestones beside a curving river. It was the clearest body of water Stacy had ever seen. It reflected the stars above so vividly it was like looking into the night sky.

She suddenly realized how warm she felt and caught the sweet smells in the air. "It's almost like summer here," she remarked.

Ethan nodded. "That's because it is." He pointed at a stone bridge going across the river. "See there? That's the winter side."

Stacy gawked at the sight of roofs laden with snow and people walking around in coats and boots on the other side of the river. "How is that possible?"

"The market has two halves," Ethan explained. "Summer on this side and winter over there. The river splits it down the middle. Pieces of the fae realm overlap here. With some complex magic, luck, and the right timing, one could slip from here into the fae world. Many have tried." Ethan paused. "And failed. The fae guard their world well."

"I don't know why they would want overlap here, then," Stacy commented as Ethan led them toward the bridge.

"They don't exactly have a choice. It happens sometimes. Worlds are connected by the same lines of magic and exist in parallel, either side by side or stacked. Imagine the human world is a piece of paper, and the Midnight Market is another lying on top of it. The fae world is a third but shifted over. The fae figured they might as well have their influence over this in-between pocket." Ethan waved a hand. "Hence, two of their courts represented in this place. Summer and winter."

Stacy was enthralled. "So, is the river water warm or cold?"

Ethan chuckled. "You don't want to find out. Dipping into the river would be the magical version of getting an electric shock. The magical energies of the human and fae world converge here, and it happens in the river. You don't want to dip your toe in, let alone go swimming."

He tugged her onto the bridge. "I know we would both prefer to stay on the summer side, but Vi's contact is a fae from the winter court."

"We didn't dress for this," Stacy protested.

"Sure we did. What do you think the warming enchantments for our clothes were for?"

Another thing Kiera had done for them before they left. Apparently, Rowan, Kiera, Miles, and Ethan thought it best to explain little of the Midnight Market to Stacy before she went, preferring that she experience it firsthand.

At first, Stacy did not think of this place in the ways Rowan and Ethan had described it: dangerous and full of dark dealings and ominous whispers. She then remembered the cruelty of the fae world. Sure, their beauty influenced this place, but perhaps the ruthlessness of their overall kind existed here, too. *Better be aware,* Stacy told herself as they crossed the arched bridge over the river.

She felt a blast of cold as soon as they stepped foot off the bridge. The main similarity between this region of the Midnight Market and the last was the same paved black road. It shimmered and hummed with magic. Everything here did. Having been in the human world her whole life, Stacy felt she would grow sick after being here for too long.

Ethan consulted an address written on a card in Viper's handwriting, directing them toward the end of the Winter Market, where they would meet her fae contact. Stacy thought a walk through snowy streets would be unappealing, but she soon found herself enjoying every step.

Many vendors had wheelbarrows or push carts loaded with supplies in addition to booths along the narrow streets. Everything from spiced drinks to sweet treats to unnamed bottled liquids at an obscene price were available. Stacy felt like she could spend all night merely looking at everything.

They entered a different part of the winter side. Here, various colored lights flooded the buildings. Blues, greens, pinks, and purples leaked onto the streets and glimmered off the icicles hanging from roofs. Pulsating music flowed, and Stacy spied several dancing figures through windows hazy with colored smoke. The clubs.

Ethan pointed to a particular place. "Viper's den used to be here. It's now a fighting ring organized by a group of shifters. We definitely won't be going in there tonight."

Several figures stood outside the buildings, pressed close in the shadows, and engaged in what appeared to be covert dealings. Anyone who caught Stacy glancing in their direction scowled.

At the end of the street, Ethan veered left down a pathway lined with smaller buildings, quieter music, and patrons speaking in hushed tones. "Here we are," Ethan stated at last, halting before a tall building with a line of people outside that wrapped around the corner. The building was nondescript, with no sign indicating what attracted all these people.

"Fortune teller," Ethan clarified at the puzzlement on Stacy's face.

"That's who we're here to see?" She waved a hand at the crowd. "We'll be here *forever*. This guy is popular!"

"I meant the fortune teller is why all these people are here. Vi's contact also works inside this building, but he conducts other business. Something a little darker. He's a secrets seller."

Stacy arched a brow. "Whatever the hell that means. Can we get through this crowd?" They strode forward but soon needed to nudge people aside. Many did not appreciate this.

"Hey, watch it!"

"Back of the line, bitch."

"What do they think they're doing? They're cutting!"

Ethan ignored them, but Stacy felt inclined to give one or two a piece of her mind. Ethan pulled her by the hand through the crowd, and soon, they were ducking into the dim building. It smelled like spices and sweet-scented smoke. The odors were so strong that Stacy coughed as soon as they entered. A staircase led to a second floor, where soft voices could be heard. A hallway bathed in red light led to a back room where, instead of a door, a tapestry separated it from the hall.

Many were loitering in the hall, smoking and laughing. Not everyone was having an amusing conversation, though. Stacy's gait slowed as she caught words between two figures standing in a darkened corner. "Europeans, I heard. A faction of them come over here to piss all over us. No one's seen them yet. Won't be long, though."

The other figure cursed. "Blood-sucking motherfuckers. Why couldn't they stay where they came from?"

A chill darted up Stacy's spine. News of the creatures had reached this place, too. That was good for their meeting, at least. The secrets seller was bound to know something.

They reached the tapestry, and Ethan pulled it aside so they had room to step in. The next room seemed small and empty at first. An ornate chair sat behind a round table covered in woven cloth. Upon the table were several strange trinkets, all reeking of ancient magic. Stacy thought she and Ethan were alone until an oily voice spoke at her neck.

"You aren't supposed to be in here."

Stacy spun, gaping at the sight of a tall, thin figure wearing a red robe. He was fae, but she could only tell by one pointed ear. The other was missing. His smooth face was the color of ivory, and his crystal-blue eyes seemed to read every emotion that crossed Stacy's face. Though not a wrinkle was visible on his skin, his eyes revealed his age. They spoke of years of gathering knowledge. Secrets, she remembered.

"I'm closed tonight. Come back another time," the creature added stiffly, brushing past Stacy.

Stacy was undaunted. She cleared her throat, allowing gold into her green eyes. "We've come to see Alban. A friend of Viper's? She sent us. Perhaps you could make an exception."

The fae male arched a delicate brow. "I wouldn't call that snake my *friend*, but I am Alban. Viper wouldn't have sent you here for shits and giggles." He fluttered a hand, and two chairs appeared. "Have a seat." Alban did the same, taking the chair behind the table and folding his unusually long fingers.

He wore a different ring on each one. All of them were old. Some were simple bands of gold or silver with strange etchings, and others bore large, bright jewels that flashed in the candlelight.

"Are you friends with Viper?" the fae male asked.

"I'm...acquainted with her," Ethan admitted. "My name—"

Alban waved him off. "Your names don't matter. I simply would like to know why you've come here and why Viper, of all people, would send you to me."

"She thought you might have heard something no one else knows about the vampire threat," Stacy replied. "We're trying to do something about the creatures, but we keep hitting dead ends."

"Ah, I see." Alban leaned against his table, folding his hands. A cold smile spread across his lips. "I do know the secrets of the vampires, but I will not hand them out. Not even to...*acquaintances* of the snake shifter. Secrets are expensive, you know. I doubt you have the coin to pay for ones such as these." His soft, whispery tone made chills erupt on Stacy's arms.

"Maybe I do, maybe I don't," Stacy returned lightly. She knew to tread carefully through the conversation. It was like playing chess with a grand master. "Won't the vampires become a threat to you if they aren't dealt with?"

Alban gave a throaty laugh. "That rhetoric won't work on me, young witch. I don't care what happens to anyone, and the vampires won't touch me. I know their secrets, and that's dangerous to them. I doubt they'll risk it."

Irritation bubbled inside Stacy. She had to switch gears.

Alban leaned farther toward her, his blue eyes glittering. "I can see you're a determined person, Miss Drakethorn."

Stacy gasped. "How the hell do you know my name?"

Alban smiled. "I know many things, witch. I knew the second you stepped in here that both of you wore glamours. Done by a fae, I see. Who is she?"

"That doesn't matter," Ethan cut in.

"I know your name, too, but I don't care." Alban eyed Stacy again. "I am interested in you because I know a Drakethorn is bound to have some fascinating treasures. You do have the coin. My previous comment was simply bait." A wicked smile. "Which you took quite delightfully, I must say. I've always heard witches were easy and gullible."

Stacy clenched the arms of the chair. This guy was too good. She wanted to punch him in the face.

"The vampires seek two things," Alban continued in the whispery voice that made Stacy's skin crawl. "Those are the secrets I can sell you. One will cost you some of your blood—"

"No fucking way," Stacy interrupted.

Alban sighed. "Very well. The other is obtainable at the cost of a treasured keepsake. What do you have, Drakethorn? A pair of scales?"

Stacy wished it were that easy. Having anticipated this part of the deal, she nodded. She dug around in her bag until her fingers brushed a small ivory box. She withdrew it and set it on the table. "This belonged to my mother, Catherine Thorn. A witch, as you probably already know."

"Ah." Alban reached for the box and traced its edges with long, sharpened fingernails. "And why would I want this?"

"It's old, for one." Stacy fought the temptation to rip the object from his grasp and forget they'd ever come here. Instead, she explained, "Inside it are several trinkets my mother collected over the years. The keeper of my estate claims that, when put together, they form a device to collect and keep memories.

Nothing is more precious, in my opinion. You're obsessed with secrets, after all. What's got more buried secrets than people's memories?"

In theory, it seemed wrong to hand it over, but the fae wasn't aware that one piece was missing, rendering the device unusable. Still, it sent a twinge of pain through Stacy's heart. Handing anything over that had belonged to her mother would feel the same.

She pulled out another object and tossed it to the faerie. "And this is water taken from one of the sacred trees on my estate. It has several healing properties. Both of those for telling me what the vampires are doing here."

Alban considered the items, then a slow smile spread his lips. "You came well prepared, Miss Drakethorn. I'm not easily impressed by patrons coming to me for information. Most are desperate enough to give me their blood. You are not desperate, but you might soon be."

"No blood," Stacy replied in a near growl, gold flaring in her eyes.

"Fine." Alban waved a hand over the ivory box and glass bottle, making them vanish from sight. Illusion magic, no doubt. Then, he lowered his voice. "These vampires are a trio, though they have several others working for them. They're younger than most vampires. Their desperation to climb the ranks of power has brought them across the sea. They prowl in the shadows, looking to build what they call a New World with them at the top."

"What are their names?"

Alban clicked his tongue. "Ah, I cannot say. I can only tell you that they have been working here for some time, setting things into motion long before anyone became aware of them. Peer into the recent past, Miss Drakethorn. You might find something there worth your consideration."

"What else?" Ethan demanded as Alban leaned back.

"That is all, witch."

"Do you know more you're not telling us?" Stacy asked, desperation slipping into her tone.

Alban shrugged. "Maybe I do. Maybe it overlaps with the second secret you were unwilling to purchase."

Stacy stood. "Fine. I guess we'll be going now." Without bidding the secrets seller goodbye, she marched out of the room. Ethan followed. Stacy didn't care who saw her as she tore through the hallway and the front door, where the crowd was still lined up around the building. She heard murmurs of, "Hey, that's the girl who went in ahead of us!"

She ignored them.

"Stacy, wait," Ethan called as he caught up to her. His hand brushed her elbow. She swung to face him.

"What was the point of that? We got nowhere. Another dead end! That guy might as well have told us a riddle. I gave my mother's box away for nothing!"

"Stacy, I—"

"What was Viper thinking by sending us here? We shouldn't have listened to her. This was a bad idea."

Ethan put a hand on her shoulder to comfort her, but she shook him off. "Don't, Ethan. We wouldn't have wasted our time coming here if you hadn't contacted Viper in the first place." As soon as the words were out of her mouth, she regretted them when hurt flashed in his eyes. "Oh, fuck. I'm so sorry. That was unfair. You were only doing what you could to help, and I was the one who pushed you to reach out to her."

They stood in the middle of the street now. "I don't know why I've been feeling like this lately," Stacy went on. "I almost bit Miles' head off yesterday because he was humming outside my window. It's not normal girl stuff. Something else."

Her words stalled, and she stiffened as she noticed two nearby people looking and listening too closely.

Ethan noticed it, too. "I think we should go, Stacy."

She agreed. "I'm sorry for what I said."

Ethan managed a small smile and took her hand. "Don't worry about it. We'll go home and get a good night's sleep. Then tomorrow, we'll see if Amy found anything."

Stacy hoped so. It felt wrong to crawl into a comfortable bed, knowing people out there were suffering at the hands of their abductors. *One step at a time,* she told herself. *One of these days, we'll stop running into dead ends.*

CHAPTER ELEVEN

The house was quiet except for the buzzing of crickets outside the open window, the shuffling of papers, and relentless keystrokes.

Amy Greentree didn't plan on going to bed anytime soon. Kiera and Miles had retired for the night. Rowan was waiting up elsewhere in the house for Stacy and Ethan, who had left for the Midnight Market an hour ago. Amy hoped their journey to the mysterious place gave them insight into the vampire threat, especially since she'd been working at this all day and had yet to glean anything useful.

Amy sat back in her chair, rubbing her eyes. She'd been in this study for hours, clacking away at her keyboard and rifling through papers. Stacy had hoped she would find a pattern, and Amy was beginning to wonder if she had ever been a good journalist to begin with.

There had to be a connection here. Amy felt it was one good search away. So why the hell couldn't she find it? She gave herself a brief break before diving back in.

She reorganized the papers so the files were in chronological order. The first vanishing occurred three weeks ago. She hadn't heard of it then because they'd been so busy dealing with Hines and Voss. She wondered if the targets were intentional or if the vampires simply abducted whoever looked tasty to feed on.

She thought of calling the families of the people who had gone missing, but the police had already questioned them at length. Suddenly, an idea came to her. The police would have asked several questions, but there was one they wouldn't have thought of.

Amy's heart raced. It was too late to call most families, especially since she wasn't law enforcement, and they wouldn't be inclined to speak to her. Her question couldn't be posed to just anyone, either. She had to call someone she could trust. Someone who wouldn't mind answering questions from a person who worked for Stacy Drakethorn.

Amy dialed the number Stacy left for the elder of the Shinnecock nation, hoping the late hour wouldn't impede her quest. A deep voice answered after a few rings. "Hello?"

"Hello, my name is Amy Greentree. I'm calling on behalf of Stacy Drakethorn."

"Ah, greetings, Ms. Greentree. Does Ms. Drakethorn have news for us?" the elder replied.

Amy said unfortunately, no, but she had a question regarding the missing young woman from their reservation. "Did she ever show signs of magical potential?"

"All our people do," the elder replied. "But yes, she had a growing bond with the land. What you call magic, we refer to as simply *being*. She has a particularly strong connection with her inner power."

"Thank you," Amy replied. "This has helped me. Stacy will be in touch if we have further developments." She bid him goodnight, then hung up and whispered, "I'm onto something."

The young woman from the Shinnecock reservation had been taken only a few nights ago and was the most recent victim of the vampires' scheme. "As meticulous as it is macabre," Amy murmured, imagining the phrasing she would use if she wrote an article about the case.

She remembered another victim, a young man, who was abducted after a shift at the Pack House, a bar owned and run by werewolves. A quick search later, she discovered the young man was the son of the wolf who owned the place, therefore also making him a werewolf. That was two paranormals out of a dozen people. Was it pure coincidence, or had the vampires targeted people with magic?

With new pathways opened to her, Amy continued her search.

An hour later, she stared at her screen, mouth hanging open. "Holy shit. I don't believe this!"

She heard the front door opening from the floor below, then Stacy and Ethan's soft murmurs. *They need to see this,* Amy thought. She was about to call them up when she heard their footfalls on the stairs. They noticed the light in her study and came to her door. Amy was standing behind her desk when they entered. "Any luck?" she asked.

Stacy sighed. "Hard to tell yet. Viper's contact told us a fucking riddle. Honestly, I think it was a complete waste of time." She plopped into a chair while Ethan hung back, grim-faced. Amy's gaze darted between the two, realizing that something had happened between them. The tension in Stacy's shoulders and Ethan's face was unmistakable.

"Please tell us you've had better luck," Stacy pleaded.

Amy spoke with excitement and dread. "Well, I've found *something.*"

Sensing the import of Amy's tone, Stacy nodded. "Go on."

Ethan leaned against the wall, his exhaustion temporarily forgotten with renewed interest in the case.

"The vampires aren't hunting at random," Amy began. "It's a coordinated effort. I know you guessed that already, but I have two pieces of evidence confirming it." She explained her call to the elder and what she'd discovered about the werewolf at the Pack House.

"It's only two out of the dozen, but I think if we keep searching, we can determine whether the others are also paranormals. If that's the case, these vampires are selecting their targets as some kind of...grand design." The words tumbled from her as she gestured at the open documents scattered across her desk.

Ethan frowned, the gears in his mind turning. "So, it's not only about survival? There's a purpose behind it?"

"Yes, exactly," Amy replied, her eyes bright. "There's a pattern, a profile to these disappearances, and not only with the paranormal side of things."

"What's the other evidence?" Stacy asked, leaning toward the desk.

"I did some further digging after I discovered they might all be paranormals. I searched the names in relation to various underworld groups to see if the victims were connected to anyone there. Then, I discovered a grant program for paranormals seeking aid with school loans, businesses, and the like. Guess who ran it?"

"Who?" Stacy asked, dread rising in her voice.

"Gregory Hines."

It was like a small bomb had been dropped.

"Every single missing person was on that list. All recipients of one grant or another from him," Amy told them. "I believe the vampires got these names from Hines. Maybe Hines was involved before he died, maybe he wasn't. If he was, he could have easily pinpointed 'suitable' victims under the guise of grant access."

"Cutting down the time it would take to find the right type of victim," Ethan inserted. "Fucking hell."

"Indeed," Stacy muttered. "But what are the vampires ultimately after? What's the endgame here?"

The excitement in Amy's eyes faded. She dropped into her

91

chair, her exhaustion obvious. "That's just it. I don't know yet. I'm close, Stacy. If we can understand their strategy or find where they're hiding, we might predict their next move."

A light came into Stacy's eyes. She stood suddenly, almost toppling her chair.

"What is it?" Ethan asked.

Stacy spun toward him. "What Alban said! To peer into the recent past and see what might be worth my consideration. Maybe he was talking about Hines!" Her excitement grew. "He might have meant other things, too. Maybe this whole shitstorm is much bigger than we realize."

Ethan straightened as the impact of the revelation hit him. Seconds later, a weary resolve settled on him. "We keep digging, then. We consider what Alban told us in his veiled, secretive way, and we look for other clues. Were there any other names on that list, Amy?"

"No. All the names so far have already been abducted."

Stacy thought she would feel better hearing this, but it made her feel worse. If the vampires were finished capturing their victims, it meant they were one step closer to their end goal, however bloody and horrifying that might be. She shuddered.

"That doesn't mean there aren't others they plan to take," she commented. "Hines' list may only be the beginning."

She caught Ethan glancing at the door and remembered he hadn't been in his shop for a full day of work all week. She laid a hand on his arm. "Go get some rest, and don't worry about us tomorrow. I'll keep you updated on anything we find."

With a nod of gratitude, Ethan bid them goodnight and exited, leaving Stacy and Amy to ponder the chilling puzzle before them. "Bedtime sounds great to me, too," Amy confessed. "You should rest. I can tell you're tired."

Stacy offered a weary smile. "You've done great work tonight, Amy. I can't imagine what sort of shit we'd be in if you hadn't discovered this."

Amy nodded in appreciation. "Whatever I can do to help." She rose, intending to shower and go to bed, but paused before she reached the door. "What was that between you and Ethan?"

"What do you mean?"

"The super-obvious tension? You know, the kind you can cut with a knife?"

Stacy chuckled. "I should know better than to think anything gets past you. I was frustrated with how things went at the Market, and I sort of...snapped at him."

"Yikes."

"I apologized, but it hurt him. He'll need time."

"Of course." Amy paused, then added, "Maybe if you kiss him again, he'll be happy."

A grin spread Stacy's lips. "About that. There's something I haven't told you yet."

The next morning, Stacy went to Rowan's study and told him about Amy's discovery.

The dryad was equally as shocked as Stacy to hear of Gregory Hines' involvement. Stacy half wished Kiera hadn't done away with him. On the other hand, she had to admit Hines being alive would have complicated current matters.

"Amy's timing is impeccable," Rowan observed after she'd finished. "Mr. Gray called last night before you were back and asked me to pass along word that his wolf spies have tracked a vampire or two to a manor outside the city on the other side of us. They seem to be hiding out there, though no signs of the taken victims are in the area. I asked Kiera to look into it, and she discovered, no surprise, that Gregory Hines owned the place when he was alive."

"The twists keep on coming," Stacy mused. "I'm tired of not having the full picture."

"We can start by having Kiera go there and keep watch tonight."

Stacy nodded. "A good plan. I'll go with her."

Rowan hesitated.

"What's wrong?" she pushed, trying not to show her budding irritation.

"Must you go, Stacy? Kiera can handle a stakeout on her own."

"I want to. I can't sit around here waiting for a bomb to drop."

"But—"

"Look, Rowan, this is my decision, and I don't want to argue." She spoke more sharply than she had intended, but she'd already started, so she barreled on. "I'm sick of being left out of the loop, too. If I'm going to know what's happening, I have to go."

Rowan's brows furrowed. "Stacy, what do you mean? Of course you're in the loop."

She threw her hands up. "You're always going behind my back and making plans without me, commanding this person and that person to go wherever you deem necessary. Then, I find out about it after the fact!" Several incidents came to mind. She hadn't known Kiera was being sent to Adrian until after the fact. She hadn't known the elf queen's true reason for wanting to meet her until later. What else was Rowan keeping from her?

Rowan blanched at her outburst but remained calm in a way Stacy couldn't. "I thought you trusted me to do what is necessary. I have never worked behind your back. I thought I was simply keeping as much off your plate as possible. If I need to keep you more in the loop, Stacy, I will. All you need to do is give me the word."

Stacy's features softened. "What I said might have been a tad too harsh. I'm sorry, Rowan." Inwardly, she wondered what the hell had gotten into her. She'd snapped at Ethan last night, and despite a good night's sleep, she'd awoken feeling like she wanted to throw her fist into the wall. It wasn't only the ordeal with

Alban that frustrated her. It felt like every small annoyance over the past month wanted to bubble to the surface.

As the frustration between them diffused, Kiera strolled in. She instantly picked up on the lingering tension. "What's wrong?"

"Nothing," Rowan responded hurriedly, pasting on a smile that convinced neither Stacy nor Kiera. "Stacy and I were discussing your mission for tonight." He gave her a look as if to say *If that's what you still want.*

Stacy nodded, and Kiera raised a brow at her. Stacy forced a grin despite the tension in her chest. "Ready to stalk some vampires?"

"Always," Kiera returned. "Is that even a question?"

"Good. I hope you're up for company tonight because I'm going with you."

CHAPTER TWELVE

<u>One year ago</u>

The female vampire stood in a catacomb, surrounded by the remains of dead humans. They'd come down here through an illegal entrance, but frankly, she didn't care. Not as long as they reached the end of this damn tunnel, and she found what she was looking for. She'd been rooting around Paris for a decade now looking for the damn artifact, and she refused to leave the network of catacombs until it was safely in her hands.

"Are you sure it's this way?" she asked the druid leading her.

The male druid turned, frowning. "You paid me to take you to the place, Ms. Gravescend. It would do you well to listen to my instruction and follow my lead."

Lenora Gravescend shut her mouth despite the plethora of profanities she wanted to hurl at him. Making the druid her enemy now wouldn't help matters. *We're close,* she thought. *So damn close.* Her hands itched as if the artifact might appear out of thin air, and she could snatch it.

She'd paid the druid handsomely for this information and for leading her into the catacombs. She'd been hunting around in the underground network for years, but with how vast the catacombs were, she'd had no success.

Until a few days ago, when she stumbled across an old series of letters written by the druid who stood before her now. They'd led her to him, and a bag of gold coins and much persuasive chatter later, they were here. Somewhere dark, cold, and smelling of the dead. *My favorite,* the vampire thought.

The druid led her through several twisting passageways, holding a torch above his head to light the way. Lenora lost count of the bones she saw. Many had died here. Had any come to this place searching for the artifact? The pair continued in silence, with Lenora debating what she would do when she had the artifact in hand. The druid would lead her out. But did she need him?

I've tracked where we came from, she thought. *I can leave him here forever.* That way, not a soul alive would know she had found the artifact.

Finally, the druid halted before a curved stone wall.

"A fucking dead end?" Lenora snapped.

The druid glared at her. "Not a dead end." He traced lines in the wall with his finger, leaving a trail of magic. He murmured words in a language Lenora did not know. Before long, the wall was glowing with whorls of magic. It hummed in the air. Lenora held her breath. This was a doorway, and the druid had used his magic to open it. Finally, the wall vanished from sight, revealing a small room with a low ceiling.

Both the druid and Lenora ducked to enter. She gasped at the sight before her. The room was dusty and dim and would have been empty if not for the waist-high stone pillar in its center and the small, golden chest on top of it.

Lenora was breathless as she approached, fingers reaching.

"Stop!" the druid hissed.

She spun to face him. "It's my right to open it!"

The druid frowned. "It's not about rights, Ms. Gravescend. If you try to open it now, you'll fucking kill yourself." He approached her and the box. "Complicated webs of magic overlay the trunk. Touch it without undoing the spells, and you'll lose a hand, maybe even your life."

Was he lying? "I don't sense warding over it."

"It's subtle, which is what makes it so deadly," the druid explained with the exasperation of an adult trying to deescalate a toddler's tantrum. Some vampires could be *so* hot-headed.

Lenora turned her attention to the trunk and what lay inside. The artifact had once belonged to her great-grandmother and all the women in her family who'd come before her. If anyone had the right to retrieve it, it was her. "Well?" she demanded. "Can you undo it?"

"I can, but it will take time."

Lenora grumbled incoherently and stepped back. She watched the druid for what felt like an eternity as he parsed through the spells and enchantments, undoing one at a time through murmured, coaxing words. Strain showed on his face. The veins on the sides of his head bulged with effort. Sweat glided down his brow. His skin paled, and his breathing grew shallow.

She wondered if he would faint. It made sense. If touching the spells would kill her, surely it would make someone undoing them feel sick.

Finally, the druid stepped back, breathing deeply. "It's finished."

Lenora felt like a child on Christmas morning. She lurched toward the trunk and flung open the lid. Lying against a velvet interior was a gold chain and an iron charm with a large, glittering blood ruby at its center. She picked it up with as much care as she could muster, marveling at the beautiful necklace. It did not look like it had been hidden deep in the catacombs for centuries.

She couldn't believe it. *I did it! I found the answer to all my problems!*

She replaced the artifact in the box and turned, still smiling. "Thank you for bringing me here."

The druid nodded. "Now that you've found it, we can go. Back this way, through—"

He'd hardly turned for the doorway when he glimpsed flashing silver. His eyes widened with horror a split second before she drove the knife into his chest. He released a pained gasp and slumped forward.

Lenora twisted the knife. "I think I'll find my own way, thank you."

She pulled the knife free, snatched up the necklace, and headed for the exit. She wove through the catacombs as if she'd been here a hundred times. When she reached the misty streets above to find it still deep into the night, she allowed herself a pause. Victory danced in her chest. She had the artifact, but it was only the first step in their plan.

I've been in Paris for too long, she thought. It was finally time to reunite with her allies. Lenora produced one last smile before heading down the street, keeping to the mist and shadows where no one would spot her. As eager as she was to leave Paris behind, unfortunately, it wasn't time to leave Europe yet.

"Time to make a trip to Rome," she murmured, then vanished into the mist.

The room was spinning.

Probably because Valen Sanguine had had one drink too many, and some guy who was a friend of a friend had handed him what he *thought* was a joint but turned out to be something else entirely. He coughed through a cloud of colored smoke and headed toward the back of the room, which happened to be the part of his living room where the windows overlooked the streets of Rome.

One of his friends stood behind a table with a DJ set before him. "Can you play anything other than this shit?" Valen asked. The DJ had been playing some obscure indie rock artist for the past hour, and no one but him knew any of the songs.

"What?" the DJ boomed.

"I said, can you play anything other than this shit?"

"Oh!" The DJ looked perplexed. *"I guess?"*

"Anything!" Valen boomed back.

He turned and spotted a tall blonde leaning against his built-in bar. She was looking at him with intoxicated lust in her eyes. She smiled and fluttered her fingers. *Okay, that looks fun,* Valen thought. He was halfway across the room when he tripped because he thought the floor and the walls had switched places. Suddenly, the wallpaper pattern swirled on the tiled floor. "Whoa…"

Someone smacked him on the shoulder. "Hey, Vay! Nice partay!" The young man laughed.

Valen wasn't sure who'd said that but knew their voice was too loud and too close to his ear. "Yeah, yeah. Thanks, man!" He pushed through a circle of women dancing in a glow of purple light and finally reached the blonde. Her smile made him dizzier.

"Hey there," he drawled, then belched. Embarrassed, he hurried to add, "Excuse me!"

"What's your name?" the girl asked.

"Valen!"

She laughed.

"What's funny?"

"You're not Valen! Valen's the guy who threw the party."

"Yeah, I know. I'm Valen, and I'm the guy throwing the party!"

The girl frowned, confused. Gods, what was wrong with people tonight? Suddenly, Valen felt more frustrated than interested in taking this girl to his room. The girl made an excuse about seeing her friend across the room and bolted. Valen swayed, then gripped the edge of the bar for support. Tonight wasn't going as well as he'd hoped.

He sighed, tipped the bottle he'd forgotten he was holding to his lips, and finished the beer off. He'd no sooner set the bottle on the bar's surface than his front door blew open. Who the fuck was it? Everyone he'd invited had already arrived.

Valen squinted at the female figure, trying to figure out if he recognized her. Her gaze scanned the room, looking for someone. For *him*. He knew this the second their eyes met, and recognition flickered in hers. She marched toward him.

Oh shit, Valen thought. Recognition hit him with enough force that he wondered if he'd walked into a wall. Despite the dread spiking in his chest, he pasted on his biggest smile and threw out his arms. "Lenora! What the hell are you doing here?"

She halted in front of him and got in his face. "I've been calling you all night, and you wouldn't fucking answer. So I came here to see why." She gestured at their surroundings. "I see now. You're partying while I was digging around in dirty catacombs. I fucking knew it!"

He pinched her cheek. It left a large red mark on her otherwise ivory skin. "Nah, just admit you wanted some fun, darling."

"Don't call me that," she hissed, shoving his hand away. "We need to talk." She studied him. "I can see you're in no condition to do that, though."

"N-no, I can talk. Comeonletsgotomyroom." This last part was so slurred Lenora hardly understood him.

"I'm not going to your room."

"We can talk here, then."

"It must be private!"

Valen threw his hands up. "I don't know what to do, then."

Lenora growled, then took his arm. "Fine. Your room. Will anyone hear us?"

Valen smirked. "Not if we're quiet. I heard you were loud in be—ow!" She'd pinched him this time and not in the friendly way he'd done to her cheek. A minute later, they had pushed past two couples making out in the narrow hallway in a cloud of smoke and reached his bedroom. Lenora shut his door behind her and locked it, not caring what anyone thought they were doing.

Valen's room was a disaster, and he was slightly embarrassed. Clothes were everywhere. His trash can was overflowing. He sank onto the edge of his rumpled bed, wearing a drunken smile. "All right, Le, you can do whatever you want to me now."

"I'm not here to sleep with you," she cut in sharply. "I found the artifact."

Valen stilled. "Shit. Did you really?"

"I swear it."

"Show me."

"I can't. I have it in a safe place. I didn't want to risk bringing it here where there'd be so many people. All we have to do now is go to London and find Cassius. Then, we can move on with our plan." A rare excitement shone in her eyes.

Dread tempered Valen's own excitement. It had been five years since the three of them were last together, a clandestine gathering of younger vampires frustrated with their lack of advancement within the traditional vampire power structures. Valen wasn't the biggest fan of Cassius, their leader, but no one else was as naturally equipped to become the unofficial head of their new group.

Since coming together five years ago, the trio and their allies had worked together on several small yet successful rebellions against their elders across Europe. However, their success on this continent was limited since using paranormal blood in the rituals they sought to gain more power was forbidden.

In America, they could do whatever the hell they wanted. That was what Cassius said, anyway. Valen was less certain. They could go to Cassius now, but Valen had a lot of questions. Like, would Lenora go insane if she used the artifact? Valen had heard rumors of her ancestors being driven mad. That was why they'd hidden it.

Valen wondered if his sense of dread was because he'd been a vampire for a far shorter time than Cassius and Lenora. Cassius had turned fifteen years ago, and Valen only seven. Lenora had been born a vampire. Valen had been restless for years and was as dissatisfied with his low rank as Lenora and Cassius were. If she truly had the artifact, they had a chance to climb.

Finally, he thought.

He stood, swaying. "Alll rightletsgotoLondon."

Lenora shook her head. "You're making no sense, Valen. How about let's get you to bed? I'll be back in the morning, then we're leaving."

Valen didn't remember lying down or her leaving. He didn't remember falling asleep, only the harsh sunlight the next morning when Lenora came back and poked him awake. *To London,* he thought. *And Cassius.*

It was raining in London, as it did most days.

The vampire sat inside one of the many pubs he owned, watching the sky empty itself on the solemn streets. This particular pub was open only to special guests. Right now, he was alone in a back room. One person was working since only those the vampire deigned to meet with tonight would be permitted inside.

The vampire called for a drink. The only other two men in the building were his bodyguards.

It took Cassius Marlowe three flicks of his lighter before he brought the flame to the end of his cigarette. He placed it between his lips and smiled. It was almost time. Lenora had sent word that she and Valen would arrive tonight, artifact in hand. Perfect. His plan was falling into place exactly as he had intended. A good thing, too, since London's underworld was beginning to feel too small. The vampire council's strong regulations weren't helping matters.

Lenora and Valen were equally irritated, or so they had communicated through various means over the past five years. Lenora had said as much in bed with him on the rare occasion they crossed paths in Paris and returned to Cassius' hotel.

Cassius hadn't seen Valen since their first meeting. If he had to convince anyone, it was the younger vampire. Valen was ambitious and cunning, but he was not one to easily give up his personal comforts, even if it meant scaling a ladder to higher success. *I'll convince him,* Cassius promised himself.

He stewed over these matters until he heard murmuring in the front room. The bodyguards led a pair of younger vampires into the back room. Cassius stood, smiling and extending his arms. Lenora reached him first, her lips crashing into his before he could utter a word of greeting. He melted into her and issued a sound of deep satisfaction.

"Should I come back later?" Valen drawled. "I didn't realize I was attending a lover's reunion."

Cassius and Lenora parted, and the former cast the other man a roguish smile. "You're more than welcome to join us, Valen. You've done it before." He brushed hair from Lenora's face. "Le here tells me she found you partying in Rome. I hope it was a good time because you will have to put that side of yourself away for a time."

Valen slid into a booth. "Depends. Are we leaving Europe anytime soon or what?"

Cassius and Lenora sat—too close for Valen's comfort—and Cassius' dark eyes glittered. "We are. Now that you two have brought the artifact, we can enact the second phase of our plan."

"I don't know how you intend to do it," Valen muttered. "After we're there, we must put everything into place quickly. And how the hell are we supposed to do anything without the Codex?"

Cassius waved for the barman to bring two more drinks. "Relax, Valen. I'm figuring it out. You clearly need a drink."

Valen eyed the glass of whiskey. "No thanks."

"He's still hungover," Lenora crooned, taking his glass for herself.

"Whiskey lover now, Le?" Cassius asked.

"I like the wine, too," she replied, reaching for the glass he'd ordered for her.

Cassius took his arm from around Lenora and folded his hands on the table, leaning forward in the dim light. "You're right about the Codex, Valen. We still need to find it, but I have clues about where it might be. I've made connections in New York who will be instrumental in our efforts moving forward."

"What sort of connections?" Valen asked, his expression guarded.

"One is a man named Gregory Hines. He is searching for prime targets within the city for our rituals. We need people ripe with magical blood, you know."

"I'm aware," Valen replied tersely. "Can this Hines person be trusted?"

Cassius shrugged. "If he turns out to be a snake, we'll cut off his head." He tipped the glass of whiskey to his mouth. "I have every confidence Hines will help us. He's as ambitious about climbing to the top as we are. He'll provide the proper sacrifices, and all we have to do is find that damn Codex. It's somewhere in New York's underworld. It's only a matter of finding it."

Hines didn't know about the Codex. After he helped the vampires to the top, they could get rid of him. Cassius knew about the Circle in New York's underworld. It was a cheaper version of the vampire council in Europe. He thought infiltrating it would be easy. It wouldn't have been fifty-plus years ago when the Circle sought to kick vampires out. Now, it was full of enough ambitious, greedy, and, most importantly, *desperate* men.

Piece of fucking cake, Cassius thought. He was convinced he'd addressed all Valen's concerns, but the younger vampire leaned toward him. "And what of the dragon? Rumor has it one still resides there."

Cassius laughed. "Mere rumor, Valen. You know better than to listen to them. A dragon hasn't been seen in that part of the world in centuries. If there is one, he's probably a fat old worm by now."

Valen didn't look so certain. Lenora reached across the table for his hand, her face pleading. "Go with us, Valen. We need you for the rituals. It takes three, and there's no one else Cassius and I trust the way we trust you." Lenora was a damn good liar, but she wasn't lying now. Cassius nodded as she added, "We're almost there. All our dreams, so close to coming true."

Valen relented. "Of course I'll go. I never said I wouldn't, but we must be careful. When we're there, we can't be flashy like we have been here. Vampires are not welcome in America's supernatural world."

Cassius' lips split into a cruel smile. "Then we will make ourselves welcome."

CHAPTER THIRTEEN

Stacy parked the car three blocks from their destination. It was close enough for a quick getaway if they needed it but not so close that a vampire watching from the building ahead would wonder why it was there. Thanks to Kiera's illusion magic, they moved toward the vampires' hiding place without being seen.

"Ready for this?" Kiera asked as they exited onto the street. "Honestly, this work is boring. I don't know why you wanted to come."

Stacy smiled and lifted a dark hood over her head. "I'm happy to do the boring work for once. A nice change of pace."

Kiera chuckled. "Whatever you say." She took the lead, stealing through the streets with a silence that awed Stacy.

Will I ever be able to move like that? she wondered.

Kiera used muffling spells within her illusion magic to make Stacy quieter and shield them in shadows pulled from the night. The streets in this area were dark and quiet, with rows of houses standing still and silent.

Ahead, Stacy spotted the manor house. It was small in comparison to her own and appeared far older. Not because it was older but because it hadn't been cared for in the past several years. Gregory Hines hadn't put time or resources into maintaining the place. After his death, it had fallen into further disrepair.

I guess vampires don't have a knack for gardening, Stacy thought. *Or even mowing the lawn.*

The house was a square block of stone on top of a hill, surrounded by trees. An iron gate ran the perimeter, and Stacy sensed wards inside when they were a few paces from the gate. Kiera slid farther into the shadows, concealed by trees along the road. She knelt among the dense foliage. Stacy followed, not taking her eyes off the house.

Stacy didn't notice she was fidgeting until Kiera laid a hand on her bouncing leg and whispered, "You're high-strung, Stacy. That won't do if we're attacked. You need to calm yourself."

Stacy knew Kiera was right, but the words made her bristle anyway.

Kiera eyed her. "You've been high-strung for a few days now."

Longer than that, Stacy thought, sighing. "I snapped at Ethan the other night for no reason and did the same to Rowan this morning. I don't know what's gotten into me. I guess this whole thing with the vampires has been stressing me out." She kept her voice to a whisper.

Kiera replied, "That might not be it. You've been in more stressful situations before. Your dragon nature was shut away for too long. You haven't shifted form since that night you killed Victor, right?"

"Right."

"That's your problem. Your dragon half isn't happy about being caged. You need to blow off steam, Stacy. Literally."

Coldness washed over her. *But I don't want to.*

"You're afraid of your other form," Kiera whispered. "I understand."

How could she? Kiera wasn't a shifter. Those bright amber eyes met Stacy's, and her response made Stacy wonder if Kiera could read her mind. "I may not have another body like you, but I transformed when I became an assassin back in the fae world. I wasn't recognizable, even to myself.

"I thought I was doing the right thing during the rebellion, and though I still consider my father the most arrogant prick in the universe, rebelling against him got a lot of people killed." Kiera swallowed. "Including my younger siblings. Children who were innocent."

Stacy's heart ached for her.

"I get being afraid of a power within you that you feel you can't always control. It'll only grow worse if you keep it caged," Kiera advised. "Before long, you'll find snapping at Ethan or Rowan will be the least of your worries."

Kiera was right. Stacy needed to use the land allotted to her and shift, practice being in her dragon form. Blow off steam. *What if I burn trees on accident?* she thought. Well, it was better than accidentally burning down her whole home when her magic got the best of her. This was something she could go to her father for. *Later,* she thought. *After we've dealt with these shits.*

Stacy's attention returned to the manor house on the hill. They'd come here to watch the vampires' coming and going. To observe the place so they could make tactical decisions their team could use to infiltrate the place.

Kiera spied a light flickering on inside the house. "Look there. At least we know someone is home."

Stacy wanted to see more than that. She scanned the perimeter and the gates, searching for weak points in the wards. Hines hadn't bothered maintaining the grounds, so Stacy had a hard time believing the security was up to par. She summoned a small amount of magic, intending to reach out and test the wards.

She never began her probing. The instant the magic rose to her fingertips, strong arms grabbed her from behind.

A hand slapped across her mouth, cutting off her cry of alarm. Her face stung where she was hit. Her hood was forced over her eyes. Two pairs of hands wrapped around her arms and shoulders and dragged her through the woods. Stacy thrashed against them to no avail. She heard the distant sounds of struggle—Kiera and a third attacker.

Shit! Stacy couldn't change form in such an open space.

Roots and rocks scraped against the back of her body as they dragged her down the path. The hands lifted her, then she went flying. Stacy landed hard on the ground, not so much as a groan issuing from her lips. The impact was hard enough to knock the breath from her for several seconds. She saw stars. Literally. The night sky through the trees was spinning, the stars wheeling in a broad circle.

How had they been attacked? How had neither of them sensed the approach from behind? Had the light in the house been a signal? *Fuck, it was,* Stacy thought. Her thoughts vanished from her mind when one of the figures slammed something cold and hard around her right wrist, then a second encircled her left.

A sudden heaviness came over her. They weren't chains intended to bind her. Not physically, anyway. Stacy tried to pull on her magic, but it was too muted. One of the attackers hauled her up and yanked the hood from her face. Stacy tried to jerk away, but his grip on her was too firm.

The second figure chuckled, and a deep male voice rumbled out of him. "We knew they'd come snooping around here soon. I didn't think Drakethorn herself would do the job. Don't have enough people to do your dirty work, girl?"

Where was Kiera? Was she chained, too?

Stacy couldn't make out the second figure since a hood shielded his face. The first man, who was holding her, got in her face. His skin was pale, and several scars flecked his face. He opened his mouth, revealing rows of gleaming white fangs. A vampire. "You will make a perfect gift to my masters on the hill," he crooned.

"Where did you take the people you kidnapped?" Stacy demanded, her voice slurring. Damn, the chains were like a drug.

The vampire simply smiled, and Stacy could have sworn his breath smelled like blood. "Wouldn't you like to kn—"

A knife entered him through the back of his neck. He fell, releasing Stacy. An arrow whizzed through the air, hitting the second vampire. He dropped with a stifled cry. Kiera materialized from the shadows, panting and disheveled. "Those shits put up one hell of a fight!" She drew her knife from the first vampire's neck but left the arrow she'd released from her crossbow in the other.

Kiera caught sight of Stacy's manacles and cursed. "They tried to put the same on me, but they got my knife to their guts instead."

"Can you take them off?" Stacy pleaded.

Kiera's brows furrowed. "Not my wheelhouse, unfortunately. Rowan or Miles will have to do it. Now, we need to *run.*"

Stacy realized why the instant the words were out of Kiera's mouth. The sounds of hot pursuit weren't far behind as more vampires crashed through the foliage. "How many?" she asked.

"A lot," Kiera retorted.

"So much for a boring night," Stacy huffed as they took off through the trees. She still felt groggy from the manacles but fought through the brain fog to go, go, *go.* As long as she remained on her feet and kept away from the damn vampires, she could make it.

Kiera zigzagged through the trees as if she had done this a hundred times before. She probably had. It wasn't long before the thugs broke through the tree line. They came from all sides. *Shit!*

All lesser vampires, Kiera had told her when they started running. None of them were as good as Voss was, but in their numbers, they posed a real threat. Heart thundering, Stacy raced with Kiera through the forest. She was several paces behind, but Kiera used her shadow magic to conceal them both.

We can't run forever, Stacy acknowledged. They needed to get back to the car.

The clash of powers echoed through the night. Magic flew toward them, but Kiera deflected, her shadows lashing out with enough force to send the vampires reeling. Stacy's body burned to do the same, but no matter how hard she yanked and pulled, she couldn't grasp a single thread of her magic.

I would do anything to become a dragon right now, she thought. Ripping off the manacles was impossible. The magic in them ran deep. Her only choice was to stay close to Kiera and hope the fae woman had enough power to protect them both.

"The car is in the opposite direction," Kiera got out when Stacy had caught up. Stacy realized Kiera had slowed for her. It made her heart pound faster. She couldn't drag her friend down.

Ever the strategist, Stacy nodded. "I know. I've chosen this path deliberately. We have to mislead them, then make a break for the car when they're confused."

"Ah. Okay, on it."

Kiera summoned her illusion magic, and a copy of Kiera started running east. Hopefully, it was enough to fool their pursuers. "I'll make another in a few minutes," Kiera panted out. Doing such a thing wore on her. It required a lot of her magic.

They kept running. Stacy evaded boulders and fallen trees, avoided tripping on protruding roots and low stumps. All the while, Kiera's shroud of darkness encased her. They charged into a clearing seconds later and were making for the other side when three figures launched from the trees. The vampires formed a circle around them, closing in. "Fucking hell," Stacy breathed.

Kiera whipped shadows at two of them. Stacy went for the third. She didn't have magic, but she'd learned a thing or two at the dojo. She struck, but the vampire evaded her blow and ducked, going for her waist. Stacy twisted away, shooting her fist out. She made contact with a shoulder.

Not enough. The vampire bared his fangs and snarled. Stacy

growled and swung again. She missed. *These fucking manacles are slowing me down!* She drew her knife and slashed, opening skin. Bright blood on white flesh. A scream followed.

Nearby, Kiera was battering two vampires with her magic, folding in and out of darkness, knives flashing in arcs of silver. As she cut down the two vampires, Stacy finally pinned the third to the ground. She chose not to kill him. Instead, she left him bleeding from a gaping wound in his side and hissed, "Tell your masters a dragon is waiting for them."

Kiera yanked her up. "No time for grandiose warnings. Let's *go*."

Stacy felt close to fainting as she charged out of the clearing with Kiera. The strain on Kiera's face said she'd expended more magic than she should have. But they were still being pursued. Stacy heard footfalls behind them and commands uttered from one vampire to another. Persistent thugs. They needed a way to shake them.

"I have to make another copy," Kiera panted.

"You can't. You'll pass out!"

"No other way."

Kiera managed it about thirty seconds after they'd hurdled over a small stream and reached a sharp incline. Stacy's whole body burned as they climbed to the top. There—a break in the tree line. She ran for it as the copy of Kiera's body took off in another direction. They made it out of the trees and to a hillside. They lurched down it, and Stacy realized they were on the street where she'd parked the car.

They ran for it without glancing over their shoulders. Stacy heard no sounds of pursuit. *Almost in the clear,* she told herself. They reached the car, and Stacy moved to get into the driver's seat. "No way," Kiera insisted. "You'll fucking pass out at the wheel."

Stacy relented, bolting to the other side as Kiera slid into the driver's seat.

When they were speeding away, Kiera laughed and shook her head. "I can't believe that happened."

Stacy remained grim. "I don't plan on repeating that experience. I think it was a trap. The vampires conducted the kidnappings to lure me out to find them. It fucking worked."

"We escaped," Kiera reminded her. "Be glad of that."

For now, Stacy thought. "We should get home so I can get these damn things off."

Eleven months ago

"This is it?" Lenora asked, one brow raised with arms crossed and booted feet planted firmly on the cement. The gate before them was closed, and the manor house looked as though it had been empty for years. Not exactly the sort of accommodations she had been expecting when coming to America.

"A hotel in the city would be nicer than this," Valen grumbled from Cassius' left.

Cassius turned his back to the gate and glared at them. "We can't stay in the city yet. Besides, this was Hines' gift to us. He promises to have better accommodations soon. In the meantime…" He waved a hand at the house and overgrown grounds. The place looked eerie in the dark, but neither Lenora nor Valen thought it would look much better in the daylight. Cassius grimaced. "Well, we can fix it up."

Valen gave him a look. "Fix it up? When the hell are we going to have time for that?"

Cassius didn't answer. He was too busy opening the gate. It shrieked as it swung open, making the trio cringe. Lenora groaned, wishing for her elegant townhouse in Paris. Even Valen preferred his cramped flat in Rome that he'd shared with too many men his age, including a bathroom no one had ever cleaned. He doubted this house was much better.

Cassius was used to nicer housing as well. Hell, he had grown up practically royal. By vampire standards, anyway. He'd never lived in a rundown place before. Whatever he thought or felt about their present circumstances, he kept it to himself.

Finally, Lenora sighed. "I suppose this helps us blend in better. No one will think to look for us here."

Cassius turned, a broad smile revealing his too-white teeth. "Exactly, Lenora. I'm glad you're finally understanding me." She scowled, but he continued. "We will stay hidden and out of the way while we look for the ritual writings. When the time comes, we can use a place like this to keep our sacrificial offerings."

Lenora produced a wicked smile. "I like that part." She breezed past him through the gate. A long path led to the top of the hill and the front of the house. "Well, shall we go in, boys? Best we see our new home." She fluttered a hand at their general surroundings. "We can keep the outside like this. Unassuming. The inside, however…well, I have plans for it."

Valen groaned. "She's going to make us go bankrupt, Cassius." He envisioned animal skin rugs, priceless art, and unnecessary marble decorations.

Despite all his riches and tendency to disagree with Valen, Cassius nodded. "You're right on this one. We'll need to keep a tight leash on her."

Leashing Lenora was like trying to leash a wild wolf. Valen wanted no part of that. They watched her flit up the hill and reach the wide porch, where she peered into darkened windows. Yes, they had much work to do, but they had come this far. What was a little more effort?

"We will keep climbing," Cassius murmured as he and Valen strode up the hill. Valen wasn't sure if Cassius was speaking to them or himself. "Until the underworld is ours, and I am on the throne."

The words made Valen cold. Above, thunder rumbled.

. . .

115

Sixteen Days Ago

Cassius was pissed off.

Valen and Lenora could tell as soon as he came into the house, and the door banged shut behind him.

Lenora was in their living room, lounging on a sofa with smoke ballooning around her. Valen sat in a chair on the other side of the room by the fire, a book opened on his lap. He had long since stopped reading it.

Cassius had left a few hours ago to meet someone. He hadn't told them who he was going to see or why. He'd been acting like that a lot lately. Both Valen and Lenora were getting sick of him keeping information from them.

Lenora rolled her eyes at the sound of Cassius stomping down the hallway. "What is it now?" she grumbled. Across the room, Valen stiffened. Whatever it was, it wasn't good.

Finally, Cassius appeared in the living room. He was dripping from the rain, but that wasn't the reason for his sour mood. "Hines is dead."

Lenora straightened. "What?"

Valen stood, echoing the word "dead."

"Two nights ago. His body was found in a fucking alley. He was drunk when it happened. Alcohol all over his clothes." Cassius stalked toward the fire, seeking to warm himself. He told his companions a dark-clothed woman and Hines' bodyguards had fought in a nearby bar. The woman had disappeared, and by dawn, they'd found Hines' body not far from the bar.

Lenora's brows furrowed. "You know who did this, Cassius."

Cassius cursed.

"I told you so," Valen muttered. "Fucking dragon."

"Not the time, Valen," Lenora snapped. She rose and walked to where Cassius stood. She didn't seem to mind his wet clothes as she wound her arms around his waist. "That Drakethorn bitch did this. We could have seen it coming."

They'd arrived in the city, thinking the only threat they'd have to remove was Corbinelli and Hines, both of whom had been on their side in the beginning. A mysterious witch with a reputation in the court system had removed Victor.

At first, none of the vampires viewed her as a threat but merely a convenient end to Victor Corbinelli's life. Cassius had planned on getting rid of Hines, too, but not this soon. They still needed him. The more they heard about Stacy Drakethorn and her lineage, the worse it became.

Cassius withdrew from Lenora's hold without so much as a brush of affection. He strode to the window and peered absently outside. The night deepened, and the storm raged. "We will deal with Drakethorn. I have a plan in mind. As long as we get to the ritual writings before her, everything will go as planned."

Lenora was pondering something. He pinned his gaze on her until she spoke. Her voice was low, like a cat's purr. "We will lay a trap for the witch. We can begin our kidnappings early, lure her to us."

Cassius nodded curtly, his dark eyes flashing with ire and resolve. "I was thinking the same thing."

"And if that doesn't work?" Valen asked.

Cassius and Lenora glowered at him. "We will make it work," Cassius growled.

"He has a point," Lenora insisted, nodding toward Valen. "It won't hurt to have friends on the sidelines. Backups in case trapping her doesn't work." She noted the fury in Cassius' face and added quickly, "But we will do what we can. Drakethorn herself might make a good addition to our sacrificial offering."

CHAPTER FOURTEEN

Ethan, Rowan, Miles, and Amy were already waiting in the library when Stacy and Kiera returned.

"You two look like you've been through hell," Amy remarked when the women strode in, grim-faced and exhausted.

Ethan spotted the chains around Stacy's wrists and rushed to her. "What the hell happened? Why are you wearing magic-muting manacles?" Apparently, they were common enough that Ethan had a name for them.

Rowan's face was a mask of concern as he ground his jaw. Miles simply shook his head, muttering, "Damn vampires."

Kiera slipped into one of the armchairs, not bothering to hide her fatigue. She dove into the story, describing where they had gone and the light they had seen in the house—a signal seconds before they were attacked. She explained how Stacy had been dragged through the woods and put into the manacles.

Stacy extended her arms. "Anyone who knows how to get these damn things off me is welcome to try anytime they want."

Ethan's brows furrowed. "They're complicated, Stacy. It will take time and a lot of unraveling complex magic."

Stacy cast a furtive glance at Rowan, seeking confirmation. It was Miles who answered. "He's right. We'll do what we can, but you must be patient."

Stacy didn't have a choice. She settled in the armchair opposite Kiera while Ethan sat to her right and Miles stooped before her. If they didn't get the chains off soon, she was bound to fall asleep.

"We can safely assume everything the vampires have done so far was a trap," Kiera surmised. "Either to get someone who worked for Stacy or Stacy herself."

"It nearly worked," Stacy muttered.

"Hold still," Miles commanded her.

Amy cast Stacy a look that said, *This sucks. I'm sorry.*

Stacy was simply glad to have her friend here. Amy's presence was a comfort.

"If it was all a trap, what the hell are we supposed to do now?" Amy asked.

Rowan cleared his throat, and all eyes moved to him. His gaze remained on Stacy. "While you were gone, Elentya reached out to me."

"The elf queen?" Amy asked. "What does she want?"

"After hearing you dared to enter the Midnight Market to seek out anything regarding the vampire threat, the elf queen was impressed. She admires your willingness to go out on a limb. She has decided to help."

Stacy sighed. "That's good, but what does it matter now? We're still no closer to finding out what the hell the vampires are doing."

"That's just it." Rowan crossed his arms and leaned against the mantle. A fire danced in the hearth, warming the room. It did little to comfort Stacy since the manacles made her body cold to the bone. "Elentya thinks she knows why the vampires are here. Part of the reason, at least."

"You can tell us any day now," Kiera nearly growled when Rowan paused long enough for Stacy to count crackles in the fire.

Rowan hesitated. Stacy was unsure why. Finally, he stated, "The vampires are looking for an ancient prophecy known as the Crimson Codex."

Miles, Kiera, and Ethan grew very still.

"Holy shit," Ethan breathed.

"It can't be," Miles murmured.

Kiera remained silent, but her face tightened.

Stacy glanced at Amy, confused. Amy turned to Rowan. "What the hell is the Crimson Codex?"

"Elentya has been researching vampires for years," Rowan explained. "Ever since a clan of her people escaped a vampire council in Europe. They informed her the vampires were after something powerful, an ancient prophecy written in a long-forgotten language. One from another world."

"Malabbra," Kiera grumbled.

"Shit," Miles muttered.

"Okay, but what *is* it?" Amy asked, mirroring Stacy's exasperation.

Rowan shrugged. "Even Elentya and her people don't know."

"But you've all heard of the Codex!" Stacy exclaimed.

"We all know it's fucking dangerous," Kiera corrected. "We know it's from the dark world where vampires hail from and that using it will make them incredibly powerful. There's a reason it's been hidden for so long."

"We know it holds the key to a ritual that could grant immense power to whoever performs it," Rowan added.

"So we find it before the vampires do," Stacy stated.

"It isn't that simple," Rowan told her. "It's been missing for centuries."

"The vampires seem to think it's here," Amy inserted. "They must. Otherwise, why leave Europe? Maybe they looked everywhere they could there, then came here to do the same thing."

"She's onto something," Kiera remarked. "The Codex was last

seen in Scotland about seven hundred years ago. The vampires would have known that and already looked there. Someone must have brought it over here."

Stacy suppressed a shudder and met Rowan's gaze. "There must be a way to find it. Did Elentya offer any clue how we could do that?"

"Nothing that would help us locate it," Rowan replied. "However, she did promise her aid with anything we might need. Anything she's capable of, anyway."

Well, it was something, at least. *I need to thank the elf queen for stepping up and telling us about the Codex*, Stacy thought.

Ethan's voice broke through Stacy's thoughts. "There is one person we could ask."

Stacy laughed. "Do you think that could work?"

Ethan shrugged.

"Maybe clue us in?" Amy suggested.

Ethan turned to face the others. "Father Angus McFadden is old enough to have heard of the Codex. He's nearly nine hundred years old and came from Scotland. He would have been there when the Codex was. Maybe he doesn't know anything, but it doesn't hurt to ask."

Rowan and Kiera shared a look. "As long as Stacy wants to, I don't see why not," Rowan agreed.

Stacy had forgotten all about her manacles during the conversation and only remembered them now because a sudden weight lifted off her. The chains thumped to the rug, and Miles grinned. "We did it." He looked exhausted. So did Ethan.

"I don't want to do that again," Ethan grumbled. "Damn dark magic. I can still feel it." So could Stacy. The coldness was receding, but she itched to reach for a blanket despite the fire roaring before her.

"Thank you both for your help." She rubbed her wrists, where her skin was ice-cold. Slowly, she felt her magic coming back. Her energy was still low. She had to remain calm the rest of the night if she expected the full force of her magic to return. She didn't want to waste time resting, though. She stood, and Ethan steadied her with a hand on her elbow. "Let's see Father McFadden and find out what this Codex is all about."

"It's already late. Shouldn't you two be resting?" Amy asked, gesturing at Stacy and Kiera.

"I want to find out whatever we can about the Codex tonight," Stacy insisted. "I can rest when we're back." She glanced at Kiera, remembering the fae woman had used far more magic than her tonight. "How do you feel?"

Kiera stood, her eyes glittering a deep violet. "Whatever your orders are, I will follow them."

Stacy directed Miles to remain behind and keep the house secure. Amy offered to stay back and keep him company. "I could do more research while you're away, too. See what I can find about the Codex myself. I know it won't be much, but it doesn't hurt to look."

Stacy gave her a grateful smile. "You're the best, Amy."

So, the team was formed. Stacy, Ethan, Rowan, and Kiera would pay the old gnome a visit. *I hope this goes better than last time,* Stacy thought as they prepared to leave.

Father Angus McFadden was overwhelmed with glee at having four visitors in his home, especially at one in the morning. So overwhelmed, in fact, that he forgot all about his bottle of liquor. He set it on the kitchen table as soon as he spotted Stacy and Ethan in his doorway with a dryad and a fae sidhe woman behind them.

"My, my! I never have anyone to my home, much less such esteemed visitors as yourselves. Come in, come in!" Angus ushered them into his tiny house. Stacy introduced him to Rowan and Kiera. Angus shook Rowan's hand eagerly and Kiera's quickly, with a hint of fright on his face. Afterward, he leaned close to Ethan and muttered, "I don't much like fae, but if she keeps to herself, I won't kick her out."

Kiera heard this, and it didn't take her fae hearing to pick up on it. She simply raised her brows at Stacy, who grimaced. She had warned Kiera and Rowan about Angus, but no amount of description could have prepared them for the real thing.

Angus invited them to sit. Since only two armchairs and a handful of cushions were in the living room, they sat around a rectangular kitchen table instead. Rowan and Ethan squeezed onto a bench against the wall. Kiera stood by the door, shadows curling around her and arms folded. Stacy selected a rickety wooden stool, and Angus also remained standing as if he might choose to flee at any moment.

Maybe bringing Kiera hadn't been the best idea.

Stacy shoved the thought away to address more important things. "Father Mc—I mean, Angus—we've come here because we recently learned why the vampires might be in the city and what they could be searching for. Have you ever heard of the Crimson Codex?"

Angus remembered his liquor and snatched the bottle off the table. Stacy had chosen the wrong moment to ask her question because, as soon as she started, he took a swig. The words "Crimson Codex" made Father McFadden spray liquor at his guests. Rowan cringed as a droplet hit his face. Ethan smothered a laugh.

"Heard of it?" Angus boomed. "Of course I've heard of it!" His agitation showed in a wagging finger and splotches of red on his face. He gaped at Stacy. "Why on earth would you want to find it?"

"Because if we don't, the vampires will," Stacy replied, staying calm despite the priest's outburst. "What can you tell us about the Codex?"

Angus paced for several seconds, muttering incoherently with his hands perched on his hips. Stacy caught phrases here and there. "Dangerous thing it is!" "Mental magicals. What are they thinking!" "Vampires and prophecies never mixed well!" "Troll-turd liars!"

Rowan cleared his throat, drawing Angus' attention back to them. "What can you tell us about the Codex?"

"It's a dark history," the gnome replied, fidgeting with loose strings on the wrists of his robes. He shook his head and finally dropped into a chair at the end of the table.

"The Codex was last seen on an island called St. Kilda, off the coast of Scotland, about seven hundred years ago," he explained. "Explorers of my kind went to retrieve it sixty-odd years later and found the cave where it was hidden empty. They attempted to trace the Codex but were unable to as soon as it left land. The sea swallowed any traces of magic. I know about the Codex because it was a Scottish sorcerer who wrote it, many ages ago."

Sorrow threaded Angus' tone. "The prophecy speaks of a blood moon ritual that requires the sacrifice of powerful magical beings under a sacred ash tree. The more sacrificed, the stronger the ritual. That's what rumor says, at least. I have never read the Codex myself, so there may be inaccuracies."

"What happens if the ritual is completed?" Ethan asked, paling as each new detail unraveled.

"The completed ritual would resurrect an ancient warlock named Malakai," Angus stated.

Stacy glanced at her companions to see if any recognized the name, but none did. Only Kiera gave the slightest reaction, a flicker of curiosity.

"Malakai was born of a human mother and a creature from a world of darkness," Angus continued.

"Malabbra?" Kiera asked.

The priest twisted to face her. "You know it?"

"I've heard of it. Malakai is a word from their language. The only word I know, actually. It means 'bringer of death.'"

"It means more than that." Angus grunted. "It means 'bringer of disaster and destruction.' Worlds have fallen prey to his methods. His home world is a wasteland, or so I've heard. Malakai has been here before. He once held dominion over the supernatural world through fear and oppression. This was centuries before I was born. Through the efforts of many good magicals, he was banished from our world. Sent back to where he came from."

"In spirit," Kiera clarified.

Angus nodded. "His body was left here. Buried." He shook his head, and his voice dropped to a whisper that alarmed Stacy more than his shouting. "A terrible mistake."

"Why?" Stacy asked.

"Because it means he can be resurrected," Rowan answered. "And those who raise him could use whatever power was left in his body when he died."

"A power we can assume was monumental?" Ethan queried.

Angus nodded. "A devastating power."

Quiet settled over the group until Rowan blew out a hard breath. He seemed prepared to say something, but Angus spoke first. "I must warn you, Miss Drakethorn. The Codex is nothing to be trifled with. The sorcerer who created it went mad putting the words to paper and burned himself alive afterward, raving that he should have never let a power such as that come into the world."

Stacy's heart pounded. "If it's that bad, we should do everything we can to get it away from the vampires before they find it and perform the ritual." The dozen missing people would turn into thousands of dead.

"You must destroy it if you find it!" Angus exclaimed in a near shriek. "It could possess you, Miss Drakethorn. You have traces of dark blood in you!"

Stacy stilled. She glanced at Rowan, whose gaze shuttered. Ethan frowned. Kiera had gone still.

What the hell did that mean?

"Where is the Codex now? Do you know anything about its location?" Ethan asked with desperation.

"If I knew, I would have found it by now and destroyed it myself," Angus snipped. "I am no expert on prophecies. You will have to speak to Adrian about this one."

Stacy's heart sank. Great. Talk to the sidhe who had a price for everything. Was anyone other than this odd gnome willing to give them information for free? People were going to be sacrificed, for fuck's sake! And that seemed the mere beginning of what their enemies had planned.

Kiera pushed upright with a sigh. "I will pay him a visit now." Before anyone could stop her, she opened the door and vanished.

It was five in the morning, and Stacy stood at the windows in her library, overlooking the garden where the sky was turning soft shades of gray. She'd come home but refused to go to bed. Rowan, Miles, and Amy were asleep, and Kiera hadn't returned from visiting Adrian.

Stacy doubted she could sleep if she tried. She was burning to know where the Codex was, and the dragon inside her was pacing.

I must shift soon, she thought.

The rustling of pages turning behind her reminded Stacy she was not alone. She turned and spotted Ethan farther back in the library. The fire had died out, and he stood in the dim light of a lamp by the table, parsing through books. Her heart ached to see him there. He had refused to sleep while she was awake.

These past few hours, they had hardly spoken. Stacy was deep in thought while Ethan searched old books for shreds of answers on the Malakai figure Angus had told them about. He had discovered cults throughout history that had worshipped such a figure but nothing about an actual person.

Finally, he shut a book and sighed, rubbing his eyes. His gaze met hers. "I'm too tired for this."

"You should go to sleep, then," Stacy responded softly.

He considered her for a heartbeat, then strode across the library and took her hands. "I want us to talk first." He paused as if searching for words. "I feel a distance between us, and I don't like it."

Stacy's shoulders slumped. "I know. That's probably my fault." She told him Kiera's theory about the pent-up tension because of her dragon nature.

"She might be onto something," Ethan remarked. "Something else is bothering you, though. What is it? You know, other than the obvious 'I got attacked by vampires tonight and found out about a ritual that could end the world.'"

Stacy smiled despite herself but sobered a moment later. "I'm bothered by what Angus said about me having dark magic in my blood. I don't know what he meant."

She remembered the alarm on Rowan's face, but the dryad was asleep. She didn't want to wake him for the sake of answering this question.

Ethan considered it, then replied, "Many dragons, though not all, came from the Dark World. Or Malabbra, as Kiera calls it. I've heard it both from witches and in books. Of all shifters, dragons are most likely to turn evil." Ethan pulled Stacy closer and cupped her face. "That doesn't mean you need to worry about it. The last person I expect to use dark magic is you, Stacy."

She leaned into him and whispered, "But what if you're wrong? Sometimes, I feel a darkness in me. I don't understand it."

Ethan shared a half-smile. "That's called being human. We all have darkness in us. We have light, too. You use yours for good."

Stacy relaxed. "Thank you, Ethan. That helps." She leaned in to kiss him, but her lips had hardly brushed his when the library door opened, and Kiera strode in, grim-faced and exhausted. She was so tired that she didn't notice she'd interrupted a tender moment between the pair standing by the window.

"You're back," Stacy observed.

Kiera nodded curtly. "Adrian wasn't happy about me showing up in the middle of the night, but because of the deal we made, he had to let me in. He was as alarmed as the rest of us to learn about the Crimson Codex. We spent hours going through several documents, both ancient and recent. It was a hell of a lot of work, but we traced the Codex through time."

"And its current location?" Ethan asked.

Kiera revealed in one look that she had the answer, but it wasn't one they would like. She sighed. "The last place the Codex was rumored to be was in the possession of Victor Corbinelli."

CHAPTER FIFTEEN

Stacy awoke in the afternoon feeling as surprised and enraged as she had when she fell asleep shortly after dawn. Of course the Codex had last been rumored to be in Victor Corbinelli's possession. The farther away from his death she got, the more of a pain in the ass he became.

She took her time in the shower, simmering in her anger. Questions ran rampant in her mind. How long had Victor had the Codex? Had he been aware of what it was? Most importantly, where the hell was it now?

She headed downstairs not long after, the questions still swarming her. The only comfort she found was in the kitchen where Rowan and Miles were seated at the small table, eating a lunch of sandwiches and pickled vegetables. They informed Stacy that Kiera and Ethan were still asleep after being awake all night.

Stacy was glad for that. They'd both worked hard and deserved the rest.

"And where's Amy?" Stacy asked as she reached for a turkey and Swiss sandwich. It wasn't as good as what Kiera would have made, but Stacy was happy with Rowan's work.

"She's been holed away in the study since we told her about Victor's connection to the Codex this morning," Rowan replied. "She's doing what she can to find out where he might have kept it."

A surge of gratitude filled Stacy's chest. Amy had started working without being asked, and it was a clear reminder to Stacy that her friend was equally important to their team as anyone else.

Along with the questions she wanted to ask about Victor and the Codex, Stacy felt restless. The sleep she'd gotten would have normally left her well-rested, but instead, she felt on the brink of a breakdown. She stuffed a sandwich down and headed toward the back door.

Miles called after her. "Where are you going?"

Stacy didn't turn back as she replied, "To let the dragon out."

Stacy inhaled deeply and closed her eyes.

How hard could shifting be?

Really fucking hard, she thought. The last time she'd done this, she'd been so enraged with Victor in his werewolf form that shifting had been as easy as putting on a coat. Now, as she stood in a sunny spot in the center of a field far from anyone, she wondered how the hell she was supposed to replicate the experience.

Breathe, she told herself, keeping her eyes closed. The dragon was awake inside her. It paced and huffed, but her magic and hints of fear chained it in place. *Break the chain,* Stacy thought. She tugged at the magic within her and remembered what Kiera said. That Stacy was afraid of her form. She wouldn't be able to change until she shed that fear.

She thought of her friends at the house, her father, and all those she had known while growing up. She thought of her friends in the city and the Shinnecock nation, especially the young woman the vampires had taken. She remembered her promise to the vampire in the forest. *Tell your masters a dragon is waiting for them.*

Stacy considered going to her father and asking him to show her how to shift. However, he'd been doing it for so long that it came naturally to him. He wouldn't know how to teach her to change. This was something she had to do on her own.

With that firm resolve filling her chest, the chain broke.

A sudden bolt of magic speared her body. She threw back her head, unleashing a cry somewhere between surprise and pain. The second shift was bound to be uncomfortable. Stacy expected her back to tear open, making way for wings, and for claws to spear from her hands.

Instead, she imagined her dragon form was standing beside her, and all she had to do was step into it.

She counted to three and stepped. Her body was suddenly larger and heavier. She opened her eyes. Everything before her seemed smaller. She was higher up, and the colors around her were far more vivid. She could see farther, too.

Stacy tested her wings. They were heavier than she remembered. She managed to lift them. Wind coursed through them, and she pushed off the ground with a mighty heave. She didn't make it far into the air before she tumbled down, but joy soared through her. She had shifted. Everything else would come with patient effort.

Keep trying, she told herself as she lifted her wings for a second time.

The sun was close to setting when Stacy returned to the house wearing her human form. She stepped into the front hall, eager to tell her friends of her shifting success, when Rowan emerged from the living room. "Ah, there you are. Better come in here. Amy found something."

Heart thumping, Stacy followed him into the adjoining room. Miles was pacing, and Ethan was sitting on the sofa. Kiera had perched in the window.

Amy started explaining when they came in. "I discovered Victor had a team of people hired over the course of thirty years who he'd sent across the world to find various magical artifacts. Reports showed these artifacts, when brought here, were given to Victor.

"The reports don't mention they are magical, of course, but I had a hunch they were and asked Ethan and Miles about it. They have confirmed nearly every object. The communications between Victor and these artifact hunters indicate the artifacts were placed in Victor's personal vault. If Victor did have the Codex, he would have put it there. Only problem is, we don't know where the vault is."

"Could it be in one of his houses or offices?" Ethan asked.

"I doubt it," Rowan replied. "Victor was smarter than that. He would have put something as dangerous as the Codex in a place no one would associate with him."

Kiera snorted. "If he was even aware of what the Codex was."

"He must have had some inclination." Miles shuddered. "We've all heard of the damn thing. We didn't think it would end up in our neck of the woods, though."

Stacy turned to Kiera. "You said you and Adrian traced the Codex through time. Where was it before it got into Victor's hands?"

"It's hard to tell," Kiera stated. "We know of several places but not the order they were in. We can safely guess Victor had it most recently since it was obvious in the texts we cross-referenced that the Codex wouldn't have gone anywhere else after Victor found it."

An idea came to Stacy, and she took out her phone. The

others watched, perplexed, as she called a number. "Hello, Mr. Gray. I hope I'm not bothering you."

"You could never bother us, Ms. Drakethorn. What can I assist you with?"

"My team and I are investigating the issue you called about last week, and we've discovered something that might be connected to Victor Corbinelli. We need to know where a vault he might have kept prized possessions in might be." Stacy was careful not to mention the Codex; no need to alarm the Graytails, especially over the phone. "Did you ever hear something about a vault when Victor sought your services?"

Mr. Gray reported that, unfortunately, no one among the Graytails had heard of a vault, let alone its location. Stacy had expected this answer. "Thank you anyway, Mr. Gray," she told him, trying not to sound disappointed. She hung up a moment later and turned to her friends. "Shit, I've killed everyone who could help me. Ain't that a bitch?"

"There is one person we could talk to," Ethan suggested, meeting Stacy's eye. "I know you don't want to see him again, but Alban is the one person who would know. I'm certain now that the other secret, the one he wanted your blood for, had everything to do with the Codex."

Amy whipped her head toward Stacy. "I'm sorry, he wanted your *blood*?"

Stacy sighed. "Don't ask me why. I didn't bother asking."

Amy shook her head. "I don't want to know."

Miles frowned. "Alban wasn't willing to give up the information for nothing before. What makes you think he'll change his mind merely because you guessed the secret?"

"That's not it." Ethan stood and paced. "Alban knows he could get banished from the Midnight Market for hiding something as catastrophic as knowledge about the Codex. All we need to do is send someone with influence to the head of the Market's council and report him for having proof that the vampires are looking for the Codex."

"We don't have proof. Not exactly," Kiera reminded him.

"We also can't shove Stacy in front of the council and hope it'll work," Rowan inserted. "They won't like a Drakethorn flaunting their power."

"She's the only one of us with that kind of influence," Miles argued.

Amy's gaze held Stacy's. "You could ask one of your allies. The wolf pack queen or Elentya. They both have influence and have promised to help."

"I'm hoping I won't have to ask either of them," Stacy replied. "Alban might get scared enough by the threat and tell us what he knows about the Codex and where it is." She eyed Ethan. "Do you think we could get him to meet us on neutral ground? I'd prefer not going back to the market."

Ethan nodded. "I'll talk to him and see."

"Are you sure you want to do this?" Rowan asked.

She nodded. "Alban pissed me off last time, and I'd like to never see his face again, but I think it's our only course of action. Unless you know someone else who could tell us where Victor's vault is."

Rowan glanced at Amy, who was quick to add, "I doubt other members of the Circle who know will give up the information."

"I could always torture it out of someone," Kiera suggested as if it was the obvious course of action.

"We'll try Alban first," Stacy interjected before anyone encouraged Kiera's idea. "Let's leave torture as a last resort."

Kiera sighed. "If you say so."

Ethan said he would make the appointment and squeezed Stacy's hand on the way out. When he was gone, Stacy noticed the looks on her friends' faces. "What?"

Amy shrugged and grinned. "You two are cute."

"*Very* cute," Miles emphasized.

Rowan merely smiled. With nothing else to discuss, Amy went to straighten up the study while Rowan and Miles returned to their estate duties. It was strange to Stacy how their lives worked. A never-ending ebb and flow between facing their enemies and dealing with everyday necessities.

Kiera lingered in the living room. "You seem relaxed, considering everything we just talked about."

Stacy smiled faintly. "I had time to myself today. It helped."

Kiera nodded. "Good."

Stacy didn't need to tell her she'd shifted. Instead, she rubbed her belly. "I'm starving."

Kiera grinned. "I'll have dinner ready soon."

It was a rundown, seedy-looking establishment, but the bar was better than returning to the Midnight Market.

Dinner at the estate had been cut short when Ethan brought news that Alban was willing to meet them in the city to discuss "the findings."

"This soon?" Amy had asked at the dinner table. "How lucky!"

"Ethan can be convincing," Stacy told her.

Amy had waggled her eyebrows in response. "What else is he convincing about, Stacy?"

Rowan drove Stacy and Kiera to the location of the bar, where they met Ethan outside. Miles and Amy remained behind, saying they were eager to hear what came of the meeting. "Of course he chose this place," Stacy murmured. "He seems eager to make us as uncomfortable as possible."

"Better than the Market, though, right?" Ethan quipped.

Stacy nodded. "Thank you for arranging this." She inhaled deeply, facing the building with determination. "Let's get this over with."

Raucous laughter, loud conversation, and music thumping

from speakers filled the interior. It was Saturday night, and the bar was packed. Not ideal for the conversation they needed to have, but Stacy would take whatever they could get.

Ethan led them through the crowd to a curtained-off partition. He moved the curtain to reveal a small back room with booths and tables. Alban was sitting at one, basking in the glow of neon lights.

They stepped into the room, and Alban stood, eyeing Stacy with no small amount of contempt. "You won't fool me, Drakethorn. I—" Whatever threat he was going to make never left his tongue as Alban's eyes met Kiera's. Something changed in his face. Contempt turned to fury, surprise, and recognition.

Stacy turned to Kiera to ask whether they knew each other. She didn't have time to ask. Kiera slammed into the male fae, throwing him against the wall and hissing in his face, "I told you never to come here, Cyprian!"

CHAPTER SIXTEEN

Stacy was so surprised at Kiera's sudden outburst that she stood gaping for several seconds.

Rowan moved first. He brushed between Stacy and Ethan, grabbed Kiera's arms, and hauled her off the fae. "Stop this, Kiera," he muttered into her ear. She struggled against him, but at Stacy's firm command to stop, she stilled. She didn't relax, though. Stacy had never seen Kiera stiffer.

Alban—or Cyprian, as Kiera had called him—straightened his clothes. His face was red with fury. "Good to see you too, Adrilonziglia."

Ethan and Stacy shared a puzzled look.

"That's not my name anymore," Kiera hissed. "Why are you here? I told you that if I ever found you here…"

Stacy stepped in, arms folded. "How about one of you tell me how you two know each other?"

"Seems like you need a catch-up," Ethan remarked.

"Let me go," Kiera muttered to Rowan. He gave her a look. Exasperated, she added, "I won't touch him!"

Rowan released her, and Kiera moved away from him and

eyed Stacy. "Cyprian was part of the assassins' guild on the fae world. He left me for dead during the rebellion."

Alban wiped Kiera's spit from his cheek with the back of his hand and spoke, his voice roiling with contempt. "You were royal! Once a fae royal, always a fae royal. You were never a true ally to us, and you proved it that day when you let half our guild get slaughtered!"

Stacy had expected the meeting to turn sour or Alban to be difficult. She had not expected it to reignite a centuries-old feud between fae assassins.

"Did you lose your ear in the rebellion?" Ethan asked dryly, gesturing at the disfigured side of Alban's face.

"Yes, and you can thank her for it. She's the reason her damn royal bastard of a brother cut it off," Alban snipped and whirled toward Kiera. "My name isn't Cyprian anymore. I chose another when I came here two hundred years ago."

Kiera didn't seem to care. She gestured at the place where his ear had been. "If you don't start explaining why the hell you came here to begin with, you'll lose something more precious than your ear." She gave the spot between his legs a pointed look and slid her hand toward the knife at her side. Stacy could have sworn that Alban paled.

"Kiera," Rowan growled in warning.

She drew her hand away from the knife but cast a glare in the dryad's direction. Stacy wasn't sure how this would have ended if not for Rowan's intervention. Kiera was too high-tempered at the moment to listen to anyone else.

"I was banished, like you were," Alban spat in Kiera's direction. "Your prick of a father sent all of us from the rebellion who survived to other worlds. I ended up here."

"But the rebellion was five hundred years ago, not two hundred," Kiera replied.

"Yeah, he kept us in prison for three hundred years!"

Kiera shook her head. "For once, I wish my father had used a more severe punishment."

"He did," Alban growled. "What do you think was done to us in those prisons for three centuries? None of it was pleasant." The look on Kiera's face said she felt sick even thinking about it.

Alban looked at Stacy. "I learned my skills as a secrets keeper in those prisons. Of course, my assassin training helped, but you hear a lot of things people don't want you to know when you're sitting in one place for three hundred years."

Stacy couldn't imagine sitting in a fae prison for three *days*, let alone the length of time Alban had endured. She still thought he was a jerk, but at least now, she understood where it came from.

Kiera decided it was time for Alban to stop yapping and turned to the others. "Alban taught me everything I knew in the assassins' guild, then sold me out at the end. He told my friends, the family I'd built for myself, that I was a traitor. They all turned against me. I was lucky to escape with my life and went to the only place I knew I wouldn't be killed. My father's stupid palace."

"Wouldn't the fae have more reason to kill you, though?" Ethan asked.

Kiera scoffed. "My father is too creative and controlling to simply kill someone. He wanted me to live a long fae life. He wanted me to be miserable. Apparently, he thought living in the human world would make me that way. I was miserable for a long time, but not because I was here. He doesn't know the favor he did me by sending me here." She twisted, pointing at Alban. "I'm glad you rotted in prison. It makes me feel slightly better about all my friends believing I betrayed them."

A distant sorrow on her behalf shone in Rowan's eyes. Stacy and Ethan eyed Alban, waiting for an explanation.

The fae male's eyes burned with ire, nearly red instead of amber. "I'm not sorry for it."

Kiera launched at him, but Rowan saw it coming and grasped

her arm. "Let's go for a walk, shall we?" He escorted her from the room while casting Stacy a look that said, *Sort this out yourself.*

Stacy nodded. She and Ethan could handle this.

Alban dropped into the booth, head in his hands. It gave Stacy some satisfaction seeing him like this. He wasn't the one in the power position anymore.

"We're wasting time," she told him. "Whatever happened between you and Kiera doesn't concern me at the moment. We need to find the Crimson Codex."

"Don't try to act like you don't know," Ethan added. "We know Victor Corbinelli had it last, and it's inside a vault somewhere."

"What makes you think I'd know the location?" Alban asked, glancing at them. His expression had cooled somewhat, but not enough for Stacy to drop her guard. She'd learned better about doing that around powerful fae.

"If you don't, you will find out. If anyone can, it's you," Ethan replied coldly. "Don't tell us, if that's what you really want, but we will go straight to the Market council and report you."

Alban stilled, and Stacy wondered if they could have threatened to unleash Kiera on him instead. If anything would work to get the information out of him, it was her. However, Stacy wasn't interested in spilling unnecessary blood.

She said as much to Alban, whose white cheeks turned red at the thought. He sighed. "I know where Corbinelli's vault is. However, I cannot guarantee the Codex is still there."

"What do you mean?" Ethan demanded.

Alban shrugged. "Others have paid handsomely for the same information. They will not like it when they learn I told you as well. Especially for free."

Stacy didn't give a rat's ass. "Who did you tell?"

"I won't share that information, no matter what you threaten. Telling you is practically suicide on my part."

Stacy believed him. Her heart sank, but she didn't push it.

"Then tell us where the vault is, and we'll figure out the rest," Ethan prodded.

Alban hesitated, and Stacy decided she was done waiting. She had one card up her sleeve. If this was the time to pull it out, so be it. Stacy bent to Alban's ear and whispered something to him.

Alban's eyes widened, and he nodded slowly. A combination of surprise and satisfaction morphed his features. "Corbinelli's vault is hidden deep within a series of catacombs under an abandoned church on the outskirts of the city." He withdrew a small card and pen, scribbled an address on it, and handed it to Stacy. "Good luck getting in. It's warded as well as it can be."

Stacy decided to worry about that later. Her heart thumped faster. Finally, they were getting closer. She felt like she had the end of a ball of string and was close to untying the knot at its center. She had other questions, though. Ones she was certain Alban would answer now. "Why was Victor involved in finding the Codex?"

"Isn't it obvious?" Alban commented. "Victor Corbinelli always intended to side with the vampires and was building an army of manufactured werewolves to make it happen. He wanted to remake the underworld with himself as king."

"Glad I could squash his dreams, then," Stacy replied dryly. She was unsurprised to hear Victor's plans had been bigger than she'd realized. She dreamed of the day when she would no longer have to hear his name.

Alban rose as if to leave. No doubt, he wanted to flee the building before seeing Kiera again. "I must warn you, Miss Drakethorn, this situation you're meddling in will come with consequences."

Stacy's voice was calm. "Is that a threat, Alban?"

"No. I simply mean to tell you these vampires are not the same as your past enemies. And the Codex...well, even my kind wishes it never existed."

Another warning. Stacy was beginning to wonder if she was

too deep into this mess. *If no one stands up to them, we can count on the whole city going under,* she thought. "I appreciate your discretion. I assume you will keep this meeting confidential."

Alban's eyes glimmered. "That's my specialty, Miss Drakethorn."

He strode from the room, and Stacy hoped she wouldn't have to see him again anytime soon. She nodded toward the exit. "We should find Rowan and Kiera. Tell them what we learned."

Ethan went with her. He waited until they were outside, past all the clamor of the bar's patrons who'd been unaware of the meeting taking place. "What was it you whispered to…" Ethan started, but Stacy interrupted him.

"We need to get to that church as soon as possible." She spotted Rowan and Kiera across the street, waiting by the car. Kiera leaned on the hood, arms folded tightly. She was muttering something to Rowan. She seemed calmer than before, but Rowan's rigid back told Stacy their conversation wasn't a pleasant one.

Stacy and Ethan reached them in four strides, and Rowan turned. "What did he tell you?"

Ethan repeated the information but left out the part where Stacy had acted cryptically. He glanced at her with a look that promised he would ask about it again later. Rowan read the address on the card Stacy handed him. "Shit."

"What is it?" Kiera asked.

"I know where this is," Rowan replied. "The abandoned cathedral has had problems for years. It was abandoned because of ghosts over sixty years ago."

"We need to go there now," Stacy insisted.

Kiera's brows furrowed. "Is it wise to go tonight? I think we need a plan first."

"I agree," Ethan spoke up. Rowan, as always, was inclined to plan before going anywhere, much less to a haunted church with an underground vault warded by strong magic.

Stacy sighed. "Fine. We'll go home and plan." As they got into the car, Stacy wondered at herself. She had never been the type of person to barge into action. She'd always been a meticulous planner. What changed?

Must be the dragon in me, she thought. This wasn't the time for the Drake side of her to open its eyes. She leashed it again. Tomorrow, they could visit the church. Stacy hoped the Codex would be there, and the vampires didn't reach it first.

CHAPTER SEVENTEEN

"I don't mind ghosts, but I avoid them when I can," Ethan murmured from beside Stacy. He was on her left while Kiera stood at her right, hand perched on the hilt of a long dagger at her side.

Rowan stood beside Kiera, his features grim as they faced the abandoned cathedral. "It's only the church that is considered haunted, not the catacombs beneath."

Kiera shot him a look. "Where do you think the ghosts came from? The people who died in the catacombs."

Stacy felt a chill and wasn't certain if it came from Kiera's words or the night wind brushing the back of her neck. She had braided her hair, the bangs loose over her forehead. Though the braid hung down her back, the mark of the tree wrapped in thorns showed. Like Kiera, Stacy wore black fighting leathers. Ethan and Rowan wore neutral browns and greens to blend in.

Stacy resisted the urge to shiver as she surveyed the old stone building before them. It certainly looked like no one had been inside it for over sixty years. The grounds were overgrown, and the steps leading to the wooden doors were cracked, with weeds springing up between them.

According to Amy's earlier research, the church couldn't be demolished because it was a historical site. The government hadn't decided what to do with the location. Amy had also pinpointed the location of the catacombs' entrance. She'd found all this information that morning while Stacy, Rowan, Kiera, and Ethan made other plans and preparations. Now that they were here, Stacy was itching to move.

Rowan led them past the church. None of them dared to glance at the darkened, arched stained-glass windows for fear of seeing a gaunt, translucent face peering out at them. No matter how old she got and how many fearsome enemies she met, Stacy would feel jumpy about spirits floating around. She feared the unseen and the unknown, which was why her back was rigid when they passed the church. She imagined the spirits haunting the building were looking out at her, gauging whether she was a threat worth driving from the grounds.

Behind the church was a small graveyard littered with headstones so old the names carved into them were faded. Several were laden with moss. Rowan headed for the back of the graveyard, where a tall stone crypt stood against a low wrought iron fence. He halted at the crypt's entrance, noting how it was sealed. The entrance to the catacombs. Now, the trick was in opening the damn door.

Magic flickered at Rowan's fingertips. He traced various parts of the door until sigils glowed on it. The door opened with ease, a signal that the warding was farther below. Great. Wards to undo in the dark.

Rowan glanced over his shoulder at his companions. Stacy nodded.

Before them, a staircase descended into darkness. Rowan summoned an orb of green magic to his palm and took the first step. Kiera was second, with Stacy on her heels and Ethan bringing up the rear. About twenty steps later, they reached the bottom and found another doorway. This one was laden with wards. The magic over it shimmered and hummed.

"This one will take more time," Rowan muttered. He set to work, but ten minutes in, he confessed he couldn't do it alone. Strain showed on his face and in the hunch of his shoulders. Ethan joined in, and before long, Kiera and Stacy gave their assistance.

The wards formed a complex web over the door with threads difficult to find and more difficult to unravel. Stacy felt like they kept running into knots that needed delicate untying. Finally, Rowan stepped back, sweating. The door opened to a dark, narrow tunnel leading farther down. "Watch for traps," he warned them as they headed in.

They traversed several twisting passageways, with Rowan using his elemental connection to navigate. Kiera, close behind him, remained alert for signs of danger. Her knife was half drawn from its sheath in preparation for a sudden attack. She was still wary after what happened to her and Stacy the other night.

The deeper they delved, the stranger the sensations became. It wasn't merely the cold dampness of being underground or the walls being so close. The air felt heavy, and walking through the stone passageways felt like sloshing through thick mud. The dark magic lingering in this place was oppressive.

Stacy glanced back at Ethan, whose face was grim. "You feel it, too?" she whispered.

He nodded. "Of course I do. It's awful down here."

Stacy had felt the same magic when investigating an abandoned cottage on her grounds where Isadora Voss had hidden while attempting to assassinate her. She could have sworn ancient voices whispered around her. "You don't seem as affected as I am," Stacy murmured to Ethan. She noted the same about Rowan and Kiera. Their gaits had not slowed. If the magic was weighing on them, they didn't show it.

"You've had magic for less time," Ethan reminded her. "Dark magic is bound to affect you more."

That made sense. Ethan had magic since he was a young boy but had only been alive for twenty-seven years. Rowan and Kiera, who were easily five hundred years old, had encountered dark magic more times than they could count.

"Does it ever get better?" Stacy asked.

"Not better, but easier. You get used to it."

Stacy shuddered. It was hard to imagine getting used to this sickly feeling.

"I don't like how it feels either," Ethan began, but Kiera hissed at him to be quiet. She sensed danger ahead. Kiera and Rowan had halted, eyes wide with concentration.

A blast of magic exploded from down the tunnel, throwing Rowan and Kiera back into Stacy and Ethan. Rowan was hit the hardest and issued a pained groan. Kiera pushed past him, her shadows at the ready. She blasted back at the attackers ahead.

If Stacy thought the dark magic lingering in the air was bad before, she wasn't ready for this. It hit her like a wave. She saw only black for several seconds before Ethan's hand on her shoulder jerked her back into the tunnel. With the space so narrow and their attackers coming at them from the opposite direction, they had no choice but to retreat. They'd come so far already.

Her vision cleared in time to see Ethan weaving a protective shield over them. Rowan was back on his feet and surging toward the coming attackers with twin swords in hand. Kiera was behind him, flinging shadows with one hand and drawing her knife with the other.

Stacy's heart hammered. She summoned flames to her fingertips but wished she could shift. *Not here*, she thought. Impossible underground. She cursed and flung the magic forward, Ethan's shield still around her.

Kiera was closest to the attackers by this point, but Stacy was close enough behind to see they were vampires. Her heart lurched. They had made it here first.

She had no more time to consider it. Kiera slashed her knife in graceful arcs, switching hands with ease. Her shadows curled around her, bellowing in blasts down the tunnel. Rowan was at her side, a force to be reckoned with. He called out incantations, and the earth responded, rumbling to disorient the vampires.

There had to be at least a dozen coming from that end of the tunnel.

Stacy heard Ethan's cry of alarm before she felt the second blast of dark magic. It came from the direction they'd already ventured, hitting her with enough force to extinguish the flames from her hands and send her flying into the wall. Ethan had taken a harder hit and was on one knee, breathing hard.

Steeling herself, Stacy ran for him. Four more vampires appeared, wearing cruel smiles. Stacy dodged another blow of magic, flinging up her shield since Ethan's had dropped with the summoning of dark magic. She covered both herself and him. Ethan was on his feet, speaking spells as he lunged with his magic. Stacy was at his side, flinging orbs of flames.

We're surrounded! Stacy thought. *And these tunnels are too damn narrow.* She had expected traps but not active attackers.

The four vampires who'd come at them from the other side soon realized they had no chance. One screamed as Ethan's binding magic wound around her, cutting into her skin. Another turned and fled. A third tried to but met Stacy's blast of fire and was incinerated. The fourth didn't bother trying as another spell from Ethan cleaved his chest.

Stacy turned to Rowan and Kiera, breathing hard. They stood beside a pile of vampire bodies. In addition to dark magic clinging to the air and the coldness around them, the tunnel now reeked. Now that the fight was over, cold realization struck Stacy. "Fuck. They got here first. The Codex..."

She took off down the passageway with no real inclination of what direction to go. Rowan and the others followed, shouting after her. More vampires could be this way, but Stacy didn't care. She would find that damn vault.

Finally, she skidded to a halt at the sight of an opening in the wall and a room beyond. Her heart sank. The vault had been broken into. No doubt the Codex was missing. She hurried into the room anyway.

Rowan, Kiera, and Ethan ran in seconds later. Stacy searched the room with wild fervor. Everything was missing. Trunks and vessels were open, but they were empty. *No, no!* Stacy turned to the others. "Alban said he sold the information about this vault to someone else. Whoever it was got here first."

Ethan was listening, but something on the wall distracted him. While standing at the right angle and holding magic over it, he glimpsed a pattern etched into the stone. He stepped closer, gasping. A message was written in a language Stacy didn't know. Ethan did, though. It had been written in a combination of magic and blood. "I've seen this before," he murmured.

"What does it say?" Stacy asked, heart hammering.

Ethan turned, blanching. He swallowed. "It's mocking you for being late. It speaks to 'the witch dragon' specifically."

Stacy stiffened. Rowan and Kiera glanced at each other.

Ethan continued. "I've seen messages written this way before. From Viper."

Stacy sank to her knees. *Of course.*

"We were betrayed," Ethan murmured.

Stacy felt like crying, screaming, or both. Instead, she fell into a dismal silence. Rowan stood beside her, clasping a hand to her shoulder.

"She must have gone to Alban the second she knew we wanted to deal with the vampires," Ethan continued. "She probably already knew about the Codex. Fuck."

"Then she sent us to Alban so we would waste our time," Stacy muttered. "That's why he was so smug when we went to him. He knew what Viper was up to. I'll make her pay."

"You think Viper broke in here?" Kiera asked.

Ethan nodded. "She saw an opportunity to make something and took it. She's probably going to sell the Codex to the vampires for a few precious fangs or whatever the hell she wants." He dragged a hand down his face. "We should have never told her anything."

A familiar pang of failure hit Stacy's chest. *It was my idea to bring Viper into this. Ethan warned me, and I didn't listen. This is my fault.*

"She would have found out about the vampires being here and gone for the Codex regardless," Rowan reminded them. "Don't worry about not coming here last night. That message is at least a few days old. Viper probably had her hands on the Codex by the time she sent you to the Midnight Market."

"Odds are she's already sold it, too," Kiera inserted.

Stacy felt like everything was unraveling. That traitorous bitch. She would make the snake pay for what she'd done. Finally, Stacy stood, her eyes burning gold. Nearly all the green in her irises was gone. "We have to find where the vampires have taken the Codex. Before they raise that fucker Malakai from the dead." Stacy turned to Kiera. "You have my permission to go to Viper's home and do whatever you want to get the truth from her. And then some."

Kiera nodded grimly. "I doubt she's there, but it doesn't hurt to pay a visit."

CHAPTER EIGHTEEN

The following morning, Stacy went with Rowan into the dining room and found Amy and Miles waiting for them, both eager to learn if the Codex had been found.

"Located, yes," Rowan grumbled as he sat at the end of the table. "But not by us."

Amy looked at Stacy, who sat at the head of the table. "What happened?"

Stacy explained the situation in the catacombs, prompting disgruntled sounds from Miles and disappointment from Amy. "Surely there has to be a way to track the vampires," Amy proposed, ever the optimist.

Stacy wished she felt the same. "Not exactly, but I have tasks in mind for each of you." She hoped at least one of the avenues she wanted to explore would lead them to answers. It had taken her hours to fall asleep last night, thanks to the thoughts rumbling around in her brain. They'd been so close but hadn't made it in time. *After all that looking around and two vampire attacks!*

Stacy drew herself back to the present and shared what she had assigned Kiera to. Kiera had gone to look for Viper and to find out where the vampires might have gone with the Codex. Late in the night, Kiera reported to Rowan that the manor house they'd tracked the vampires to before was empty, and she was heading to Viper's shop. They hadn't heard from her since.

"What we need to focus on now is finding out where the ritual might be held. The blood moon is only a few days away," Stacy pointed out. "All we know is that it needs to be done under a sacred ash tree."

"We can rule out the entire concrete jungle. That's a start," Amy returned. "That's about it, though. There's like nine hundred million ash trees in the state of New York alone!"

"How do you know that?" Miles asked.

"Used to be a tree girl," Amy replied with a shrug. "Plus, you learn a lot of random facts in journalism."

Rowan's voice rumbled across the table. "I'll make contact with our allies today and see if they've heard anything. With the vampires having the Codex, they'll be busier. Someone has to know something. I plan to speak to Elentya this afternoon."

"I've been wondering about her," Amy spoke up. "The elf queen?"

"That's right," Rowan confirmed. "What about her?"

"I wonder why Kiera doesn't handle that side of things. Aren't elves and fae nearly the same?"

Miles chuckled. "Don't ever say that in front of Kiera. She'll bite your head off."

"They're like cousins," Rowan clarified. "Similar, but with key differences. Elves are far older and have inhabited many worlds. Fae came from a line of elves that broke off from the most powerful of their kind. Their history is long and torrid. I suggest asking Ethan about it, though, not Kiera. You'll hear profanities you didn't know were invented if you ask her."

Amy grinned. "That might be more amusing than Ethan's bookish talk."

Stacy cleared her throat, a signal to bring the attention back to the matter at hand.

"Sorry," Amy murmured.

Miles coughed to disguise a laugh, but it didn't work well.

Stacy eyed the groundskeeper. "Miles, I want you to spend today fortifying the estate's defenses in whatever way you can. I wouldn't be surprised if we were assaulted by both vampires and traitorous members of the supernatural community. The vampires' influence has spread farther than we thought." An image of Viper's face flashed through her mind. "Amy, please keep your ears and eyes alert for anything new in the human world."

Amy stood and saluted. "Aye-aye, Captain."

Stacy finished breakfast and left the kitchen. As she started toward her office on the back portion of the property, she noticed clouds gathering overheard. Sprinkles of rain fell on her face. She pulled her phone from her pocket. *I've got one more favor to ask.*

In the shadows of early morning, as rain drizzled onto the street, Kiera entered Viper's shop. She went in through the back door, where no one could spot her. She found it unlocked, which ignited a new sense of caution within her.

The place was in disarray, as if the person who was last here had scrambled around, searching for their possessions and stuffing them into a bag before fleeing. Kiera's keen gaze swept the room as she kept to the shadows, out of sight, in case she was not alone.

She spotted broken glass on the floor by the counter and, not far off, large pieces of what had been a vase and spilled flowers. A small puddle surrounded it. Viper must have knocked it over in her haste. Kiera noted other things. An overturned bookcase, a slight dent in the wall, and a large tear in curtains closed over a window. A realization came to her. A person couldn't have done the damage here. Something larger had caused this.

"Fuck," Kiera got out half a second before a large mass of scales exploded from a dark room behind her. Kiera hit the floor and rolled, avoiding the strike of fangs and a long, lashing forked tongue. The body of a large snake swept over her.

Kiera rolled again, this time to the side. Glass crunched under her. She cursed and got to her feet. The snake was easily twice Kiera's size. It twisted, its tongue flicking. Viper's eyes were large and yellow, her fangs as long as Kiera's hand. One bite and the viper's poison would have Kiera writhing on the floor, inching toward death.

"I never liked snakes," she muttered.

The viper's sleek green body glowed. She struck again, hitting the wall behind Kiera as the sidhe fae flung herself into shadows. Kiera appeared on the other side of the room, wishing someone had dealt with this bitch before she decided to shift.

"Where is the Codex?" Kiera demanded, lunging for the snake with her knife drawn. She slashed out, but Viper twisted out of her way.

"Sssomewhere you'll never find it," the snake hissed.

"Traitorous bitch!"

The snake twisted again and would have taken Kiera out if not for the fae's quick thinking. She jumped up on the counter, and more glass crunched beneath her boots. Instead, Viper crashed into the glass display case on the counter. It fell on the other side and shattered.

The place wasn't in disarray because Viper had been attempting to flee. She had simply shifted and waited for prey to show up. The mocking message in the vault made more sense. Viper had expected Stacy to come here, and now she was pissed off that Kiera had come instead.

"I'm not the only traitor," Viper replied. She twisted toward the hallway, and Kiera was certain she would strike again. Instead, she slithered at a speed Kiera could hardly fathom through the building and out the open back door. She vanished into vapors.

Kiera stood in the shambles of the shop, breathing hard. Viper was too good, and Kiera knew better than to waste her time hunting it down. It was better to return home and see what progress the others had made.

Kiera headed toward the back door, intent on returning to the Thorn estate, when another idea struck her. She couldn't get revenge on Viper for her betrayal tonight, but she could make another pay for letting this happen. Kiera didn't bother sheathing her knife. It was time to pay Alban another visit.

Ethan returned to his shop, intending to sleep as long as he could. He'd decided it wasn't worth opening his shop for the day. They had too much going on with the vampire ordeal. He didn't like that Stacy was paying him for all his work, especially now that romantic feelings had sprung up between them, but he needed to pay the bills somehow.

He'd thought he would lead a quiet life as a bookshop owner. Now, he was practically dating the heiress to a large estate and helping her hunt enemies across the city. *This is my fight, too,* he thought. The vampires wouldn't stop until they controlled the entire city and its paranormal inhabitants. That included him.

So get to work, he told himself.

The moment Ethan saw Stacy's name on his phone lock screen, warmth surged through him. He had a guess as to what she was calling about before he answered. By the time their conversation ended, he'd agreed to delve into the extensive library of arcane tomes in his shop and search for a way to counter the resurrection spell in the Crimson Codex.

"There has to be a counter-spell. This can't be the first time in history someone has tried using magic to resurrect someone," Stacy had insisted over the phone.

Ethan agreed. The sorcerer who'd created the Crimson Codex couldn't have done so unless other resurrection spells had come before him. Every spell was a development from another, and they were all integrated. *Like the covens that wield them,* Ethan thought. *Or, in this case, a cult of bloodthirsty vampires.* He had shared these thoughts with Stacy.

"There has to be one that will work before the shithead is resurrected, right?" she replied.

Ethan wasn't certain but agreed it was worth looking into. When they were off the phone, he hunted through his collection, remembering he had once cataloged books containing death and resurrection spells. The magic was rare and dangerous but known enough that books had been written about it.

Rain pattered against his shop windows, and Ethan soon found a collection of three leather-bound volumes at the back of a dusty shelf customers almost never glanced at. He opened the first and discovered it was a book for bringing dead plants or small animals back to life. It was mostly natural and herbal rejuvenation, unhelpful for their current situation.

He opened the second to find a series of journal entries from an old Irish druid who had spent half his four-hundred-year life searching for the hidden, buried body of a woman he'd fallen in love with as a youth. The journal entries indicated that she had died in a shipwreck and her body was buried off the coast of Ireland. The druid had sought her body and a way to resurrect her.

Ethan found the story heartbreaking and sorrowful. It wasn't right to bring someone back from the dead, was it? They couldn't possibly be the same after years had passed. Even so, Ethan imagined one of his loved ones dying and what he would give to bring them back. His parents. His grandparents. He imagined it happening to Stacy, and his heart twisted.

He refocused on the task at hand. At first, the sad tale of a druid seeking his dead lover seemed irrelevant, but then Ethan stumbled on an interesting piece of information. One of the final journal entries spoke of a cult off the coast of Ireland and their dark leader, a mysterious figure shrouded in shadows. Ethan stilled as his eyes caught on one word.

Malakai.

Was this the same warlock the vampires were attempting to raise?

The entry told Ethan this cult had taken the druid in, promising him his dead love to resurrect if he dedicated the remainder of his life to their dark lord. The words on the page became scattered, suggesting the person writing them had either been afraid or emotional when he'd penned them. Probably both, judging by the page's contents.

They brought me to the center of their sacred forest, where a clearing spanned several feet, and they had drawn ritual lines in the ground. A great ash tree stood at its center, and beneath it, a pile of bodies. So many I could not count them. The sight was horrifying enough that I fled, and they followed me.

I knew their secrets and what they planned to do with me. They'd spoken of my service to their dark lord but had failed to mention the part where they carved up my body for ritual sacrifice. I should have known.

I've hidden in a cave far from that place for days now. It storms, and the rain will not let up. I fear they will find me, for this Dark Lord and his servants do not cease searching. I must act quickly. I must find a way to counteract the ritual before the bodies of the dead they've taken are used for malevolent purposes.

Ethan's heart thumped. When he'd first come across this book, he thought it was merely a sad tale of a man losing his love and encountering evil on the way to right a wrong. It was far more than that, he saw now.

Had the druid found a way? Ethan turned the page and found a series of strange figures marring the page. It was all that remained in the journal. He traced them, his breath growing shallow. "It's a code. If I can crack it, I'll know the counter-spell."

Questions barraged him. Had the druid ever had a chance to test it? Had it worked? Ethan swallowed. Most importantly, could it work again?

"I'm sorry, Anastasia, but your father is out of the country at the moment on business. He will not return for a few more days."

Stacy's heart sank with Reginald Blackguard's words over the phone.

"Is everything all right, Anastasia?" Reginald asked.

"Not exactly, but nothing for you to worry about. Please remain at the estate and have everyone else do the same. Secure it in whatever way you can. This vampire threat is no joke."

"Call us if you need help," Reginald replied. "We are here for you always, Anastasia."

His words and tone touched her. "I will, Regi. Thank you. Please have my father call me when he returns."

After she hung up, Stacy sank back in her chair. It was late afternoon, and with the sun moving toward the horizon, she felt like the day had swept by. Disappointment over her father's absence weighed on her. Why did he have to leave at the worst times? He knew what she was dealing with here!

Stacy shoved the thoughts away. She needed to figure this out on her own. Khan wouldn't be around forever. *Right?* she thought.

Stacy sat at her desk. Seconds later, Rowan stepped into her office. He was wet from the softly falling rain, and his features were somber. "What is it?" she asked, setting her pen aside. Her paper was full of pointless scribblings anyway. She'd been trying to decipher the code Ethan had sent her to no avail. It was outside her skillset, and she only hoped Ethan could crack it.

"Reports are coming in from other supernatural factions about betrayals," Rowan told her. "It seems Viper wasn't the only one. Elentya reported first, saying there's been a traitor among the elves. One of her war generals and a handful of warriors have betrayed them, and several elven children were kidnapped."

Stacy cursed. "To take to the vampires, no doubt. They want paranormal blood for their ritual."

Rowan nodded grimly. "The Codex requires one of each paranormal kind to raise a powerful being like Malakai. Elentya and the rest of her people have gone into hiding but will fight at your side if you need them."

"We must save the people they took." Stacy had felt anxious before, but desperation clamored inside her now. *Keep calm,* she told herself. *You'll never figure this shit out in a panic.* "Who else?" she asked, struggling to keep her voice even.

"Small groups here and there," Rowan replied. "Some shifters. Others are small covens. A few gnome councils."

"Has anyone else been taken?"

Rowan nodded. "I'm afraid so. The vampire cult has the Codex. We can't doubt that. All they need now are enough powerful paranormals to sacrifice."

The blood moon would be soon. Stacy's heart beat faster at the thought. How the hell were they supposed to figure it out in time?

Rowan continued. "It seems the vampires carrying out these abductions have a powerful weapon. An artifact capable of controlling the minds of weaker paranormals. Elentya witnessed it happening to one of her soldiers as she and her people were fleeing. I've heard of it before. It's an ancient blood ruby imbued with powerful dark magic and linked to a chain many believe was forged on Malabbra."

Dread curdled in Stacy's stomach. "Is there anything we can do about it?"

"We can trace the dark magic from where the artifact was last seen and try to find the vampire wielding it," Rowan replied. "That's the only way. I've already sent word to Kiera."

Stacy stood. "We must warn our other friends of this threat before anything happens to them."

Rowan swallowed and blanched.

"Rowan, what is it?"

"The Graytails sent in a report, too. The young woman they recently initiated as their sovereign magical protector has been taken."

CHAPTER NINETEEN

The mansion was much nicer than the last one they'd stayed in and farther outside the city.

The room they were in now was the picture of comfort with deep maroon carpet that matched the draperies hanging from floor-to-ceiling windows. Ornate furniture graced the room, and though none of it matched, it all seemed to belong here. A fire roared in the hearth, a welcome change to the chill pressing against the windows outside.

Despite the comforts, Valen was wary. He wasn't certain coming here had been the best idea.

He turned to Lenora, who lounged on a loveseat, her feet propped on one of the arms with her elbow on the other. She stared at the dancing flames and tapped the back of the couch with her long fingernails. Valen glanced at a grandfather clock in the corner, then remembered it didn't work and checked his watch instead. Any minute now.

Several minutes passed, and Lenora sighed. "Where the hell is she? She was supposed to be here already."

Valen's heart thudded. Maybe Viper had been discovered and wouldn't make it home. The snake shifter had sent word that she needed to stop by her shop before she came here to the mansion she owned outside the city.

Viper's house was decadent, full of strange and beautiful artifacts. It was no wonder she'd been interested in finding the Codex. However, she did not come to this house often. She preferred living in the city, where she could keep her yellow viper eyes on everyone, including the witch who was a friend of Drakethorn's.

Valen didn't mind that. The snake shifter made him nervous, though he tried to hide it. The less she was around, the better.

He glanced around the room, comparing it to his previous accommodations. Hines' mansion had felt too empty and cold. Valen's own flat back in Rome hadn't been much better. He knew they would not be in this house long. Viper never did anything without a price. Cassius had promised them a better home after this when they'd completed the ritual, and Malakai was with them.

Valen wondered if their new home would include himself, Lenora, Cassius, and the warlock, and he half-wished Viper was going to live with them instead of Malakai. He'd heard only tales of the warlock and all the power he had displayed. He was too young to have been alive when Malakai ruled. Lenora was, too, though she'd learned about firsthand experiences from her grandmother.

Finally, the front door opened and closed. The light patter of footsteps and the sound of something being dragged across the wooden floorboards followed. Viper appeared, eyes dancing with delight despite the thin line of her mouth. She wasn't in snake form, at least. Valen had caught one sight of her snake body the night before and almost pissed himself.

You're a fucking vampire, he thought. *Get a hold of yourself.*

Viper wasn't alone, though the other person was clearly unconscious. Valen realized the figure was a paranormal. The pointed ears said enough.

Lenora raised a brow. "Where the hell did you find a fae?"

"Elf," Viper corrected. "Brought to me by a general of the elven queen herself."

Though Viper was small, her strength was considerable. She dragged the elven warrior to the middle of the room, disregarding the mess his bloody, rain-soaked body made on her rug. "Don't worry. I didn't poison him. Do with him as you wish." She waved a hand in Lenora's direction.

Lenora straightened, eyeing the elven warrior with glee. Valen didn't take his gaze off Viper. "What happened to you? You've been in a fight."

Viper's yellow eyes pinned him. "I ran into the fae bitch who works for Drakethorn." She was clearly bothered by the fact that she hadn't managed to kill her. Valen wasn't sure if this comforted him. On the one hand, the fact that someone could evade Viper in her snake form was a relief. On the other, he didn't like knowing someone that skillful was on their enemy's side.

Cassius and Lenora should have listened to me when I told them we'd have to deal with a dragon, he thought.

It was too late. Valen didn't see a way back. They'd climbed this far, and he was as determined as the others to lead a comfortable life where they had power over this city and its supernatural factions. All of them. He watched the elven warrior, who stirred. Viper dropped into an armchair to watch Lenora's work.

Lenora stood from the loveseat with a gracefulness that made Valen jealous of both her skill and the fact that Cassius shared her bed. Lenora slid a chain from under her shirt. The dazzling ruby of the artifact glowed against her chest, the dark magic within rising to the surface.

Her fingers hovered around it, drawing out the energy. She harnessed it, and her eyes turned from amber to red. Valen had seen her use the artifact only a few times since coming here.

Most of those instances had been practice. However, the wicked smile on Lenora's face said this was no mere practice.

The elven warrior realized he'd been taken somewhere he did not recognize and struggled to his knees. Sweat poured down his face, and terror shone in his eyes. "Pl-please let me go home."

"Oh, you poor dear," Lenora crooned in her French accent. "I'm afraid that won't be possible."

The artifact's magic floated around him and settled on his neck, slowly forming a vice. "I need you to tell me what you know of your people and where they have gone," she murmured. "Where is your little queen hiding?"

Valen wondered why. The elven warrior was enough. They could sacrifice him on the night of the blood moon and be done with it. That wasn't what Lenora and Cassius wanted, though. They were convinced they needed the most powerful people in the city for their sacrifice, including the elven queen, who had gotten away.

The guard could help them find her.

"Tell me," Lenora whispered in a lover's cadence. "Tell me where your queen has gone."

The fear still lurked in the warrior's eyes, but so did defiance. "*Never.* I won't betray her."

His scream sliced the air as Lenora's magic poured from the artifact and surrounded his head. "Tell me," Lenora repeated, her voice cool and calm.

The warrior continued screaming.

Viper sat nearby, watching with grim satisfaction. Valen glanced at her, not bothering to hide his wariness. Had it been wise to side with someone like her? They would soon have enough bodies for their ritual and the Codex, thanks to her. *Whatever it takes,* Valen thought. *But I won't let that snake slither to the top.*

He returned his attention to Lenora, who knelt before the warrior and held his head between her hands. His screaming ceased, and he stared blankly beyond her, his lips moving but no sound coming from them. His pupils and irises disappeared, leaving only the whites of his eyes. Finally, Lenora let him slump to the floor, unconscious again. She stood.

"Well?" Viper asked. "Did it work?"

Lenora nodded. "It did. I know where the queen is."

"Where?" Viper demanded.

The look Lenora gave the snake shifter made Valen wonder if they were about to rip each other's throats out. Finally, Lenora stated, "I will speak to Cassius about it first."

Valen didn't care where the elven queen was. Fetching the ritual sacrifices wasn't his job. He stayed here to guard the Codex while Lenora did her work with the artifact. He was fine with that.

Viper hissed but didn't push. Instead, she glanced at the warrior and produced a satisfied smile. Without a word, she stood and sauntered from the room. Valen didn't realize how rigid he'd become in her presence until she was gone.

Lenora whirled toward him. "Thanks for nothing."

"What?"

"You could have helped me with Viper."

Valen shrugged. "You had it handled, Le." She bristled at the use of the nickname but soon forgot it when the sound of the door opening came again, and their leader joined them.

Cassius strode in, wearing a blank expression. The sight of the elven warrior on the floor made him pause. He whipped his head to Lenora, who simply nodded.

"I'll take care of the elven queen," Cassius announced. "Valen will stay here with the Codex."

A chill moved through Valen. Guarding the Codex was the job he wanted, but not when it was only him and Viper in the same house. "And you will go after a new target," Cassius continued, gesturing at Lenora.

Lenora played with the artifact. The glow had vanished after the elven warrior blacked out for the second time. "But it's so much easier when they come to me."

"We're finished with Hines' list," Cassius responded curtly. "We go after them ourselves now. I've seen a group of our kind after a new target. The magical protector of a pack of werewolves who happen to live near the Drakethorn bitch. You will join the other vampires, Lenora. What is it the stupid humans say? Kill two birds with one stone?"

Lenora grinned. "You want me to get the little magical pup and Drakethorn at the same time?"

"If you can." Cassius' eyes gleamed. "With that pretty necklace of yours, we'll soon have an unstoppable horde of paranormal beings at our command. Warriors first, sacrifices later." Pure hunger and bloodlust gleamed in his eyes. Valen felt another chill when Cassius added, "The Drakethorn girl won't stand a fucking chance."

Rowan's revelation had hardly left his mouth before Stacy's office phone rang. She answered it, then blanched after listening to the voice on the other end. The conversation continued for a few minutes before Stacy hung up. "The Shinnecock people have had three more members go missing. Same as before. Fang symbol at the site of the abductions." She felt sick merely saying it.

During her call, Rowan checked his phone, his brow furrowing. He cursed. "It's a joint attack. I have distress calls from another group of supernaturals I'm connected with in the city, and there was a hit on the Midnight Market last night, with several taken."

Stacy's heart hammered. The vampires weren't trying to be subtle anymore. The kidnappings from before had only been the beginning. Her personal phone rang. This time, it was Ethan. She answered on speakerphone. "Please tell me you have good news about a counter-spell and not something else."

"Unfortunately, it is something else." Ethan informed her that he'd heard from the witches of his former coven about two of their members disappearing in the night. Taken from their beds with signs of violence left behind. "The witch who leads the coven says she almost caught up to those who took the others and saw a flash of red light, then they vanished."

Stacy frowned and addressed Rowan. "Please reach out to all your contacts, especially Elentya, and make sure they are safe. If Elentya needs a place to go, she can stay here."

Rowan's curt nod was all the confirmation she needed. "What will you do?" he asked.

"I plan on helping the Graytails find their missing member and rescue her. They're our closest allies. I have the best chance of helping her over anyone else." Stacy gestured around. "I can't sit in here any longer without doing something."

"Very well, then," Rowan replied. "Please take someone with you."

Amy couldn't go. It was too dangerous. They needed Miles at the estate to maintain security. Kiera had not returned from going after Viper.

"I'll be at your house soon," Ethan stated. "Don't leave without me."

Stacy thanked him and told Rowan, "Some of the Graytails will be with us, too. I'll be safe. Well, as safe as one could be when chasing down vampires."

Rowan hesitated but finally relented.

Within half an hour, Rowan was making calls with Amy and Miles in his study, doing what they could to help him reach out to the supernatural community. Ethan arrived, and he and Stacy took her Bentayga to meet the Graytails. By this time, the sun was setting, and the hues of dusk stained the road. At least the rain had dissipated.

"Her name is Luna, and she's only sixteen years old. The youngest protective magical the pack has had in generations," Stacy explained as she drove toward a small town near her home that bordered the Graytails' land.

Mr. Gray had reported that Luna was patrolling the borders with some of the pack's guards and had vanished early that morning. Since then, the pack had been searching their lands and the town nearby. "They've picked up traces of her," Stacy added. "Mostly her scent mixed with vampires. Apparently, vampires have a distinct, repugnant smell that the wolves have no trouble picking up on."

"Then we shouldn't have trouble finding her, right?" Ethan asked.

Stacy sure as hell hoped so.

She stopped the car on the outskirts of the town, where she spotted two gray vans parked beside a small forest. They got out, and she and Ethan glimpsed the vans' drivers, members of the Graytails she recognized. Stone and Warden were sons of the pack's alpha and head of the patrolling sector. They'd also been the ones to last see Luna.

"Poor pup disappeared out of nowhere," Warden muttered to Stacy when she approached.

"We've picked up her scent going into town," Stone inserted.

"Be wary," Stacy warned them. "Those vampires are ruthless motherfuckers."

The werewolves nodded. They didn't need to hear about Stacy's encounters with the creatures to know that. Stacy remembered her battles with Isadora Voss and wondered if she would come up against a vampire of the assassin's caliber anytime soon.

If I do, I'm prepared for it, she thought. *Those fights with Voss weren't for nothing.*

Stacy and Ethan rode in one of the vans with Warden, Stone,

and three other patrolling werewolves. When they reached the town, Warden pulled into a gas station and parked.

In their human forms, the wolves looked more like bodyguards than creatures who could shift into beast form and tear someone to shreds. Stacy supposed she was similar. No one who spared her a second glance would guess a dragon crawled beneath her skin.

Ethan was the least suspicious-looking. He'd shown up in his normal attire—a cable-knit sweater and jeans. However, his alert expression and the magic humming at his fingertips assured he could handle himself.

The small town was quiet since most places closed after dark. Stacy noted a small bank, a few restaurants, a second gas station, and a tiny church on the main road, with neighborhoods fanning out. One diner down the road appeared open, with warm light in the windows and patrons venturing in and out.

The group exited the van under the guise of going into the gas station when the wolves paused, sniffing the air. Ethan stilled. "I sense dark magic," he whispered. The wolves had caught a scent. Luna's or the vampires? Probably both, Stacy thought.

She turned as a wave of something in the air hit her. Her body suddenly felt heavy. "Damn dark magic," she muttered. It was coming from the gas station.

Through the windows, Stacy caught sight of a flashing red light and remembered what Ethan had told her earlier about the coven witches. Her heart thundered. "Luna's in there!"

The wolves were already taking off toward the building. Fur bristled at their knuckles, and their jaws tightened and elongated. Ethan and Stacy strode after them, magic simmering at their fingertips in case they needed to summon quick shields. The closer they drew to the gas station, the heavier the sensation of dark magic became.

Thunder rumbled overhead, and drops of rain spattered. The lights inside and outside the gas station flickered.

Warden signaled for the wolves to surround the place, then stepped toward the front door. Stacy peered inside but saw only overturned shelves and flashes of red magic. The other lights went out. A man cowered behind the counter, whimpering. A cloud of smoke from the area of the red magic concealed the figure who stood there. This vampire wasn't like the others. She was powerful and could wield magic.

Like Voss did, Stacy thought. Through the haze, she glimpsed a figure half-turned into wolf form on her knees on the gas station floor. Red magic surrounded her head, and her face was tilted toward the ceiling. A scream wrenched from her throat. *Luna!*

The damn vampire had taken control of her mind!

The rain fell harder, but Stacy didn't care about getting wet. Warden broke down the door, and Stacy was intent on barging into the place after him and confronting the vampire.

As she lifted her shield on instinct, a sudden shattering of glass and an explosion of magic from inside the gas station threw her back.

CHAPTER TWENTY

Stacy hit the ground hard and groaned.

One side of her face was scraped and bleeding, and her eyes stung with tears. Slowly, she peeled herself off the pavement. Her hair was plastered to her face, and she swiped it aside to peer at the gas station.

The blast of magic had come from inside but not from the vampire who'd dug her red, tentacle-like magic into Luna's mind.

Luna was standing now, a shield of blue magic glowing around her. Stacy spotted the vampire groaning from where she'd been thrown into a shelf of camping and outdoor essentials by the broken window. Shards of glass scattered the ground outside.

Stacy spotted the other werewolves struggling to their feet. Where was Ethan? She didn't have time to look for him before the vampire rose, and red magic flared from the ruby on a chain around her neck.

Stacy realized what the vampire was about to do. "No!" she cried, though her voice wasn't loud enough for the vampire to hear.

She lurched for the gas station building and the gaping hole in the wall where the werewolf had thrown her magic. Glass crunched under her boots. Rain pelted her. She ignored both. She was halfway across the lot before another blast of magic exploded inside the building. This time, it was red.

Stacy flung up her shield. The vampire's magic collided with it, rattling her body. Damn, this one was powerful. Beyond her, Luna was once again on her knees. The blast had hit her hard. It had also collided with Warden and Stone, who had attempted to get inside again.

The female wielding red magic stalked toward Luna, intent on seizing her mind once more.

"Hey, stop! Leave her alone!" Stacy shouted.

The vampire halted and turned on her heel. She was beautiful in the same way a new, sharp knife was. Sleek black hair hung in a braid down her back. She had sharp features, silver eyes, and blood-red lips. Stacy wondered if it was truly blood. The vampire's pale skin shimmered with roiling magic.

The vampire didn't seem to think much of the drenched woman who'd called out to her. Stacy summoned her magic into flames, holding them above her palms with her shield protecting them from the rain. If the vampire took one step toward Luna, Stacy would burn her body to a bloody crisp.

A sneer parted the vampire's lips, then recognition crossed her countenance. Instead of growling with contempt, she laughed. "I was wondering if you would show up, Drakethorn."

Stacy didn't have time to react. The vampire, whoever the hell she was, sent another blast of red magic. Stacy didn't move. Her shield was strong, and she conjured a wall of fire to meet the vampire's blaze of power.

When both the flames and the red energy vanished, the vampire stared at Stacy in shock and dismay.

Stacy didn't understand why until the vampire clutched the ruby around her neck. Its glow had diminished. "No one has ever been able to resist this!" she screamed.

Resist what? That damn ruby necklace?

Realization hit Stacy. The vampire was using the necklace to take control of magical minds. Not weak minds, either. Luna was as strong as any member of her pack. Something else had made Stacy immune.

"That's what happens when you come after a fucking dragon and her friends," Stacy growled. She didn't want to send more fire toward the vampire or turn into a dragon. Otherwise, the poor gas station owner would be out of a job and a building.

The female vampire seemed to forget all about Luna and sauntered into the rain. A wicked smile parted her lips. Stacy jerked her head at Warden and Stone to help Luna. They cast wary glances at the vampire as they went in to collect her.

Footsteps splashed through puddles, and Ethan appeared at Stacy's side.

"You should go with the wolves. Get Luna to my estate," she murmured to him.

"Not a chance," Ethan replied. "I will fight with you."

"But—"

"You asked me to join your coven and lead at your side. This is my responsibility, too."

Stacy couldn't argue with that.

Ethan's shield gleamed around him. "I've got you," he added, his shield extending to cover her so she could focus her magic into the spells she needed to bring the vampire to her knees.

The vampire's red magic unfurled from her hands like whips. Stacy braced herself for a tough confrontation. Then, the vampire's expression seized. She stilled, seeming to recall something, then turned and vanished inside.

"After her!" Stacy called to the wolves closer to the door. When she hurried into the gas station, the wolves reported that the vampire had vanished.

"Into thin fucking air," Warden growled. He had Luna's arm slung across his shoulders. The young werewolf did not appear wounded on the outside, but her expression was blank. She sagged against Warden.

Stacy's instinct was to chase after the vampire, but they had no idea where she'd gone, and Luna needed their help.

Ethan laid a hand on Stacy's shoulder. "Let's go home. From there, we can figure out what to do next."

"We need to find out more about her shiny mind-controlling necklace," Stacy returned coldly. "But you're right. We'll go home first."

In the van, they headed to the road where they'd parked the other vehicles. The rain still came down in a torrent, leaving them all soaked. Stacy didn't care, even when they got into her car and dripped all over the seats. As she pulled off the road, she told Ethan, "Remind me to donate to the repairs for that gas station."

"One step at a time, Stacy," he replied. "Let's take care of Luna first."

***

Stacy changed her clothes, found something for Luna to wear, then met the others in the library.

Ethan had changed, too, but he was practically drowning in the clothes Rowan had lent him. Amy sat by the fire, smothering a laugh at the sight of him. She invited the young werewolf to sit beside her. Luna had been freezing since the vampire's magic pierced her mind, and it helped to settle by the fire.

"I have an herbal salve Kiera made to help with your scratches and cuts," Amy told her. Luna seemed at peace by Amy's side, especially when Amy began gently applying the salve to her small wounds.

Rowan, Miles, Warden, Stone, and the three other werewolves focused on Stacy as she scanned the room. "Where's Kiera?" she asked Rowan.

"She returned while you were gone. She had a run-in with Viper but no success in taking her down or getting any information out of her," Rowan explained. "She's been sleeping since she came back."

Stacy wondered if Kiera had gone somewhere else after visiting Viper's shop. She'd been gone all last night and today.

"The damage was more to my mind than my body," Stacy heard Luna admit to Amy as she strode across the room and took the armchair across from the werewolf.

"Luna, I would love for you to tell me what happened, but I understand if it is difficult to talk about," Stacy invited.

"It is difficult," Luna admitted after a few silent seconds. "But not because of the pain. Don't get me wrong, it was horrible. The problem is that it's difficult to describe."

"Do your best," Stacy urged gently. She sat back as if to communicate with her body that they had time, though truthfully, they didn't.

Luna began, hesitant at first but gaining confidence. "It was like the vampire got into my mind. I heard her voice in my head. Horrible whispers. She wanted to know about my power and where the alpha was. I don't think I told her anything, but I felt cold all over, and like my head was full of needles. She might have seen something in my mind without me knowing it."

At the pained expression on her face, Stacy assured her, "You've told me enough, Luna. Thank you." Stacy couldn't help but feel for the young woman. She was only sixteen and carried a far greater burden on her shoulders than Stacy had at that age.

It may be best to wait a few years before we ask her to join our coven, Stacy thought. The poor pup needed to finish growing up first. Despite this, Luna had an endurance and determination that Stacy admired. The pack was lucky to have her.

Despite Stacy's insistence that she stop there, Luna continued. "There's another thing. She told me her name. I don't know if she meant to or if the fusing of our powers let me glimpse into her mind, too."

Stacy and Ethan shared a glance, remembering Luna's blast of power. The werewolf was young, but she had potential. It would be remiss for anyone to underestimate her.

"Her name is Lenora, and she's working with two other vampires named Valen and Cassius. From what I gathered, Cassius is their leader," Luna revealed.

Stacy looked at Rowan. "Have you heard of those names?"

He shook his head. "Vampires in Europe usually go by last names. The families there are patriarchal, and they hold onto their last names as if it is their sole identity."

Stacy thought of Kiera and the fae, who were not much different. She nodded at Luna. "Thank you. I'm sure everything you've told us will help."

She turned her attention to Rowan, Miles, and Ethan, who stood side by side. Rowan towered over the other two with crossed arms and a grim expression. Stacy hoped for the day when she'd find Rowan smiling more often.

"We need to find out more about the artifact the vampire used on Luna," Stacy directed. "And find a way to stop them before they can complete the ritual."

"If we knew what was actually in the Codex, I could come up with a counter-spell for the ritual," Ethan commented.

"I know what's in it," a voice from the library doorway announced.

Kiera stood there, her shoulder propped against the frame. How long had she been there?

She strode into the room, her expression tired and grim. "I went after Viper and failed to catch her. She went into snake form. Which, by the way, is fucking huge."

"You made it out alive," Miles pointed out. "That's something."

"Barely," Kiera replied. "I decided I wasn't coming back here until I got some information, so I paid Alban a visit."

Rowan and Stacy shared a look. Stacy wondered if the fae male was dead or possibly missing more than his ear. She decided it was better not to know.

"Alban knows what's in the Codex. He told me what the ritual entails," Kiera continued as she scooted onto the edge of the large table, her legs dangling. "The ritual requires the sacrifice of several bodies, all with magic in their blood. The more powerful the being, the more powerful the ritual.

"Those conducting the ritual must make a smaller sacrifice to give them the power to make the larger one. The second sacrifice involves spreading the mind-controlled bodies of those being offered around a sacred ash tree, then carving through the hearts one at a time so the blood pools around the tree."

Stacy felt sick, and Luna blanched.

Kiera seemed to notice and skipped the details. "It all boils down to one thing. A lot of people die, and the elemental magic of the tree is enough force to reawaken the soul or body of another being. In this case, Malakai.

"The final step is to speak an ancient incantation only found in the Codex. I won't dare speak it now, but Alban wrote it for me." Kiera produced a small roll of parchment. She moved to hand it to Stacy, but Ethan reached for it instead.

"I can use this to create a counter to the ritual." He looked at Stacy. "I'll need time to work on it."

"How much?" Rowan asked.

"As much as you can give me."

"The blood moon is the night after tomorrow," Miles reminded them.

Ethan nodded. "There's another thing. Stacy, I think you could craft a counter-spell to destroy that vampire's artifact. You were probably immune to her attack because of your dragon heritage."

"Makes sense to me," Kiera inserted. "Dragon blood comes

from the same world where an artifact like that would have been made. Only you will be able to destroy it."

Me or my father, Stacy thought. But Khan had been away for some time now, and she had no idea when he would return. *I need to do this without him, anyway,* she thought.

"It might not be a bad idea to visit our priest friend," Rowan suggested. "He may be able to tell you more about the artifact."

Stacy wasn't exactly inclined to make another visit to Angus after the evening she'd had, but Rowan was right. "All right, then. Rowan, you and I will visit Angus. Miles, you and the wolves will stay on guard here. Amy will take care of Luna, and Kiera will rest."

She turned to Ethan, and he spoke for her.

"I'll work on a counter-spell for the ritual."

With everyone knowing their tasks, they dispersed from the room.

Stacy felt like they had something to work with, but the urgency weighed on her. She clutched the locket around her neck, taking comfort in its warmth. *Here we go again,* she thought. *Another journey into the city.*

CHAPTER TWENTY-ONE

"You think this will be enough booze to lubricate the gnome's memory?" Stacy asked after hauling a barrel of the best liquor the estate had across the armory floor.

Rowan cast the barrel a rueful look and grunted. "Memory or goodwill?"

"Both."

"If that doesn't work, I don't know what will. I suppose you expect me to carry it?"

Stacy grimaced. "Be a dear and haul it to the car?"

Amy, who stood by the stairs leading to the main floor of the house, giggled. "Stacy and I want every excuse to see your muscles, Rowan."

Rowan glowered as he hauled the barrel onto his shoulders. "I thought you were past crushing on me, Amy. Aren't I supposed to be your grumpy uncle now?"

Amy shrugged, amusement still shining in her green eyes. "Good looks are still good looks."

Stacy groaned. "Please don't let Kiera hear you say that."

"Kiera?" Amy glanced at Rowan, mouth dropping open. "Are you two…"

Rowan glared at Stacy before heading up the stairs, barrel on his shoulders.

"Oops. Guess I wasn't supposed to voice my observations." Stacy smirked.

Amy caught her arm as Stacy headed for the stairs. "Hey, be careful out there. Those vampires know you mean business, and I wouldn't be surprised if they were watching your every move."

Stacy had thought of this already. "I will. And Rowan will be by my side the whole time." She had hoped to take Ethan and Kiera as well, but Ethan needed to work on the counter-spell for the ritual. Kiera would help him by supplying knowledge about the Codex, but then she was on strict orders to spend the rest of her time sleeping. They needed everyone in prime condition for the fight ahead.

Outside, Rowan loaded the barrel into the car. Stacy wore her combat suit in case she needed it but hoped their visit to Father McFadden's home would not involve being assaulted on the street. Amy hugged her goodbye, whispering, "I'll see you soon," then waved the pair off.

Half an hour later, Stacy and Rowan stood outside Angus' home. The gnome opened the door, glaring until he recognized Stacy. "Ah, the dragon comes again! Next thing you know, you'll be goin' to the church durin' the day to confess your sins."

Stacy hoped not. "We need your help again, Angus. This time, we brought a gift. Consider it a thank you for last time and a request for help tonight."

Angus eyed the barrel Rowan carried and ushered them inside.

Stacy explained what had happened since their last visit. "As a gesture of our ongoing goodwill, we brought this." She gestured at the barrel. "Your favorite liquor, if the bottles on your shelf are any indication."

"Yer not tryna poison me, are ya?" Angus demanded, his snow-white brows drawn together.

Stacy blanched, glancing at Rowan, then back at the gnome. "Of course we aren't!"

"Traitors all over the damn city," Angus muttered. "Don't know who ta trust."

Rowan grabbed a nearby empty cup that looked clean, filled it from the barrel, and swigged. "Not poisoned."

Finally, Father McFadden seemed convinced. "You wanna know 'bout the artifact, don't ya?" he asked as he poured himself a large tankard. With the roaring fire and the wooden table and benches they sat on, Stacy felt transported back in time to some European tavern serving mead.

"That's right," she answered, explaining what she'd seen Lenora do and relating Luna's description of the artifact's power.

The longer she spoke, the deeper the wrinkles in Angus' face became.

"Have you heard these vampires' names before?" Rowan asked.

Like Rowan, Angus had not and cited the same fact about last names and vampire factions in Europe. *I'll put Amy on the name-searching job,* Stacy thought. She wondered if it would matter. Either the vampires would succeed in bringing their beloved warlock back and doom the whole damn world, or they would die. Hopefully, thanks to Stacy's fire or Kiera's knife in their guts.

Stacy didn't particularly care how they dealt with the vampires. However, they needed to destroy the damn artifact first.

"I've heard of it," Angus amended at last. "Ah, lass, this artifact ye speak of, it's a dangerous relic from a time best left forgotten. Its power is not to be trifled with."

Stacy's heart sank.

Angus considered the barrel, then added, "But with this fine barrel of liquor, I reckon I can share a bit more. It's gone under many names, mostly popularly 'the vengeance stone.' It's been in this world for centuries but came from another."

"Malabbra?" Rowan asked.

Angus nodded and shuddered. "Don't like that name bein' said in my home. Not while I'm sober, anyway."

Rowan and Stacy exchanged a look, convinced that Angus hadn't known sobriety in years.

"But yes, lad, the artifact comes from that world. Passed down through vampire families ever since. I suppose this woman you saw usin' it was one of 'em. Dangerous and dark. I'd hate to see it myself." He shuddered again before taking a swig from his tankard.

"Do you know a way to destroy it?" Stacy asked, impatient but trying not to show it.

"Destroy it?!" Angus stood from his stool so quickly it toppled over.

"Yes, destroy it. What the hell else am I supposed to do?"

Rowan shot her a warning look. He didn't have a problem with her being firm, but if Angus caught a tone he didn't like, they were as good as thrown out.

Stacy softened her features. "Please, Angus. The artifact didn't work on me. Don't get me wrong, I'm glad the vampire can't control my mind. I have a feeling my dragon blood makes me immune."

"You're right, lassie," Angus amended at last. "Not many could destroy it. Use your magic to counteract its power."

"How? Is there a spell?"

Angus was quiet for another moment, considering. For once, Stacy wished he would keep talking. Finally, he nodded. "I know a few you could try."

Stacy didn't have time for experiments, but seeing no other option, she asked if Angus could write them down. Moments later, she had a yellowed piece of parchment with the gnome's handwriting scribbled across it. For a scatterbrained, intoxicated individual, the priest had some of the most elegant script Stacy had ever seen. "Thank you for everything, Angus. Your knowledge has been invaluable to us."

Angus simply motioned at the barrel. "Bring one of these every time you come for a visit, and I'll tell you anything I can."

When they returned the car, Rowan murmured, "Should I add a line item in the estate budget for liquor gifts to our dear priest friend?"

Stacy hoped they wouldn't have to keep coming to Angus for information, but she nodded. A grin pulled at her lips. "Might as well. We should be keeping our allies happy."

Alex waved goodbye to his friends as they piled into an Uber outside the bar.

He'd promised them he could walk home since his apartment was only a block and a half away. Besides, the bar had been too warm inside, and the fresh night air already made him feel better. He watched the Uber pull away with three of his friends jostling one another in the back seat. An Elton John song floated out the windows.

Alex stood in the neon lights of the bar, laughing. He turned to light a cigarette before heading down the street. It was better not to join his friends anyway. He was a witch, and they were not.

The alcohol had led him to accidentally cast a spell earlier that got the bartender's attention and earned him another drink. Thankfully, none of his friends had noticed, though a werewolf in the corner had rolled his eyes. Alex wasn't inclined to have his accidents witnessed again. Better to go home and get into bed. "A shower first," he muttered. What time was it?

He checked his phone only to find it had died. It had to be past midnight.

He glanced toward the horizon for hints of dawn. The sky

was inky black, and he was certain this direction wasn't east, anyway. Whatever. His head was spinning.

He recalled his friend Kyle's parting words. "Sure ye'll be good, man? Bunch of people been goin' missin.'"

Alex knew it. He was determined to make it a block and a half without being abducted.

He rounded the corner of the street, and his apartment complex came into view. He took a drag of his cigarette and hummed a line of the Elton John song, unable to remember what it was called, then halted mid-hum as something skittered up his spine. He shivered.

It wasn't the night air. Alex had the sensation he was being watched. He glanced over his shoulder, but no one was there. The sensation was more in his magic than anything else.

"It's the beer," he muttered, walking again. "Shouldn't have drank so much." He recounted how many he'd had. It wasn't enough to normally make him feel this way. *Was I fucking roofied?* he wondered.

He could have sworn the shadows ahead had taken on strange shapes, not the block formations of the buildings on either side of the street. A new sensation washed over him, leaving him cold and heavy. Dark magic. He'd felt it before.

Alex glanced over his shoulder again. This time, he caught glimpses of those strange shadows—all sharp, moving lines. Someone was following him. His heart beat faster as he picked up his pace. His apartment was a few hundred feet away.

He never made it that far.

Within a hundred feet of the building, Alex stilled before an open alley. He hadn't meant to, but a sickly sensation washed over him, and he couldn't resist a command for his body to halt. A voice entered his mind. *Hello, witch. You're exactly what we hoped to find tonight.*

The voice was feminine and alluring, but the dark magic slicing through him made Alex wish he'd never heard it. Two figures materialized from the shadows. One was a tall, grim-faced male. The other was a woman with a glowing ruby around her neck. Her cruel smile told him it was her voice in his mind.

Alex tried to run, but he couldn't move. He screamed as magic blasted through his mind, and he knew no more.

Valen couldn't help himself. He was either too curious or too bored. He couldn't decide which. He only knew he was sick of sitting around in Viper's library, reading old books he didn't care for and feeling suffocated by the fire's warmth.

The lowest level of Viper's home might have once been a series of cellars, but it was now several dimly lit dungeons. What the hell had she used this place for before Cassius brought them here? He wondered this but didn't actually want to know.

He wandered several twisting passageways before reaching a wide, open room with stone walls and cement floors. On either side of the room were rows of closed cells with their captives inside. Most of the prisoners were unconscious. The few who were awake muttered and groaned, rocking back and forth in their torrent of emotions. Desperation. Pain. Anger.

Valen didn't care. This was what it took. Right?

He couldn't deny the pity piercing him inside. He approached a cell holding a young woman with dried blood matting her hair to her face. She was awake, but her expression was blank, her eyes far off. Thanks to Lenora's mind control.

Lenora and Cassius were out in the city tonight, hunting for more prey. They had plenty of vampires to do the work for them but wanted a night of hunting for the two of them. It was an interesting idea for a date, he thought. Valen was glad they'd left him behind, no matter how boring it was here.

Valen examined the woman, then straightened. As he did so, a voice behind him sent spikes of ice through his body.

"Getting cold feet, bloodsucker?"

Valen twisted, hoping the alarm didn't show in his face. Viper sat in a dark corner, watching him with those eerie yellow eyes. How long had she been here? Was she already sitting there, or had she followed him down? It didn't matter, he supposed.

"No," he answered brusquely. "Of course not."

Viper laughed. "Whatever you say. I've seen people like you before. Young magicals looking to prove themselves. You think the only way to climb is by going through with this ritual." She cocked her head, and Valen half-wondered if she would shift into her snake form simply to see him piss himself. "I was like you once."

Valen didn't find these words comforting. "And now, here you are. You're powerful. People fear you," he replied evenly.

"Is that what you want?" Viper whispered in a lover's voice.

"I want..." Valen trailed off. Damn, Viper was right. He wanted to prove himself. To Cassius and Lenora, to the vampires in Rome and all of Europe. To himself.

"That's right," Viper purred. "Exactly as I thought."

Valen's face hardened. "Don't pretend you can read my mind."

Viper chuckled. "No, but I can read your body. Every damn thought you have crosses your face. You should work on that. You won't last long in this city's underworld if they know everything you're planning."

Was that one of the reasons Cassius and Lenora always left him behind? Because their plans were so damn obvious when Valen was involved? Gods, he hoped not. He was tired of this conversation and half afraid of where it was going. He turned on a heel and stalked up the stairs.

Viper's low laugh followed him through the dark.

It was past midnight when Stacy and Rowan returned to the Thorn estate. Miles and the werewolves had gone to bed. Ethan was still in the library, working on finding a counter-spell for the ritual. Kiera was somewhere on the estate, probably concealed by shadows and sharpening her knives. Amy had waited up for them.

"You didn't have to do that," Stacy told her when she entered the house and found Amy sitting on the living room sofa.

Amy gave her a wan smile. "I wanted to. Besides, Luna couldn't sleep for a while, so I was up for her."

"And now?" Stacy asked.

"Sleeping like a baby."

"She deserves it," Rowan inserted.

"I dove into my research after she fell asleep," Amy added. "I think I've pieced together where the captured paranormals are being held. There's a small estate outside the city. The Graytails were able to track the vampires' scent there. The property records show it's owned by a Violet Parselton. Ethan confirmed that's Viper's legal name."

Stacy went cold. "The vampires are working with Viper in more ways than one. Great."

"I'll have Kiera scout out the place for weakness," Rowan suggested, already knowing Stacy was weaving a plan to rescue the captives.

"We might be able to do two things at once," Stacy mused. "Rescue the people they took and destroy the artifact."

"Not until after you rest," Amy insisted. "I know you, Stacy. You want to go to Viper's house now and tear it down brick by brick. Well, you can barely stand, let alone fight off a horde of vampires."

"You don't know which spell to use to destroy the artifact yet anyway," Rowan added. "You can spend tomorrow figuring that out while Kiera scouts the location."

Stacy knew they were right but found it difficult to admit. She pictured the prisoners in pain and anguish, not knowing if they would be rescued. If their minds were still intact enough to consider rescue as an option.

Amy squeezed Stacy's arm. "Please promise you'll go to bed?"

Stacy gave her friend a grateful smile. "Only if you promise to do the same."

"I'm going to fall asleep about two seconds after I lay down, so you don't have to worry about that." Amy headed upstairs, and Rowan promised to speak to Kiera about scouting Viper's estate. Stacy started toward the library in search of Ethan. Bed was a priority, but she wanted to see him first.

She didn't have to walk far. Ethan met her in the hallway.

"Any luck?" she asked.

"Getting there. You look tired."

Stacy nodded. "I think I'm about to fall over."

Ethan chuckled. "Let's get you upstairs, then." He draped an arm around her shoulders, and they took the stairs together.

Up here, the house was mostly quiet. Stacy heard Miles snoring from one room and knew all the others were full of sleeping werewolves, including the guest room Ethan normally used.

"Stay with me tonight." Stacy tugged him toward her door. "Please."

Ethan kissed her brow. "I was hoping you would say that."

Stacy didn't care what jokes might come the next morning. She changed her clothes and slid onto the bed. Ethan's troubled eyes met hers.

"What's wrong?" she asked as she stroked a thumb across his cheek.

Ethan placed his hand over hers. "Viper. It's my fault we trusted her."

"No, it isn't. You warned me, and I didn't listen."

"Stacy—"

"No, please. Listen to me. I feel like I failed, and—"

"I do, too."

Despite herself, Stacy flashed a tired smile. "Let's not allow this feeling of failure to get in the way."

Ethan nodded. "You're right." He kissed her lightly. "Let's go to bed."

Stacy curled up beside him, grateful for his warmth and comfort. She hadn't imagined their first time sharing a bed being as simple as going to sleep, but it was what she needed. She liked knowing he was there and never intended to leave her side.

That's what I'm fighting for, was Stacy's last thought before she slipped into slumber.

Rowan located Kiera among the trees at the back of the estate. "I thought I might find you here."

"Needed a moment," Kiera murmured, her back to him. He approached and stopped at her side. Inches separated their arms. "I know you're unhappy with me, Rowan."

"I'm not un—"

Kiera cut him a sideways glance. "You hardly looked at me when we were in the library earlier. You didn't like that I paid Alban a visit."

Rowan's tense face was a dead giveaway. Kiera had always been able to read him when no one else could. "I was only wondering why you did something Stacy did not order."

Kiera bristled. "I did what Stacy wanted in spirit. Sure, she didn't command me to question Alban, but she wanted information. I couldn't get it out of that damn snake, so I went to the next best person. It worked out. We know what's in the Codex now." At the dread pooling in Rowan's eyes, she added, "I didn't kill him or remove his favorite extremity. Though I very much wanted to."

The relief on Rowan's face was unmistakable. Kiera turned to face him. He was beautiful in the moonlight with his silky silver hair. She yearned to run her hands through it, to trace the planes of his face and his sharp jaw with her fingers. She imagined his groan of resistance, and the urge vanished.

He'd been resisting her for weeks. What about her made him hold back?

"Your perception of me is askew sometimes, Rowan." Her voice was quiet but firm. "I'm not a mindless, loyal dog to be ordered around. I follow Stacy's orders because I believe in her. She's the only person I've ever come close to following blindly." Her voice choked at this.

"I know that, Kiera," Rowan murmured. "I only want to understand why—"

Kiera wasn't finished. "I'm a killer, Rowan. I've been trained as one since I was a child. It's in my fucking *blood*. I see the way you look at me when I come back from a job. Ones you send me on, no less!" She flung her hands out. "If you can't accept what I am, maybe we shouldn't be..." She gestured between them. "Whatever *this* is."

Rowan seemed briefly at a loss for words, then resolved his feelings. Kiera expected an objection, but he surged toward her, closing the distance between them before she realized what was happening. His lips crashed against hers. It wasn't the gentle, prodding kiss he'd last given her but something fiercer.

It was Kiera who groaned, opening her mouth to him. His tongue swept in, and his hands grasped her hips, hauling her closer.

When he pulled back, breathing ragged, he muttered, "Whatever this is?"

"Yes, I..."

"You're more than a killer, Kiera. So much more. I only wish you saw what I see in you. You're loyal and fierce and far more moral than any of the damn people you were with in your world.

That place made you who you are, but you escaped it and became your own person."

He was right. She had changed her name, for fuck's sake. Kiera couldn't help the tears that came to her eyes.

Rowan could count on one hand the number of times he'd seen her cry since they met hundreds of years ago. This was one of those times. He grasped her face, eyes wide and earnest. "And 'whatever this is' between us, it's killing me. It always has, Kiera. Since the day I met you."

Kiera drew back, shaking her head. "Th-that can't be. You came here to work for Catherine. You never followed me."

"After everything fell apart, I went away because it hurt too much to see you hate me," he reminded her. "I've wanted you ever since, Kiera. I hoped we could heal what happened between us with time. That…" He was breathing too hard to continue.

"I never hated you," she whispered.

A deep silence passed between them, lasting several heart-beats. Kiera's eyes met his, and she wiped a tear from her cheek. She closed the distance between them, taking his hands in hers. He bent his head to lean his brow against hers.

"I never hated her, either," she admitted, her voice breaking.

"I love you," he murmured, his warm breath filling her.

Kiera kissed him softly this time. "Then let's stop acting like this. All this circling each other. I'm done with it."

A smile of relief graced his lips. He reached to kiss her again, but she stopped him. "Rowan?"

"Yes, Kiera?" Gods, the way he said her name filled her whole body with warmth.

She held his gaze. "I love you, too."

CHAPTER TWENTY-TWO

Stacy was beginning to wonder if the spells Angus gave her were a practical joke.

"They don't fucking work," she muttered after speaking one over a heavily warded piece of jewelry Rowan had brought her. There was no way of telling which spell would work until she had the artifact in hand and could try it. For now, she had to experiment on the next best thing.

The late afternoon sun flooded the library where Stacy had gone to be alone. Elsewhere in the house, Amy was hunched over a computer, continuing her research but coming up with little else to help them.

Kiera was sleeping to prepare for her nighttime mission, Miles was working the grounds as usual, and Rowan was keeping in touch with his contacts throughout the city. Ethan was on the other side of the library, figuring out a counter-spell of his own. He didn't seem to be having much luck. Every now and then, Stacy heard his soft cursing.

We must figure these damn spells out, she thought. Otherwise, the abducted paranormals would never be freed. More had gone missing in the night, according to the reports Rowan received. He'd come to her during breakfast with the news, his expression as grim as ever. It was safe to say Stacy's appetite fled after that.

Exhausted by her efforts, Stacy decided to check in on Ethan. She strode across the library, and sprites hopped onto her shoulders for a ride. They were so common in these spaces that Stacy sometimes didn't notice their movements. One hid in her hair from another, its giggle like tiny bells ringing.

She wished she could have an afternoon of peaceful silence. One where she could sit with Ethan in the garden and watch the sprites play in the fountain. Damn, she wished they could go on a date and feel like they were living normal lives. Her movie night with Amy over a week ago felt like some distant dream.

"Any luck?" she asked when she reached Ethan.

"Getting there," he replied. He didn't elaborate, but his expression showed the stress he'd been feeling for the past forty-eight hours.

Stacy reached for his hand, remembering with a surge of warmth how she'd awoken that morning, nestled in his arms. She'd hardly kissed his neck before Miles pounded on the door to let them know breakfast was ready. *We'll have time for that later,* Stacy thought. "Want dinner?" she asked now.

Ethan gave her a weary smile. "I would. Anything to give me a break from this." He gestured at the pile of books he'd been consulting and the papers he'd scribbled on. Despite the urgency of destroying the artifact and stopping the ritual, the day seemed to stretch endlessly.

We won't know anything for certain until tonight, Stacy thought. *When Kiera scouts out Viper's home and lets us know how we can attack.* She decided to focus on a quiet meal with Ethan. They needed these moments to feel like they had a good life to fight for.

Kiera arrived home from her mission sooner than anyone expected. It was only nine at night when she met the team in the library to report her findings. "The location Amy found in her research checks out. It's heavily guarded by lesser vampires and wards. It's as though the trio Luna mentioned knows we're coming. We should be prepared for them to expect us."

She laid out what she'd learned about the place's weaknesses. The wards were strong, but nothing Miles couldn't take care of if Stacy permitted him to join their mission.

"Do you think Viper will be there?" Amy asked.

Kiera eyed Ethan. "I would expect so because it's her house."

"Viper doesn't like putting herself at risk," Ethan explained. "Unless there's a great reward for her. She's a coward at heart. I expect she may defend her home because she doesn't want to give it up, but anything she does is for selfish reasons."

"I narrowly avoided detection by the vampire faction's guards," Kiera added. "They have them posted everywhere, so we will need a distraction if we expect to sneak inside."

"I have some ideas on how to do that." Miles turned to Stacy. "It's been some time since I was on a mission. With your approval, of course, I would like to join this one."

Rowan inserted himself before Stacy could answer. "We have a good team here, but our numbers are far fewer than what the vampires have. If we're going to succeed in rescuing the hostages, we'll need more help."

"We can't expect the hostages to be in their right minds or have any strength left when we do rescue them," Ethan added. "Rowan is right. We need help."

"I thought of that, too," Stacy amended. "I'll call Mr. Gray, then we can talk about what you're going to do, Miles." The groundskeeper nodded as Stacy grabbed her phone to call the werewolf pack emissary.

Mr. Gray answered after the first ring. "Ms. Drakethorn, I

cannot thank you enough for what you did for Luna. If there's anything we can do to repay you, say the word."

"That's what I'm calling you about." Stacy explained the situation and what she and her team planned to do. "If you can spare members of your pack for this mission, the help would be much appreciated. Warden, Stone, and Luna are still here at my home and can provide security for my estate. I will need others for the rescue mission, too. If possible, we would like to undertake this mission tonight."

"I will speak to our alpha and see who we can spare," Mr. Gray promised.

Stacy thanked him. "Our shared history makes me grateful, Mr. Gray. It's not often two factions like ours can work together so well. You and your pack are valuable to my team. I believe we will always stand together against common threats."

"We remember all you do for us," Mr. Gray replied. "We'll stand with you in this fight. Those vampires will think twice about coming after us again."

"I hope so."

They ended the call. Now, they only had to wait until the reinforcements showed up. Stacy shared the news with her team, who had only been half-listening to her end of the conversation.

She headed to the table, where Kiera had laid out a drawing of Viper's estate, its defenses, and marks where the guards were. "We will be taking some of the Graytails' pack with us and leaving the rest here to guard the house so Miles can join us."

Miles beamed.

Stacy directed her attention across the table to Amy. "I want you to stay here and watch for movement in the city while commanding the security of our home."

Amy's eyes widened. "I don't know anything about your security measures, Stacy. I can't control magic or wards."

"It's not about that," Stacy answered. "You know how to lead, and you know this home as well as the rest of us. Miles can walk you through everything before he leaves, and Luna, who will be staying behind with you, can control the magic if needed." Amy didn't seem convinced, but she made no further objection. Stacy smiled at her. "You've got this. I know you do."

Kiera, who'd been sitting on the table, slid off and tugged Stacy's elbow. "Let's suit up, shall we? Like old times."

The first time they'd "suited up" together was less than a few months ago, and to hear "old times" from the lips of a centuries-old sidhe fae made Stacy laugh. "I'd like that," she replied. "But only if you let me borrow one of your knives."

Kiera grinned, her violet eyes sparkling. "Only for you, Stacy Drakethorn."

It was the moment of levity Stacy needed. She snapped back to her serious, determined self when they were in the armory, strapping on armguards, belts, and vests and sliding into boots. "Ready to hunt some vampire bastards?" Stacy asked when Kiera handed her a sleek knife with an ivory handle. Stacy felt magic humming through it.

Kiera's smile was answer enough, but she still replied, "I thought you'd never ask."

The trees along the edge of the property looked like they had not seen life in years. They were scraggly, contorted shapes, gloomy in the night. Silver moonlight bathed the grounds of Viper's estate. The house was tall and imposing, its dark façade made of a substance that reminded Stacy of scales. The windows at the highest point in the house glowed yellow with the light, like Viper's yellow eyes.

Stacy suppressed a shiver as she and her team concealed themselves in the shadows and counted the guards. Four at every corner of the estate, all vampires dressed in deep-red cloaks and matching boots.

She remained hidden with Rowan, Kiera, Ethan, and the four werewolves the Graytails' alpha had spared for tonight's mission. Miles was the one who stepped forward, his hands already crackling with the magic he would use to provide a distraction.

On the other side of the estate, a great groaning, creaking sound echoed as the trees started moving. Exactly as Miles planned, the vampires jerked their heads in that direction. Three at the closest corner moved toward the sound, while one remained behind.

Miles glanced over his shoulder at Kiera and nodded.

Kiera needed no further encouragement. She surged forward, unfolding from the shadows behind the lingering guard and dispatching him in one swift move. He hardly made a sound as he slumped to the ground. *They don't call her Swiftshadow for nothing,* Stacy thought as Kiera moved back into the darkness where they were hiding.

Miles only had a few minutes to make his next move, maybe mere seconds, depending on when the vampire guards returned. The earth moved according to his command, and Stacy watched in awe as a tunnel opened leading into the lower levels of Viper's home.

The groundskeeper beckoned for them to follow. Stacy went first, with Ethan close behind. The werewolves were next with Rowan on their tails. Kiera came last, her knife unsheathed in case they were attacked on the way down.

They made it several yards into the tunnel before they reached a wide opening and a room full of crates and supplies. Stacy wondered if the supplies belonged to Viper or the vampires. She shuddered to think of meeting Vi in her snake form anywhere, but especially in an enclosed space like this, where the snake shifter had the home advantage. Kiera had described her form as massive.

You're a fucking dragon, Stacy, she reminded herself. *That's almost the same thing! Get a hold of yourself.*

Groans of pain from somewhere nearby alerted Stacy. She took off through the room toward a doorway, where she gasped in horror at a large space full of cells populated by prisoners.

"This setup isn't recent," Ethan told them. "Viper has had it down here for a while."

What the hell had she been using it for? Stacy felt sick at the thought. She decided it was better not to know. She approached one of the cells, where a young woman was rocking back and forth, her expression blank and eyes far away. Her clothes were tattered and dirty. Dried blood caked much of her skin.

"Hello, there," Stacy murmured.

The woman turned her head, and fear filled her eyes. She scrambled into the far corner of her cell, trembling.

"Don't worry. I'm not here to hurt you. I'm going to help you escape."

The woman began crying, but not from relief, as Stacy first thought. She was terrified.

Rowan came to Stacy's side. "They're under the artifact's influence and are incapable of viewing anyone as something other than an enemy."

Stacy glanced around. The few who were conscious wore the same blank, dazed expression. Those who were unconscious were bundled heaps on the floors of their cells. She counted quickly. Fourteen? The vampires had taken far more. Where were they? Stacy's heart thundered, but she couldn't worry about that now. She had to get these prisoners out first.

"You can't destroy the artifact without actually holding it, but you can break its power," Rowan reminded her.

Stacy remembered the spells she'd read in her mother's journal. "Of course!" She turned back to the young woman, clutched the cell bars, and whispered the words. "By the power within me,

I break the hold of this ancient darkness. Let the captured be free once more."

The woman groaned and sagged against the wall. Then, she blinked and focused her gaze on Stacy. Still crying, she asked, "Wh-who are you?"

"My name is Stacy." She didn't bother with her full name. A gentle, reassuring smile was enough.

"We're here to help you," Rowan added. "What is your name?"

"E-Estella."

"Estella," Stacy repeated. "Elf?"

Estella nodded.

"We come on behalf of your queen." Rowan jerked his head toward the opposite side of the room. "We need to find a key for these cells and bring the other prisoners to consciousness."

"I'll look around," Ethan offered. Kiera dug around in a satchel for herbs she could use to wake the others.

Stacy knew what she had to do. She went from cell to cell, speaking the same words and gathering her power. The strain started to take hold. Her body felt heavy, and sweat formed on her brow. An aching sensation settled in her muscles. She pushed through the uncomfortable sensations. It was a small price to pay compared to the misery these prisoners had endured for days. For some, it had been weeks.

Stacy reached the last cell and the woman who occupied it. After releasing her from the artifact's hold, she asked where she had come from. The woman answered that she was a native of the Shinnecock nation.

Stacy's heart lurched. Thank God. She was alive. The elder and their people would be beside themselves with relief.

"Found it," Ethan called.

Stacy turned to see him approaching with a rusty iron ring of keys. "It was up by the door. I suppose they didn't think anyone would come down here. Not to rescue prisoners, anyway."

Ethan went from cell to cell, unlocking the doors. Many of

the prisoners were too weak to walk, so the werewolves helped them. "Take them back through the tunnel and to our vans," Stacy commanded. "We will tend to them at my estate and have them returned to their homes as soon as they are recovered enough to leave."

The relief on the prisoners' faces was unmistakable, and it sent a sharp, aching pang through Stacy's chest. These people had been through hell and back. She'd be damned if she'd let it happen again.

The werewolves and prisoners filed from the room and into the tunnel. Rowan regarded Stacy. "You did well. We should get back so you can rest."

She hadn't realized how drained she was until that moment. Ethan and Miles started for the tunnel first, followed by Rowan and Stacy. Kiera, as always, brought up the rear. It wasn't until they were in the tunnel that Stacy heard a commotion behind them. Alarmed cries rang out.

Panic pierced her. They'd been found out!

"The keys!" Kiera realized. "Taking them off the hook must have set off an alarm."

"That or breaking the artifact's power over the prisoners alerted Lenora," Rowan growled as he set off faster through the tunnel. He called to the wolves ahead, "Hurry!"

Miles ran toward them, intent on using his magic to dispatch any guards outside.

"Fucking hell," Stacy breathed. "This is just my luck."

Ethan's face was ashen. Stacy realized the keys had been placed there all along. A temptation. A trap. The vampires had hoped she'd come here. It was why they had chosen to hide out at the home of someone she knew. Heart hammering, she hurried through the tunnel. She heard a scream of agony ahead, and her heart nearly dropped from her chest.

Rowan had stopped short at the tunnel's entrance. Stacy realized with sudden horror that he was on his knees, head thrown back and veins pulsating. Red magic flared around his head.

Lenora stood before him, the artifact glowing on her chest.

She held Rowan's mind with her power, a laugh trilling from her throat. "You should have known better than to come here, Drakethorn. Those prisoners you freed might have gotten away, but they were so few compared to what we have elsewhere."

Rowan's back arched, Lenora's magic shooting spikes through his body and mind as another scream pierced the air.

CHAPTER TWENTY-THREE

A fire crackled in the hearth, and for a moment, Amy could pretend nothing was wrong in the world. She glanced at the other end of the sofa where Stacy had been sitting a few weeks ago during their girls' movie night. It wasn't Stacy who sat there now but sixteen-year-old Luna, holding a cup of hot cider mixed with herbs Kiera had made to progress her healing.

For the first time since coming here, Luna seemed relaxed. She watched the flames dance with a contented expression. Amy smiled. The young werewolf deserved the rest. Stacy had insisted Luna stay with them until the ordeal with the vampires was over, and Luna had not protested. If anything, it seemed like she didn't want to leave anytime soon.

Amy understood. Something about the Thorn estate made people want to stay forever. It wasn't merely comfortable. They felt safe here.

She was glad to have Luna with her tonight since the other pack members were patrolling the estate, and Stacy's team had gone to rescue the hostages. Amy tried to keep her worry for her friend at bay by engaging Luna in conversation. "You must feel honored by your new position in your pack."

Luna cupped the warm mug to her chest and smiled. "I do. My gifts come to a werewolf only once every few generations. I am lucky to have them. It's imperative that I stay safe for the sake of my pack."

Amy knew the legacy had fallen onto her shoulders without Luna having a choice. It reminded her of Stacy. Luna was so young. It surprised Amy to see someone her age holding the burden of responsibility so well.

Luna sighed. "It has its difficulties, don't get me wrong."

Amy had the feeling Luna needed a listening ear. "How so?" she prodded.

Luna sipped from her mug. "I often feel left out of the grander scheme of things because I am so young. I have much to offer, but the pack insists on protecting me at all times. I have little experience using my magic or protecting *them*, which is the whole point of my job."

Amy laid a hand on Luna's shoulder. "I don't have a drop of magic in me, but I understand where you're coming from on a human level. I felt the same way when I was sixteen." She laughed. "Sometimes, I still feel that way." She explained her desire to become a journalist from a young age and struggling to find her footing in the industry as a young adult. "Now, living here and being part of Stacy's inner circle, I often feel like an outsider."

"Because you don't have magic?" Luna asked.

Amy nodded. "Stacy has often reminded me that I have skills no one else has. We all do, and we're all needed. You're young, and you have the whole world in front of you."

Luna smiled. "Thank you for that. I feel better."

Amy nudged her with an elbow. "Magic isn't the only skill you could have in your arsenal, you know. I could teach you some things outside combat and using magic."

Luna perked up. "And I could do the same for you! Not with

magic, of course, but if you wanted to learn combative techniques, I could show you a thing or two."

Amy couldn't resist the sparkle of excitement in Luna's eyes. Training with the pup sounded better than having Kiera throw her ass to the ground. "It's a deal, Luna. But we're not doing anything until after you've fully recovered."

Luna opened her mouth as if to object, but a commotion at the front door interrupted their conversation. A grim-faced werewolf sentinel appeared in the living room. "Miss Greentree, there was a disturbance in the wards, and we spotted someone at the front gate."

Amy groaned. Great. Exactly what they needed. "Prepare your men for a potential attack," was the only command she gave. Amy's heart beat faster, fearing they would have to fight off vampires trying to seize Stacy's lands. The werewolves would have to take the brunt of the fight, but Amy was determined to give whatever she could. This wasn't only Stacy's home. *It's mine, too, and I will defend it with everything I've got.*

"I'm coming," Luna stated as she rose from the sofa.

"You're not recovered yet—"

"I'm helping," Luna insisted. "If my pack is going to defend this estate and Stacy Drakethorn, so am I."

Amy couldn't help but admire the young woman's tenacity. "Fine, but arm yourself, please. You'll put too much strain on your magic by shifting." Luna agreed. Moments later, they had strapped knives to their thighs and waist. Amy grabbed a handgun Stacy had gifted her from the safe and reached for another. "Have you used guns before?"

"Hell, yeah," Luna replied. "I learned to shoot before I learned to read!"

Amy chuckled. "A werewolf thing?"

"Not necessarily. My dad is a gun nut and insisted on teaching me."

Amy handed her a Sig Sauer P365, which made Luna grin. "Follow my lead."

They headed for the front door, and Amy spotted five of the ten werewolves sent to guard the grounds standing at the gate. A lone figure stood beyond the closed iron gate, cloaked so their face was concealed.

Amy approached, shoulders pushed back and head held high. She might not be Stacy, but she had the right to decide who came and went from her home. Her voice was cold when she demanded, "Who are you, and why have you come here?"

"You're not Anastasia Drakethorn," an annoyed female voice within the hood replied.

"Tell me your name," Amy demanded, searching beyond the figure for others. She saw no one else but had the feeling this person had not come here alone. Was this a vampire preparing to attack them or someone else?

Slowly, the woman dropped her hood, revealing a brown face and pleasant but sharp eyes. Her skin was without blemish, and though Amy could not sense magic the way her friends could, she suspected that the elven queen had used it to enhance her appearance.

Must be nice to have magic, Amy thought. *They probably don't spend any money on Botox!*

The queen was beautiful. Her clothing was simple but regal, and a small circlet of jewels sat on her brow. Amy noted the pointed ears as well.

"I am Elentya," the figure clarified. "Rowan sent word that my people and I were welcome to come here for safety. I expected to find at least him or Miss Drakethorn here."

"They're on a mission tonight, I'm afraid," Amy replied lightly. "My name is Amy Greentree. I'm a friend of Stacy's and the one in charge here for the night."

The elf surveyed the other figures, quickly gauging they were werewolves. Her gaze lingered longest on Luna as if considering who and what she was. Did the elf sense the shift of power inside Luna?

Finally, her silver eyes slid back to Amy. "I would appreciate being given a safe haven for tonight, or at least until your mistress returns. My people are distressed with many unexpected losses." The sorrow in the elf queen's eyes was unmistakable.

"Rowan told me nothing of your coming," Amy replied. "How am I to know you're truly the elf queen and not an enemy disguised and using her name?"

"Fair enough," the queen responded, though the set of her jaw indicated she was not happy. "I am more than willing to stay here and be guarded by your...wolves. We will hand over all our weapons."

Amy knew taking their knives, swords, and bows wouldn't do much. The elves still had magic.

Elentya added, "Moreover, I promise our aid to your mistress. We want vengeance on the vampires as much as she does."

Amy considered the proposition. Queen Elentya was intelligent, that much was clear. What if this was a trap? On the other hand, if this was the real elven queen, Amy would look like a jerk for not letting them in. Besides, when Stacy returned, she could put the elves to good use. "Fine. We will allow you in under your proposed conditions." Amy nodded to one of the werewolves to open the gate, then asked the queen, "Where are your people?"

Elentya raised a slender brown hand adorned with rings and waved. From the shadows and trees beyond her, figures materialized out of thin air. Glamour, Amy thought. Rowan had told her many magicals used it.

Over a dozen elves stood beyond the gate, armed with blades and bows. Each wore a dark green cloak trimmed in gold like the queen's. The elven territory colors. Amy had never seen so many beautiful people in one place before.

The elf queen smiled. "It has been pleasant meeting you, Miss Greentree. Now, I would like to introduce you to my court."

―――――――

Kiera released a blood-curdling cry and launched at the vampire. A blast of shadows went out from her, colliding with the red magic coiling around Lenora. Stacy hardly had time to register Kiera crashing into the vampire before Ethan was at Rowan's side, catching his slumping body.

Behind Stacy, Miles flung up a wall of roots, earth, and stone, blocking the tunnel so the vampires surging through it would not reach them. "*Go!*" he bellowed. "I can only hold it for so long!"

Stacy hesitated, then whirled to see Ethan getting Rowan to his feet. "I've got him," Ethan assured her, encasing himself and the dryad in a shield of magic. The wolves had escaped with the prisoners.

She turned to find Kiera and the vampire going head-to-head. Knowing Rowan was in safe hands and Miles would close the tunnel, she joined the fight against Lenora.

A sphere of red magic exploded from the vampire's hands, throwing Kiera back. Kiera's shadows vanished as she hit the ground hard.

"Leave her alone, bitch!" Stacy cried as she summoned flame.

Lenora whirled, eyes widening. She wasn't daunted and flung out her red magic, seeming to forget the artifact's power did not work on Stacy.

The distraction gave Kiera time to get to her feet and run at Lenora with her knife. Stacy threw up a wall of fire to prevent Lenora's magic from hitting her. When the flames faded, Kiera was close to the vampire. Lenora whirled, her magic seizing Kiera's wrists and holding her captive.

"No!" Stacy screamed. In seconds, Lenora could rip into Kiera's mind as she had done to Rowan.

Lenora ignored Stacy.

Heart hammering, Stacy bolted for the vampire, but Miles' groan distracted her. The tunnel's wall had collapsed, and two new figures appeared. One was a tall, broad-shouldered man with tawny skin and black eyes, his long, dark hair blowing around his shoulders. The other was a thinner, shorter man with ivory skin and short, sleek black hair.

The other vampires, Cassius and Valen, if Stacy had to guess.

The smaller of the two went for Miles, flashing a gleaming sword. It arced around and would have hit Miles if the groundskeeper had not flung up a vine in time and torn the sword from the vampire's grasp. The vampire gaped, then issued a shrill cry as a second vine caught his leg and yanked him to the ground.

The older vampire slid his gaze from Lenora to Stacy. His nostrils flared, and he released a low snarl. "*You.*"

"Come at me, motherfucker," Stacy challenged. "I dare you."

The vampire lunged. He was so intent on getting to Stacy, he didn't notice the pitfall opening in the ground before him. He stumbled and fell several feet. Roots and vines swarmed over the pit's surface. The other vampire lay on the ground not far from a stone wall Miles had quickly erected.

Stacy returned her attention to Kiera and the female vampire.

They were still fighting, Kiera's shadows leaping and Lenora doing all she could to penetrate Kiera's mind with her blazing red magic. *I must get that damn artifact,* Stacy thought.

Lenora didn't know Cassius and Valen had failed and was fighting Kiera with all her might. *This is going to fucking hurt,* Stacy thought as she lunged, tacking Lenora from behind. She might have been immune to the artifact's mind-controlling powers, but the magic still cut through her flesh when she collided with Lenora's shield.

Stacy fused her opponent's shield with her flames, melting it in seconds. Lenora screamed and twisted to face Stacy—exactly as she'd planned.

Stacy snatched the ruby, crying out as heat flared through her hand and up her arm. She wrenched the chain from the vampire's neck. The artifact burned against her hand, so she stuffed it into her pocket. The light in the ruby went out.

Lenora's bellow of rage rang through the tunnel.

We have to get out of here, Stacy thought. Kiera had decided the same thing. She was running for Miles, shadows pooling around her to prevent others from attempting to go for her. The groundskeeper was barely keeping Cassius in the pit.

"Go! Run!" Stacy shouted. She was tempted to take dragon form and end the vampires altogether. *I can't. Not yet. I don't know how to control my full power.* How could she avoid killing the innocent along with the guilty when all she knew while in dragon form was power and instinct?

Instead, Stacy ran.

She spotted the gate and the trees. Kiera was ahead of her, and Miles was behind. Stacy glanced over her shoulder to find Lenora and Valen pursuing as Cassius climbed out of the pit, dripping with rage. Stacy could practically feel it in the air. Smaller openings appeared in the ground, making the vampires too busy evading them to keep up.

"Go!" Miles cried, halting by the gate to ensure his power made the vampires fall into his traps.

Stacy and Kiera reached the gate. The vans with the wolves and the prisoners were nearby. As Stacy glanced back, a sinking feeling engulfed her. They'd only rescued a small portion of the prisoners. The vampires were keeping more in another location.

"Miles!" Stacy shouted, but the groundskeeper held his footing. Vines snaked over the ground, heading for the vampires.

"*Go!*" he bellowed again.

It wasn't until Kiera was pulling Stacy away, wrapping her

into shadows, that Stacy realized Miles intended to stay here until they got away.

"N-no!" The cry rasped from her throat.

"He'll get away," Kiera promised her. They were past the gate and down the hillside, with the manor house growing smaller every second.

Stacy hoped so, but dread filled her as she watched Miles throw up another wall of stone and earth before turning to run for his life.

CHAPTER TWENTY-FOUR

Lenora was about to raise hell.

She paced Viper's library with more fury than the fire burning in the hearth. "We must go after that bitch directly! Drag her ass to the ash tree and sacrifice her. With her power, we won't need the other prisoners!"

Cassius sat in a high-backed armchair by the fire, elbow perched on the arm. It wasn't a comfortable chair, but he'd taken it so his back would be to Lenora. He wasn't ignoring her, exactly, but he hadn't been listening closely either. He'd been deep in thought, contemplating their next move.

Finally, he glanced back at Lenora when she mentioned going after Anastasia Drakethorn. "We can't do that."

Lenora threw up her hands. "She took my necklace!"

Cassius considered telling his lover he would get her a new one, but the artifact was one-of-a-kind. A fresh wave of fury over the situation crested within him, but he managed to keep it contained.

He was about to explain to Lenora why they couldn't simply attack Stacy in her home when Valen strode into the room, grim-faced and sweating. His clothes were muddied and torn. "The warden is contained. There were plenty of cells to choose from," he grumbled.

They hadn't learned the element user's name, but Cassius didn't care. The man was an ally of Drakethorn's, and he planned to use that to his advantage.

"Good," Lenora snarled. "Next best thing. I'll carve his fucking eyes out, and—"

Cassius stood abruptly. "Enough, Lenora." His voice was dangerous enough to halt Lenora mid-sentence and for Valen to cast him a wary glance.

"Going after Drakethorn would be a waste of time," Cassius stated.

"And there's no certainty we would make it out alive," Valen drawled.

Cassius agreed with the younger vampire. "We can use the warden to our advantage. Bait Drakethorn into coming to us again. Only this time, we'll be ready."

"Come to *where*?" Lenora demanded.

"The ash tree, of course," Valen answered before Cassius could. "Tomorrow is the blood moon. We can make it obvious where we plan to conduct the ritual, then lure the bitch to us."

Lenora eyed Valen as if she thought the idea was stupid, but she relented when Cassius remarked, "It's the best course of action, and don't worry about your necklace. We'll get it back."

"Fine," Lenora grumbled. She met Valen's gaze again. "Did you find Viper? Where the hell did she go?"

Valen had had a long night. He dropped into a nearby chair and tipped a decanter of whiskey toward an empty glass. He didn't answer until he'd taken a drink. "I've looked everywhere for her, but she's gone. I don't think we'll be seeing her again anytime soon."

Cassius' jaw tightened. "Viper was only ever interested in saving her own ass. She must have known Drakethorn was coming and got out of the way."

"She could have warned us," Lenora muttered. Her eyes were glassy with tears. She'd worked nearly her entire life to find that damn artifact, and in a matter of seconds, it had been snatched from her neck. Well, she should have controlled herself better. She'd been too focused on fighting the fae woman in league with Drakethorn.

Cassius ignored her. "Keep an eye out for Viper in case she returns. In the meantime, we will finish our preparations for tomorrow." The look he gave both Valen and Lenora was enough for them to leave the room. Cassius needed some time to himself.

"Everything will be better when you arrive, Malakai," he murmured as he wandered toward the window and stared out into the deep night. When the being of the dark world was with them in the human realm, they could begin their takeover of the world. One day, if all went according to plan, the human world would be like Malabbra, the home Cassius yearned for but had never seen and could never go to.

He turned his mind to the coming blood moon and Stacy Drakethorn. He needed to send a messenger, make it obvious where they planned to sacrifice her friend's body. He could practically taste her fear and her blood. What did dragon blood taste like? Cassius had never liked human blood much, but dragon blood? It sounded simply delicious.

The Thorne Estate was fuller than ever.

With half the Graytail pack, Elentya and her small court, Stacy's team, and the diverse group of magicals they'd rescued, Stacy wondered if they would ever find room for everyone. Amy had started filling the small cottages around the estate, then the many bedrooms inside the main house. The children of the elven court set up smaller beds in the library.

The place was a flutter of activity despite the late hour.

Seeking solace, Stacy shut herself in Rowan's small study. For the first time since she moved here, she felt her home was too small.

One thing was noticeably missing, though. The moment Stacy and her team came through the door, concern filled Amy's face. "What happened to Rowan? Where is Miles?"

Miles.

Stacy would have done anything to hear his jovial laughter and poorly-timed jokes. Instead, he was at Viper's estate or running as far from it as he could get. She did not know where he was, and anxiety filled her. *I will get him back and rescue the other prisoners*, she determined as she sank into the chair behind Rowan's desk.

Rowan was in his bedroom with Kiera tending to him. Thankfully, though Lenora had pried into his mind, she didn't have time to do much damage. Even so, Rowan was rattled.

Stacy remembered the artifact and pulled it from her pocket, careful not to touch it with her bare fingers by slipping on a glove first. Even through the leather, she felt the hum of dark magic in it. While Lenora used it, the magic had burned Stacy's skin. Strange since she could summon flame without discomfort.

She set it on the desk and stared at it as if doing so would make the damn thing combust. Stacy wished her will was that strong. It was the largest ruby she'd ever seen, dark due to its age and the fact that it hadn't been cleaned in years. Did vampires take arcane pieces like this to jewelers? Stacy doubted it.

She wanted to destroy it here and now, but her mind was too muddled with troubles to bother. Her focus was gone, and the strain of setting the prisoners free had pummeled her body. It would be at least another hour before she recovered enough to cast a spell over the artifact.

She heard murmurs and shuffling from people in the hallways as Amy led them to their bedrooms for the night. How would they feed all these people? How would they heal the prisoners? It was simply too much.

I need fresh air, Stacy thought. She crept from the room, timing it to avoid anyone seeing her. She slipped through the back door, where the fresh air and quiet of the night was a welcome change. She wandered toward the Guardians' grove, knowing she wasn't likely to be followed. However, she was not expecting someone to be waiting for her, having guessed she would come here.

She spotted the tall figure standing at the end of the grove, his back to her and his hands locked behind him.

"Dad?"

Her surprised tone made him turn. Khan smiled and waved at their general surroundings. "I thought you might come here for peace and quiet. You're like me in that respect. I hope you can forgive your old man for interrupting it."

Stacy wasn't sure what it was—everything that had been going on or not seeing him for two weeks—but she was suddenly overwhelmed with relief to see him. "I thought you were away on business."

Khan's smile widened. "Is that what old Regi told you?"

"Where were you, then?"

"Blowing off steam. I flew north for several days."

Stacy raised a brow. "Are we talking private jet or huge, scaly wings?"

Khan laughed. "Don't worry. I didn't burn any forests during my time away."

"I still don't know if we're talking about aircraft or dragons," she replied, but her smile communicated she knew it was the latter. Stacy wondered if she would ever reach the point of needing to get away, flying somewhere else and leaving her normal life behind for a while. "Wait. If you were flying north, that means you have more land, doesn't it?"

Khan nodded. "Much more. That is a conversation for another time, though." He gestured toward her house. "I see you have a lot of guests tonight. Mind filling me in?"

Stacy didn't mind. In fact, she was relieved to do so. Everything spilled out of her, from meeting Angus, Alban, and Elentya to their findings regarding the vampires. She explained their search for the vault, the missing Codex, and Viper's betrayal. She told him about the attack on Luna and her pack, followed by their rescue mission to Viper's estate.

Khan listened in attentive silence. When she finished, he drifted closer. "The weight is heavy on your shoulders, Stacy."

That much was obvious. Stacy fought off tears at the thought of Miles being captured or still running from vampire pursuers. She thought of all those still suffering at Cassius, Lenora, and Valen's hands.

"Do you recognize those names?" she asked.

Khan didn't, though he stated he might recognize the names of their fathers or grandfathers if he knew them. "It might be time for me to visit the vampire council across the pond," he mused. "After this matter here is dealt with." Khan spoke as if it was as simple as getting a car repaired or a leaky roof fixed. It wasn't that he didn't care about people's suffering or dark magic being used where they lived. It was simply a small problem compared to what he had faced before.

The world is much bigger to him, Stacy thought. *He's grown so used to the big picture that he no longer sees the smaller problems and how they affect everything.* She put this thought aside and considered her next steps.

"I know what I must do," Stacy confessed. "It's just…"

"Difficult?" Khan supplied.

"Very."

"That's life."

Stacy rolled her eyes. "Thanks, Dad."

He shrugged. "We all learn these lessons over and over, no matter how old we get. I can see you're tired, but don't let what happened defeat you." His words were kind, even gentle, though his expression was grimly detached. *That's Khan for you,* Stacy reminded herself. His duality never ceased to amaze her.

"I will be here if you need me," he added after several seconds of silence. He was close enough to place a hand on her shoulder. Their matching green eyes met. "I know this is your battle, and you will see it through. You are a dragon, after all."

Yes, I am, Stacy concluded. *And those blood-sucking mother-fuckers are about to feel my fire.*

Khan did not stay long but urged Stacy to return to her house and her team. "I know you have much to prepare before tomorrow."

The word sank through her. Tomorrow. The blood moon. "Any way to procrastinate cosmic events?" she asked.

Khan's eyes glittered. "If only we could." He disappeared a moment later, and Stacy could have sworn she felt a gust of wind from flapping wings and spotted a long, pointed tail swishing through the shadows above. She shook her head, chuckling. She supposed it was easier to fly home than drive.

She roamed the grove, back toward the house, and found another person waiting for her at the door. Ethan extended his hand, glove on, with the artifact in his palm. "I figured you'd want help getting rid of this." He nodded toward another section of the grounds, somewhere they could go undisturbed. "Shall we?"

Stacy smiled, gratitude surging through her. She'd felt her magic return and knew it was better to get this over with before tomorrow. "Let's go," she told Ethan.

He led the way along a narrow cobblestone path, around a fountain, and toward a small clearing surrounded by dense foliage. The stones her mother's coven had pulled power from were arranged here, smooth and clear, enchanted so age did not touch them.

Ethan handed Stacy the note with the spells Angus had given to her. "Try one at a time," he suggested as he laid the artifact in the center of the circle. Stacy stood on the center stone and pulled energy from the ley line beneath her land.

She pulled a small amount at first, wanting to test it on the artifact before going full force with a spell. She spoke the first of three incantations. The air around her shifted, but nothing else happened. Stacy tried the second. Same result. She stuffed down her irritation and tried the third.

"It doesn't work," she nearly growled. The artifact still lay there in the same condition. Stacy contemplated keeping the artifact and hiding it where no vampire could get it, but then she remembered Angus' grave warning. It was dangerous no matter where it was or in whose hands it lay. The priest might have been a borderline lunatic, but his warning had been too serious for Stacy to ignore.

The dragon within her stirred, stoking an old need to finish a job she'd started. *No, I will do this. I will fucking destroy it.*

"What if you aren't supposed to use only one spell?" Ethan spoke up. "Angus only knew the spells had been used to attempt to destroy the artifact. Maybe it didn't work before because they didn't use the right combination."

"You mean, speak all the spells at the same time?"

"It's worth a try. It might work if we're pulling considerable magic from a source like the ley line."

"All three spells?" Stacy reiterated.

"Why not?"

Stacy's brows furrowed. "There's only two of us, and I wouldn't know who else to ask." Kiera could use magic but wasn't proficient in spells unless they had to do with dismantling wards. Rowan was sleeping, still in recovery from Lenora's invasion into his mind. Miles could have done it, but he wasn't here. They needed another witch or someone adjacent to their kind.

At that moment, Stacy heard rustling in the nearby undergrowth. She turned, eyes narrowing. The wards had not been taken down. Whoever was watching and listening was supposed to be on her grounds. "Whoever you are, come out. No need to hide."

Slowly, the sheepish face of a young woman appeared. Stacy chuckled. "Luna, why are you hiding in my bushes?"

The werewolf's face flushed crimson as she scrambled through briars and leaves. "I was exploring. I liked how these stones looked in the moonlight, but I heard you two coming and decided to leave. Only I overheard what you were trying to do." She stepped toward Stacy, hesitant at first, then growing confident. Her silvery-blue hair shimmered around her face. "I know how to do spell work. Some, anyway. I could try casting the weaker of the three spells you need."

Stacy glanced at Ethan, who simply shrugged. "It could work. Why not try it?"

Stacy agreed. It was a good opportunity to see how the three of them worked together. "Very well. Step on that stone there." She pointed to one three feet from the center where she still stood. Ethan took the stone opposite Luna so they formed a triangle. It would be more effective with a full coven covering every stone, but they could work with this.

She pulled on the ley line once more, and warmth surged through her body. "Ready?" she whispered.

Ethan and Luna gave affirmative responses.

Stacy spoke the first spell. Ethan spoke the second. Luna finished with the third. Their magic collided at the center of their circle, converging over the artifact. The artifact rattled against stone, then a small shattering sound echoed from the trees. The light of their magic vanished.

Stacy smiled. "We did it."

The artifact lay in pieces, tiny shards of ruby littering the grass around the stone where they'd laid it.

"No more mind control," Ethan stated.

Stacy eyed him. Pride shone in his eyes as if to say, *You did it, Stacy.*

She turned to Luna, who was beaming. "That was fun. Next time you need to destroy something, count me in."

CHAPTER TWENTY-FIVE

Rowan was sitting up in bed when Kiera returned to his room carrying a small bowl with ground herbs. "Truly, Kiera, I'm fine. You don't have to keep bringing me this...concoction." He wrinkled his nose.

"You're only saying that because you don't like the smell." Kiera perched on the edge of his bed. "You're going to have to get over it. Nothing helps with a speedy recovery like this. What happened to you was..."

"Terrifying? Tell me about it." Rowan was weighed down by his experience but also because Miles had not returned with them. He knew Kiera felt the same, though she was doing everything possible to distract herself. "Ever had anyone pry into your mind and try to take your thoughts from you?" he asked.

To Rowan's surprise, Kiera nodded. "My father used to do it all the time." Her voice was so quiet that he almost didn't catch her words. Kiera didn't look at him. She stirred the herbal concoction as if her words held no weight.

"Kiera." Rowan's voice was rough. He reached for her hand. "Look at me."

She did. Her eyes were a hazy shade of violet. "When I was young, he would slip into my mind so he could 'teach me' how to defend myself. At the time, I thought that was the truth. Now, I know he did it merely for his own amusement.

"After we staged a coup and lost, he did it again. He stole the secrets of the assassins' guild straight from my mind and used it to root out my remaining allies. He slaughtered half of them and imprisoned the others. Apparently, those who didn't die in the fae prisons were banished to other worlds."

She paused, gathering her courage to go on. "That was why Alban thought I was a traitor. He thought I gave the information willingly. I've never had the guts to say out loud what truly happened. Until now."

Rowan's hand tightened over hers. "Why now?"

"Because…" Kiera choked on the word, her gaze distant for a heartbeat until she met his eyes. "When I saw that bitch rip into your mind, it made me remember everything and why we should never let greedy scum like these vampires have power. I hated seeing you like that, Rowan. I hated feeling it happen to me all those years ago." Kiera lifted her chin. "Perhaps if I was better at facing my damn past, I wouldn't be so fucked up now."

"You're not fucked up," Rowan admonished softly, then chuckled. "Though I might be. My head feels like it's been rattled."

Kiera managed a smile. "Then shut up and drink this damn tea I made you."

Rowan accepted the cup, now enhanced with the herbs she'd been grinding in the bowl. He winced at the taste, or maybe the temperature, but he didn't complain. A comfortable silence passed between them until Rowan broke it. "I'd struggle if I had to see that happen to you. The mind invasion thing. If I ever have the great misfortune of meeting your father, I'll carve him up myself."

Kiera gave a half-smile. "You won't have to. I'll make sure he receives a worthy punishment. Besides, he's old as shit now. He might have died already or been killed by someone who staged a rebellion better than I could." She joked about it, but what if it was true? She had no way of knowing what was happening in the fae world.

"Do you ever think of going back there and taking your vengeance?" Rowan asked after her statements had settled into him. It took him longer than normal to process words with his mind feeling like mush.

Kiera considered the question. "I think about it, yes, but I always conclude that it's not worth my time. Everything I want is here, in this world." She placed her hand on his cheek. "In a way, I'm glad I got banished. I met you."

"And Miles," Rowan reminded her.

Kiera snorted. "I was trying to be romantic, and you brought up the man I consider a brother." A distant sorrow shone in her eyes.

Gods, he hoped Miles was okay.

"And what do you consider me?" Rowan teased, drawing her closer. He wanted to distract her.

"You're still recovering," she protested.

His lips touched hers. "What do you consider me?" he asked again.

"Boyfriend" seemed too causal, considering the connection they'd shared all these years. "*Not* like a brother," she answered at last.

His laugh rumbled into her. "I'm very glad to hear that."

Kiera moved to get off the bed, protesting that it was late and they both needed rest. Rowan snagged her wrist. "Stay with me. Sleep here. Amy put Elentya in your room, anyway."

Kiera paused. She hadn't shared anyone's bed—not for sleeping, anyway—since the last time they'd lain together in a house far from here. Over a hundred years ago. Her heart ached at the thought of it.

Rowan took his empty tea cup from her hand and placed it on the nightstand. "Please."

"I want to change my clothes," Kiera insisted.

Rowan tugged at the strings on her pants. "I can help you with that."

She grinned. "I thought you said 'just sleep.'"

Rowan cleared his throat. "I did, but it won't hurt you to sleep without these on."

Stacy, Ethan, and Luna were hardly inside the house when Amy ran up to them. "There's a disturbance at the front of the estate," she reported. "One of the wolf guards has captured a vampire."

Alarm spiked through Stacy. Surely, the vampires wouldn't have dared send one of their own this late at night. Was this an attack?

"Only one?" Ethan asked.

Amy nodded. "We think he's a messenger."

Stacy wished she could go to bed. Instead, she strode across the grounds with Ethan and Luna flanking her. Amy walked ahead of them and halted at the gate, where a werewolf stood holding a vampire through the bars.

"Who are you, and what do you want?" Stacy demanded.

The vampire struggled against the wolf's hold but quickly discovered resisting wouldn't help him. "I have come on behalf of my master." He rooted in an interior pocket of his cloak and drew out a folded piece of paper, sealed shut with red wax.

Stacy tore the seal and opened the paper, reading the crudely scrawled message.

The dragon and a thorn
Ashes and blood of scorn

Meet at midnight in a storm
Of magic and might
A world opened, a new power born to blight

It wasn't signed, but Stacy had a good guess who'd sent it. Cassius, Lenora, or Valen.

"What the hell is that? Some kind of riddle?" Amy asked as she glanced over Stacy's shoulder at the message.

Stacy turned to the wolf guard. "Bring this asshole inside for questioning. Kiera will speak to him in the morning when she awakens. Don't let him see anything."

The werewolf nodded, then slapped a blindfold over the vampire's face. The creature thrashed against him to no avail. Stacy turned and spotted Queen Elentya approaching them. "It looks like a riddle, but I don't know what it means," she announced

Elentya halted before her, extending her hand for the paper. Stacy didn't see the harm in letting the queen look, though she did not know what good it would do.

"A poorly written riddle," the queen pronounced at last, handing it back. "The dragon is you, obviously, and the ash and blood speak to the location for the vampire's ritual tomorrow. The storm is a metaphor for what will come, and a new power is their dark friend Malakai."

"What does a thorn have to do with Stacy being a dragon?" Amy asked.

Elentya observed Stacy with considering eyes. "I've noticed a talisman around your home. A tree wrapped in thorns. What is it?"

"The symbol of my mother's coven," Stacy answered without hesitation. She lifted her auburn hair and turned to show the queen the marking on her neck.

Elentya's eyes widened. "I see. The vampires must know of it. Tell me, do these foul creatures have any connection to your home here?"

At first, Stacy intended to say no, then she remembered something. "Maybe. Once, long before I was born, a blight overtook part of these lands. My mother dealt with an ancient, abstract darkness. It killed everyone in her coven except her."

Elentya looked like she'd seen a ghost.

"I have no clue if it's got anything to do with the vampires," Stacy added. "Kiera seems to believe the darkness came from the world where the vampires and Malakai were born."

Elentya shook her head. "You know so little, child."

Stacy bristled. "Tell me, then."

Amy and Ethan shared a glance. Luna listened intently to their conversation.

The cool night air brushed dark curls across Elentya's face as she responded. "The elves have dealt with a similar issue in our lands. We call it the Dark Days. It comes upon us every century or so. An abstract, malevolent presence leaks through a weakness in the veil between our world and others. We have learned how to drive it off, but it grows stronger each time."

She pointed to the message Stacy held. "No doubt the vampires are aware of it, whatever it is. They must also know of your mother's history with that darkness. They bring up the thorn because they know part of your last name comes from her."

"They're daring me to face them, aren't they?" Stacy asked.

"It's obvious," Elentya returned.

"But how the hell are we supposed to know where their stupid ash tree is?" Amy inserted.

"It's in the elven lands," Elentya told them. "That's why they drove us away and took some of our people. It is why one of my generals betrayed me. They wanted us out of the way so the tree would become unguarded. Stacy, that symbol on your neck has been carved into the tree at the center of our lands for over a hundred years."

Stacy felt like she couldn't breathe.

"Granted, a hundred years is but a breath in an elf's life, but it seems long to a human," Elentya admitted. "Still, it is strange, and no one knows why it came to be there."

Stacy had a hundred questions, but now wasn't the time to ask them. "You know how to get to the tree, right?"

"I do," the queen replied.

"That's it, then. We're going tomorrow when the blood moon rises." Stacy addressed everyone. "It's time we all got some sleep."

CHAPTER TWENTY-SIX

The gate wasn't visible to those who did not have magic. To any normal human, this area was a web of twisting vines between two trees. It might have looked strange, but no one would have guessed it was the entrance to elven territory spanning several hundred acres of forest in northern New York.

The gate resembled the iron one at the Thorn estate, though this one was constructed of vines. It was as tall as the trees it attached to and shimmered with magic.

Stacy stood before it with Elentya. The queen wore elven battle gear that included leather arm bracers, fine black boots, a bronze chest plate and helmet, and a dark green, flowing, light-weight cloak. A knife hung at Elentya's side, and a bow with a quiver of arrows rested on her back. She looked as regal and beautiful as ever, but she was also the picture of a battle-worn warrior.

Stacy had seen Elentya's judicial side. Now, she was ready to see the woman's leadership in battle.

"This is my home." Elentya's voice whispered like the wind. With the sun down, Stacy could barely see what lay ahead. The forest was dense and dark, with only the magic at her fingertips to light the way. The elven queen did not take her eyes off the gate. "It has been my home since I was born. I intend to take it back."

For the first time in centuries, the elves had been driven from their home.

Stacy lifted her chin, defiance sparking in her gold-green eyes. She'd worn her usual combat gear, a black leather fighting suit that allowed her to move with grace and agility, and had enough hidden compartments to stow her knives. One thing was different, though. Ethan had helped weave enchantments through her clothing to make shifting easier.

"The dragon might come out tonight," she had warned him in a whisper before they left.

Ethan had simply handed her another knife. "Good. Rain fire on them all."

Stacy had no plans to shift yet. She wasn't interested in wrecking Elentya's home.

"We must be prepared," the elven queen continued. "Magic runs through this forest, and the vampires will use it to their advantage."

"So will we," Stacy promised.

Elentya grabbed her arm, eyes flashing. "Listen to me, Drakethorn. Several ley lines converge at one place, creating a well of power many would kill to get their hands on." That was why the elves had hidden for so long, Stacy realized. They wanted to keep their magic safe.

"The ash tree?" Stacy guessed.

Elentya nodded.

"I will be careful," Stacy resolved. She turned to face those behind her. Ten elven warriors from Elentya's court stood with bows and spears ready. Beside them, ten werewolves awaited her command, with Luna at the front. Rowan, Kiera, and Ethan waited behind the wolves, and Rowan offered a silent nod of encouragement. *We will follow you.*

Stacy addressed Luna. "Take your pack through the gate after the queen opens it. Scout out the area ahead." She gestured to the tree line, where the moon was beginning to rise. "We have about an hour or so before the blood moon is at its apex. The vampires won't be able to complete the ritual until then. We must hurry. Do not engage unless they spot you first and strike. We will not be far behind."

Luna's response was a simple nod before she shifted. Standing before Stacy was not a young woman but a silvery-blue wolf with large, shining eyes and a powerful body. The others shifted into gray wolves.

Elentya stepped toward the gate, her hands moving to undo the spells her family had placed there long ago. "This won't trigger any alarms," she told Stacy. "Only those of my bloodline would notice."

The gate opened silently, and Stacy felt its magic permeate the air. Strong, beautiful, ancient magic. Luna bounded through with the wolves on her tail. After they were out of sight, Elentya and her elves advanced in neat formation. Stacy stepped back with Rowan, Ethan, and Kiera to take up the rear.

"They'll be coming for you the hardest, you know," Kiera remarked, nudging Stacy's arm with her elbow.

"So we will stay close to you," Ethan spoke up.

"For our people," Stacy whispered. "For Miles."

"For Miles," the others murmured.

Rowan placed a hand on her shoulder and was the last to speak before passing through the gate. "Give them hell, Drakethorn."

Everyone spread out with a few yards between each person. Elentya was not far from Stacy, but several elves had gone into deeper parts of the forest. They knew this territory better than anyone, and their guidance was invaluable. They had a singular plan to reach the ash tree at the center of the forest before the moon had fully risen and destroy the vampires before they could conduct their ritual.

The forest provided a sight Stacy had not expected. The trees were taller here, outlined in a soft haze of white magic that lit their way. It was still dim, with intersecting pathways littered with protruding roots, stones, and fallen trees. A stream that glowed like sapphires under the rising moon trickled past.

Stacy could walk here all night and never grow tired of the sights. She wanted to lay in a patch of moss and stare at the stars. That was not a privilege she would have tonight.

Most of the elven homes were in underground cities. They'd once been high in the trees, connected by twisting staircases and bridges. However, in the past century, the elves had taken their homes and people underground. The forest above was for hunting and reading the stars.

Stacy wondered if a better world was possible where the elves could live aboveground without fearing for their lives. *If I have the chance, I will make it that way,* she thought.

She halted at a new sight. The smell greeted her first—rotting flesh. Animal carcasses were strewn across the pathway ahead. Deer, rabbits, coyotes.

"I see the vampires have been feeding," Kiera remarked from Stacy's right. She stood about two yards away, her face pinched with the smell.

Stacy shuddered, hoping they would not find human bodies in the same condition. As the realization that the vampires were close, Stacy heard a sudden, sharp cry ahead. It cut off almost as soon as it started. A howl followed as one of the wolves signaled they'd been attacked.

The elves rushed ahead, taking to the trees with an ease Stacy envied. They mounted sturdy branches, bows pointed ahead and below. Only Elentya remained on the ground, brandishing a spear as she scanned the path ahead. It was well worn, a sign that the elves had traversed this place repeatedly.

Ethan wove a shield around himself and Stacy. Kiera vanished into the shadows, appearing ahead where the wolves were. Rowan waited by Stacy's side.

A figure exploded from the undergrowth. A human in tattered clothes, their eyes crazed. One of the minions. Stacy had hardly registered the arrival before Rowan fired, and the human went down.

Stacy gasped.

"Tranquilizer," Rowan explained. "They'll be out for a while but not dead."

The commotion ahead morphed into pandemonium. Several figures burst from the trees. More mind-controlled humans, along with lesser vampires.

"Fire!" Elentya called. Arrows rained from the trees. Rowan and Ethan fired their tranquilizer guns at the oncoming humans, knocking them unconscious before they had a chance to meet the werewolves. Luna rose on her hind legs, releasing a howl that gathered her wolves to her. They charged as a pack toward the vampires. Snarls, screams, and the scent of blood filled the air.

With Ethan's shield around her, Stacy advanced. She plucked magic from the ground and the trees around her instead of taking from her personal stores. Flames appeared in her palms. She formed them into orbs and lobbed them into one vampire after another. Flesh singed and melted.

The lesser vampires were vicious, but with the combined efforts of the elves, wolves, and Stacy's team, it did not take long to kill half and send the other half retreating into the trees. *We keep going*, Stacy thought. *We corner them at the tree and slaughter them all.*

If only it were that simple.

A figure ahead materialized out of thin air, a shield of red magic surrounding him to prevent arrows from penetrating his flesh. Cassius wore a wicked smile. "You're too late to save anyone, Drakethorn! We sacrificed the other humans so we could gain power, including your friend."

Miles. No!

"You have escaped us before, dragon. This time, there will be nowhere for you to run," Cassius continued. "Your power will be ours, and the resurrection of our god will be complete."

Stacy didn't care that the lesser vampires had returned and were lunging at her forces. She didn't care that Lenora appeared on Cassius' right and Valen on his left. She narrowed her focus on the older vampire, a wave of rage rising within her. "For Miles," she whispered before she launched at him, her body on fire.

Rowan watched Stacy rush for Cassius. The pair collided, her flames against bolts of red magic. Lenora and Valen appeared, and the other two vampires wasted no time. Lenora lurched down the hillside, headed straight for Kiera. Stacy's shield was still intact, thanks to Ethan, so Rowan focused on Valen.

Blades in hand, he bolted forward. This wouldn't be the first time his twin swords met vampire flesh. Valen's eyes were cold and empty, black as night. He whirled with a grace one so young as him was unlikely to have. He bared his fangs and snarled, "Come at me, old man."

Rowan braced himself as Valen brought a sleek sword down. He crossed his own, blocking the blow, and threw Valen back. However, the vampire wasn't easily daunted. He came at Rowan with a series of hard parries, forcing the dryad down the hillside.

For someone as small as Valen, he fought hard, drawing on an inner strength Rowan would have been impressed by if not for the fact that the vampire was his enemy.

Unleashing a roar of rage on Miles' behalf, Rowan struck back. Valen staggered but kept his footing, advancing again. They traded blow after blow, their swords singing against each other. Sweat poured down Rowan's body. Where had this fucker learned to do this?

Valen's jaw was tight as he served another slash. Rowan barely blocked it. Valen came at him again, this time managing to nick Rowan's shoulder. The dryad growled, advancing with enough force to knock Valen off his feet. *Finally.*

As Rowan raised his sword for a final strike, he was attacked from the sides. Three lesser vampires hit him hard enough to bring him down. He dropped one sword, and Valen surged to his feet, blood shining on his teeth.

"You can't win, dryad. Not this one."

The lesser vampires clawed at Rowan. He hit one in the gut with a hard elbow jab, then struck the same vampire on the head with the hilt of his sword. He swung, using both hands to cut through a second vampire. A third launched with a knife, managing to slash Rowan's thigh but not duck before Rowan's sword sliced across his neck.

Three bodies surrounded him. Valen pounced, holding his own sword and the one Rowan had dropped. He came down with a blow that would have ended Rowan if not for the blast of magic hitting his side.

Valen flew into a tree, and blood flowed from the side of his head as he crashed to the ground.

Rowan turned to see Ethan stalking forward, magic at his fingertips. "We *can* win, and we will."

Somehow, Ethan had managed to keep Stacy's shield intact while throwing his magic at the younger male vampire.

Rowan hauled Valen to his feet, his grip as hard as iron. "Where is Miles?"

Valen laughed darkly. "Your friend is dead."

"He isn't!" Rowan shouted.

Ethan wasn't sure if Valen was lying or if Rowan was simply in denial.

Rowan shook the vampire. "Tell me where he is!"

Valen didn't answer.

A spike of something hot and sharp plunged into Ethan's side, interrupting his focus on his magic. Stacy's shield fell. *No!* Ethan screamed inwardly. He realized the sharp sensation in him was dark magic, and it had gone into Rowan, too. Though Rowan hadn't lost his grip on Valen.

"Let him go," a cold voice demanded. Lenora appeared before him, holding Kiera with a knife to her throat.

Lenora was one hell of a bitch, and she fought like it.

Kiera poured all her power into her shadows, attacking Lenora from every side. Wielding a sword that glowed with dark magic, the vampire slashed off Kiera's shadows, advancing step by step until they were close enough to feel each other's breath.

"You should never have left your world," Lenora hissed. "Fae scum should stay where they came from."

"I didn't exactly have a choice," Kiera returned, hitting Lenora with a heavy blow of magic. Lenora reeled but did not lose her footing. What Cassius had said was right. The vampires had sacrificed some of the captives and drank their blood, giving themselves more power. She did not remember it being this difficult to fight the vampire bitch before.

It was time to bring out the knives. She unsheathed one, wielding it in her right hand while her left kept using the shadows.

Lenora chuckled. "Child's play."

She vanished, leaving Kiera to gape. The next thing Kiera knew, something sharp was at her neck, and Lenora's voice was in her ear. "Got you. Should I slit your throat now, or..." She trailed off at the sound of a cry. Valen, not far away. Kiera saw a bolt of Ethan's magic hit him, then Rowan stalked toward the downed vampire.

"Not on my watch," Lenora growled and began dragging Kiera toward them.

Rowan felt like his body was caving in at the sight of Lenora holding a knife to Kiera's throat. Kiera's eyes were dark and fierce. She wasn't giving up yet.

Neither would he.

"Let him go," Lenora repeated. "Or I'll slit her fucking throat."

Rowan didn't have a choice. He released Valen, and the young male vampire vanished. Kiera jammed her elbow back, hitting Lenora in the ribs. Ethan blasted the vampire with his magic. Rowan snatched up his second sword and bolted for her.

Lenora disappeared, too.

"Where did she go?" Kiera growled.

"Be happy you're alive," Rowan panted, reaching for her. Then, he saw the horror on Ethan's face.

Ahead, Stacy and Cassius were exchanging blows, and Stacy didn't have a shield.

Ethan ran for her, and Rowan gave Kiera a nod. "Give 'em hell."

As she folded herself into the shadows, Rowan hefted his swords. He was far from finished.

Luna never felt better than as a wolf racing through the trees, launching and pouncing. The taste of vampire blood different in wolf form than in human form. Or so some of her pack had told her. This was her first time tasting vampire. She reveled in it. After the ordeal in the gas station with Lenora, Luna wanted nothing more than to tear these fuckers apart.

Her pack raced alongside her, but they did not know the same feeling of magic rushing through their blood. She was faster, more agile. She could endure longer. Above, the elves continued firing their arrows, taking out lesser vampires where the wolves could not reach them.

Ahead, Luna saw fire glowing. The ash tree and those sacrificed around it. Her heart pounded. *We're so close.* She could nearly taste their victory. If they took out the vampires, Stacy and Ethan could reach the tree in time.

A startling realization came to her. The fire and the bodies meant the sacrifice had been completed. Unless it was undone in the next half-hour, the ritual would be completed. Luna raced forward. *I must do something!*

A fresh horde of vampires were coming for them, sharp swords drawn. Five headed for her at once. Panic seized Luna. She couldn't fight them all alone, but she didn't want to run, either.

Then, to her amazement, the ground opened and swallowed all five before they ever saw the pitfall.

Luna twisted to see a figure between two tall trees, hands extending to open the ground. His clothing was torn and bloodied. He looked like he'd been through hell. But Miles Ironwood was here, and he had saved her.

The shield around Stacy dropped, but she didn't have time to see why. She could only hope Ethan hadn't fallen victim to one of the vampires. Cassius' lips curled into a satisfied smile at the sight of her vulnerable. He lurched, a black blade slashing toward her chest.

Stacy jerked back and flung up a shield of her own in the nick of time. Cassius snarled. Stacy deflected blow after blow with a sword of fire she'd summoned from her magic. Ahead, she saw other flames and the outlines of piled bodies. Beyond it, the ash tree. They were close. They were running out of time.

Kiera shouted from down the slope. "These fuckers fight like they've got nothing to lose! We need to keep pushing them back!" Stacy did not know who she was calling to. All she knew was Cassius in front of her and those he'd already killed. Only the mind-controlled humans Rowan and Ethan had tranquilized could be rescued now.

Cassius' eyes gleamed with malice as he advanced again. Stacy twisted out of his reach, sending up a small wave of flames. Cassius roared. He would have been burned to a crisp if not for the shield of gleaming red magic that appeared around him. Dark magic.

Two figures appeared on either side of Stacy. Lenora first, then Valen. Her heart sank. *Shit.* Her friends were too busy fending off the lesser vampires.

"We have you cornered now, like a rat in the cupboard," Lenora taunted.

Valen's eyes shimmered. "You can't run."

No, but she could fight.

Stacy reinforced her shield, then realized the magic around her was not hers. Ethan's. He was coming back to her. The vampires didn't need to know that, though. She swung her sword of fire, but it was three against one.

The dragon inside her roared, begging for release.

I can't, she thought. What if she damaged Elentya's home? What if she couldn't shift back in time to enact the counter-spell for the ritual? Stacy summoned every ounce of strength as she spun and whirled, fending off the vampires in the hopes someone would come to help her.

Cassius' voice bellowed above the pandemonium of the battle, dripping with menace. "You've put up a good fight, but it ends here. Your power is the key to our ascension!"

Fear and defiance filled Stacy. She moved to strike again, but something distracted both her and the vampires. They halted as a deafening roar filled the sky. Stacy looked up to see gleaming red scales and an enormous serpentine body.

Khan circled the trees, found a place to land, and hit the ground with enough force to make the forest tremble.

Stacy whirled on Cassius, Lenora, and Valen. Their faces were ashen with terror. "You don't stand a chance now," she called before lunging to attack Cassius again.

CHAPTER TWENTY-SEVEN

All around him, the trees shook.

Ethan was close to trembling himself. He'd hardly made it up the hillside, about a few hundred feet from Stacy and the vampires, before Khan's roar filled the air.

The vampires scattered, giving the elves and wolves an opportunity to regroup.

"Fucking dragon," a voice muttered.

Ethan turned to see the elf queen beside him, a sword dripping vampire blood held fast in a firm hand.

"He might be the tide-turn we need," Ethan replied. "That's Stacy's father."

"I know who it is," Elentya answered sharply.

Ethan realized why she disliked seeing a dragon here. This forest was her home. Having a creature that massive around meant her home would not be the same afterward. It wouldn't be the same regardless, he thought as he focused up the hill.

Stacy stood facing the three vampires, who'd turned their attention back to her. It seemed Khan had merely been a momentary distraction.

Stacy was fighting hard, but it wasn't enough.

She had lurched for Cassius only to be knocked back by a powerful blast of Lenora's magic. Valen's hands grabbed her. "Keep her down," Cassius commanded.

Stacy thrashed against Valen's hold, but his grip, combined with the fact that she couldn't breathe thanks to Lenora's strike, left her unable to fend him off. Down the hillside, her father was eating vampires left and right. She had to keep fighting until someone came to her aid.

Magic flared around her. A shield. *Ethan!*

"Let her go," his cold voice commanded.

Valen lifted his arm in time to block a blast of magic. It knocked him aside, and Stacy scrambled to her feet. No sooner had she stood than Cassius reached for her. She twisted away, grappling for her magic. A spear shot from the trees, aiming for Lenora. She dodged it with a snarl, then Elentya emerged.

Stacy felt her magic, but it wasn't the kind she wanted. *I can't keep a tether on this dragon for much longer,* she thought. The presence of Khan in his dragon form was doing something to her. Her blood sang to what was familiar. Stacy's eyes met Elentya's as the elf queen whirled with her spear, using it to evade Lenora's and Cassius' strikes. Realization settled in Elentya's eyes. Sorrow was there, too, but she nodded.

Do what you must, her eyes seemed to say.

It was all the permission Stacy needed. She snapped the tether within herself and shifted.

Rowan had seen Stacy's dragon form before, but that didn't mean he was any less amazed this time. With a mighty heave of her wings, she took to the sky, knocking out branches as she went.

Khan roared and joined her. Four wings in the sky, two tails whipping the tops of the trees. Stacy roared with her father, a strangled sound of rage and the unleashing of power. Rowan could hardly believe it.

They flew together, circling, then dove. Stacy snatched up vampires with her claws and threw them. Her father caught the ones that didn't crash into trees. Rowan watched as Khan *ate* them. *No way in hell vampires taste good,* he thought. Maybe it didn't matter when one was in dragon form.

Rowan spotted the last of the elves descending from the trees and joining the wolves against the remaining vampires. On the hillside, Ethan and Elentya were fighting Cassius, Valen, and Lenora. Rowan started for them, but Kiera's voice stopped him. "Let me. You go with them." She pointed to the wolves and elves. "We need to distract the vampires so someone can get to the tree."

"Ethan?" Rowan asked.

Kiera nodded. "And Luna. Do what you can to help her."

"What about Miles?" Rowan asked. "We must find his body!"

Ahead, a great groaning sound echoed. Rowan thought it might be Khan or Stacy, but he soon realized it was the ground and the trees. Relief washed through him, and tears pricked his eyes.

Kiera grinned. "I think Miles is going to be fine."

Ethan ducked to evade Valen's blade. The crazed expression in the vampire's eyes made him wonder if he should have ever come up this hill. He flung out spell after spell, stunning Valen when he could. Elentya was fighting off both Cassius and Lenora, but she would not be able to hold them off for long.

The roars of the dragons overhead made Ethan's heart soar. It didn't make the fight here on the ground any easier, though.

241

He drew in his breath to shout another spell at Valen when a vine snaked across the ground and snatched Valen's ankle, jerking him into the trees. The ground opened, and Valen went down, screaming. It did not close over him, though.

Ethan peered into the trees. Vines twisted out, and behind them was Miles Ironwood.

Shadows swirled around another tree nearby. Kiera appeared, twin blades in hand. "Go to the tree!" she shouted at him before diving for Lenora. Miles drifted closer, going head-to-head with Valen as he climbed from the hole.

Ethan hesitated, but seeing no one was better fit to fight the vampires than Elentya, Kiera, and Miles, he headed farther uphill. The ash tree was in sight. The scorched, distorted bodies lying around it made him nauseous. At least twenty had been slaughtered for the sacrifice.

He glanced toward the sky. The moon was almost at its apex. *Hurry!* a voice inside him urged.

Ethan halted at the ash tree, hands shaking as he summoned his magic. *Speak the incantation and draw magic from the tree,* he told himself. The counter-spell was as simple as sucking the magic from the tree and leaving it dead. If only it was easy. He and Stacy had planned to do this together. Ethan wasn't certain he could do it on his own.

I have to, he thought. *It's the only way.*

Ethan pulled on the ley lines converging beneath the tree. There were simply too many for him to grasp at once. He tugged on one here, then another there, hoping he could move between them fast enough to draw energy away from the tree.

A cold realization settled within him. If he drew all the magic away from the tree, it would fill him. Several ley lines of magic hitting him at once meant certain death.

His heart ached. *I will do it,* he thought. *For Stacy. For our world to be safe.*

"*Stop!*" someone screamed.

Ethan whirled to see a figure bounding through the trees, changing from wolf to human form as she came. Luna stumbled into the clearing, wide-eyed and panting. "I want to help!"

"No, Luna. It's too much—"

"I'm going to help," she growled. "This is my fight too!"

Ethan knew he couldn't resist. It might work, too. She was young and inexperienced, but he needed someone else to grab the ley lines. "This might hurt. We're going to be hit with a shit ton of magic. Are you sure you can handle it?"

"I have to," she replied, her face grim.

Ethan felt the same determination. "On the count of three," he murmured.

"One," Luna called.

"Two," Ethan added.

Then, together, "Three."

The incantation rose to his lips. But before Ethan could speak it, Cassius appeared with a sword in hand.

Ethan screamed, but it was too late. The sword arced out, and the vampire sank the blade into Luna's gut.

Kiera slashed with her knives. She folded into the shadows and appeared elsewhere. She converged her magic to create an illusion of herself. Lenora swung at the wrong Kiera, cutting through air. She snarled. "You bitch!"

"Right here," Kiera drawled, appearing from behind a tree.

Lenora lunged, a scream of rage curdling the air. She lost her focus and slipped past Kiera, who shot out a tentacle of shadow to trip her. The ground opened below the vampire. Kiera jumped out of the way as Lenora fell.

The female vampire cried out her fury. Kiera hopped down into the pit beside her, a whisper of death on her lips. "I will be glad to never see you again, vampire." She sank her knife into Lenora's chest.

———

Miles opened the pit for Lenora and watched from the corner of his eyes as Kiera jumped in after her. He spun to face Valen, striking out with vines that pinned the young male to the tree. "You've done enough damage for a lifetime," Miles stated evenly. It was Valen who had tortured him. Valen who had dragged him here and started carving his body for sacrifice. It was Valen who'd started too late, and now he was paying.

"D-don't!" Valen begged. "Let me go!"

Miles was beyond pity. The ground opened, and he let the vines drop Valen into it. The earth covered the hole, burying the vampire alive.

He turned again, this time to see Elentya battling Cassius several yards away. The elf queen was a warrior in her own right, but she couldn't continue much longer. Miles sent his vines careening toward Cassius. Kiera was climbing out of the pit where Lenora's body was bleeding out.

Cassius' eyes widened as he realized it was one against three. He roared with rage, then vanished into thin air.

———

Luna sank to her knees, gaping at the bleeding wound in her body. Pain seized her face as she clutched it.

Ethan screamed again.

Cassius yanked his sword from Luna's body and turned on Ethan. "I'll fucking kill you," the vampire hissed.

Ethan knew he couldn't defend himself and maintain the work he'd put into pulling the ley lines from the tree at the same time. *I'm going to die, too. We're both going to fucking die, and there's nothing we can do about it.*

The thoughts were banished as the wind picked up, and a thunderous wingbeat filled the air. Enormous claws swept from the sky. Cassius didn't have time to evade them. His alarmed cry was all Ethan heard before the claws snatched him, and Khan swept back into the sky.

"Shit, shit, shit," Ethan panted as he hurried to Luna's side. She lay flat on the ground, the blood pouring too profusely to be stopped. Ethan couldn't heal her. He didn't have enough strength left. "I'm sorry. I'm so sorry." Ethan clasped her hand. Her face was so pale. Tears burned his eyes. "It should have never happened like this."

"It's okay," Luna whispered, lifting a hand to his face. "I can go now."

She was only sixteen. This wasn't right.

"Stay with me," Ethan begged.

"I will finish this," she grated. "It's all I can do now."

Ethan realized what she meant. Luna wanted to speak the incantation and give her body to the ley line, provide a conduit for the magic. It would finish her. "No," Ethan commanded, but it was too late. She spoke the words.

Magic erupted through the ground, tossing him several feet away.

With tears tracking down his cheeks, Ethan knew only one thing remained for him to do. He spoke the spell, too. He felt the force of the ley lines, but it was nowhere near as strong as it would have been if Luna wasn't here. She took most of its force.

The light of the magic vanished, and Ethan managed to crawl toward her. Every part of his body ached, but he ignored it to reach Luna's side. Her eyes were open but glassy and unfocused. Her face was pale, her body growing cold.

Ethan glanced toward the tree. It was blackening, leaves and branches falling one by one. Dying, just as the young werewolf was dying beside him. Ethan gathered her in his arms, his heart breaking. This wasn't right.

The tree had been the primary source of power for the elves in this land, and now it, too, was gone. Was it worth the sacrifice?

He clutched Luna close to him, his tears falling onto her cold body.

———

Khan dropped Cassius into a clearing, and Stacy saw her moment. She beat her wings in the air and gradually landed. Cassius wasn't dead yet. He couldn't move, either, thanks to the impact against the ground.

Stacy's dragon eyes blazed gold. *You're finished,* she thought. She didn't need to say the words aloud. The fire that tore through her throat was enough. It engulfed Cassius, and in seconds, he was gone.

CHAPTER TWENTY-EIGHT

A light drizzle of rain fell in the graveyard as Stacy and Amy stood before a headstone, arms linked and bodies pressed close for warmth. Orange and red leaves were scattered around them, growing damp from the rain against the pavement. They were alone here, except for the occasional crow. Stacy found comfort in that.

"I can't believe it took me this long to come here," Stacy murmured. "I'm sorry for not doing it sooner, especially with you."

Amy squeezed her arm. "You've had a lot on your plate. I think he would understand."

Stacy wiped a tear from her cheek. "Do you think Spencer would believe us if we told him everything that happened in the past few weeks?"

Amy smiled, though her eyes were also glassy with tears. "He wouldn't believe it. How could anyone without seeing it for themselves?"

Stacy supposed Amy was right. She'd hardly believed her father was a dragon until he shifted. A heavy sorrow weighed on her heart as she remembered Spencer. She thought of Luna and the grieving pack, how it had only been four days since the tragedy in the forest. She thought of the elven territory and the ash tree that was now dead, leaving the land without its magic.

The elves were preparing to move. Stacy did not know where. Her estate was full of elves and healing prisoners. Soon, they would all be gone, and her home would feel too big again.

The vampires are gone. Malakai was not raised. That counts for something, Stacy reminded herself. Had the cost been worth it, though? She didn't know.

"Think of how far we've come," Amy murmured, her voice a comfort through Stacy's troubling thoughts. "We met only a few months ago."

"Did you think you would end up with a dragon as a best friend?"

Amy grinned. "I'm only disappointed my dragon bestie hasn't taken me for a ride yet."

Stacy patted Amy's arm. "Don't wish for that too soon. I can barely keep myself in the air."

"You should take flying lessons."

"I've been talking to my dad about it. Soon."

"Then…rides!"

They laughed. After a few more moments of silent consideration at Spencer's grave, they decided to go. The rain was letting up, and the sun was sliding from behind the clouds.

"There's a lot more we need to figure out," Stacy admitted on their way to the car.

Amy leaned her head on Stacy's shoulder. "We will. You and me, together, like we've done since the beginning."

Kiera sat on the window seat, her long legs dangling over the edge. Miles leaned nearby, his focus on the need to trim a rosebush he'd spotted through the pane instead of the conversation at hand. Ethan sat on the sofa beside Amy. Rowan stood by the table, and Stacy paced.

"Please stop, Stace. You're making us all nervous," Amy urged.

"I'm never nervous," Kiera spoke up from the window. She sharpened her knife against a whetstone for emphasis.

Miles snorted. "You're nervous whenever I walk into the room."

"Probably because you track mud everywhere you go," Rowan cut in with a grunt.

Ethan laughed.

"What's so funny?" Kiera demanded, setting her knife in her lap.

Ethan put his hands up. "Nothing."

Amy directed her attention to Stacy. "Want to share why you've gathered us all here?"

Stacy halted, taking in the sight of the library full of her friends and the bright afternoon light through the windows. The trees were abundant in color, and the air was warm. She couldn't have wished for a better autumn day.

Unfortunately, she couldn't spare much time to enjoy it. "The Codex is still out there. We must find and destroy it before anyone else gets a stupid idea about trying to raise Malakai." She dropped into a chair. "We have several places we can look. Our role as protectors of the magical community is far from over."

"Is it ever over?" Amy mused. "I don't mind being in this role for as long as we need to. Someone has to do it."

She was right. "It would be nice to have a week off every now and then," Stacy muttered.

"Then we take a week off before we go looking for the Codex," Miles suggested.

"We can't," Rowan insisted. "The longer we wait, the greater the chance it falls into the wrong hands."

"Which is any hands but our own," Ethan inserted.

"I'm already on it," Kiera stated without taking her gaze from the knife. She slid it against the whetstone, producing a satisfying sound.

"There's one problem," Rowan spoke up. "The only way the Codex can be destroyed is if it's taken back to Malabbra, which isn't possible. Not unless it's sent back with scum that also comes from that place."

"So the Codex is like the One Ring?" Amy asked.

Miles chuckled. "Not quite. Opening it won't make you invisible or pollute your mind with darkness."

"But someone could use it to raise Malakai," Stacy protested. "We have to make sure that never happens."

"We can hide it," Ethan suggested.

Stacy faced him. "How? where?"

"Adrian's library," Kiera suggested.

Stacy glanced at the sidhe fae. Kiera stood. "Only Adrian and I have access to it, and Adrian wouldn't let it escape in a million years. Hell, he doesn't like me leaving with magical cookbooks, much less an ancient prophecy that could destroy the world."

"Are you sure we can trust him?" Stacy asked.

"I am."

"Kiera's confidence is enough for me," Rowan inserted.

Stacy considered it, then sighed. "I don't know of a better solution. But if we ever come up with a way to destroy it without going to Malabbra, we will, okay?"

Nods of assent traveled the room.

"What now?" Miles asked. "Business as usual?"

There would be a funeral rite for Luna in a few days that they would all attend. Stacy planned to buy the elven territory and repair the damage so Elentya and her people could return one day. Plus, she had flying lessons with her father. *It never slows down, does it?* she thought. "Yes, business as usual," she replied, forcing a smile everyone saw through.

"You aren't fooling us, Stacy," Kiera pointed out. "Know that we're all on your side. Your wish is our command."

Kiera, Miles, and Amy filed from the room, leaving Stacy with Rowan and Ethan. "I want to extend our coven and our circle of allies. We have battles ahead, I am certain," she told them.

"Where will we find worthy people for the coven?" Ethan wondered.

Rowan cleared his throat. "It might be easier to find candidates than you think." He drew a small, white envelope embossed in gold from his pocket and handed it to Stacy. "This came for you in today's mail. I was about to bring it to you when you called the meeting."

Stacy opened the envelope to find an invitation. "Rowan, what is this?"

"Leaders within the city's supernatural community want to throw you a gala tomorrow night. It's an invite-only event in an exclusive hotel. The most powerful supernaturals in the city will be there."

Stacy studied the invitation, feeling like she was on the edge of great change. What would be the point in going? She would only expose herself more, but maybe that was what she needed to do. She'd told everyone she was Anastasia Drakethorn. Why not show them?

"Will you go?" Ethan asked.

Stacy returned the invitation to Rowan and grinned. "Of course I will. It's a perfect excuse for buying a new dress!"

Rowan dipped his head. "I'll make preparations for a car to take you tomorrow."

After he left the library, Ethan swept his arms around Stacy, nuzzling his face into her neck. "I know you're busy, Stacy, but I hope one of these days you will have time to let me take you on a proper date."

"Trust me, anywhere you go wearing fae jewelry will make you the most looked-at person in the room." Kiera handed Stacy a wooden box with ornate carvings. "I didn't bring many things from the fae world, but this was one."

Stacy opened the box, and her eyes widened. A row of shining emeralds gleamed up at her, connected by a silver chain set with diamonds. "Kiera, I can't possibly accept this."

She tried to close the lid, but Kiera kept it open. "You will accept it. I have no use for the jewels, but you do."

"Maybe I don't want to be the most looked-at person in the room," Stacy protested.

"It's going to happen anyway," Amy spoke up from the end of Stacy's bed. Stacy turned toward her floor-length mirror, wearing a glittering black dress she'd bought specifically for this occasion.

Kiera looped the chain of emeralds around her neck. "See? It brings out the green in your eyes."

Her father's eyes. Dressed in black with her auburn hair unbound and flowing over her shoulders, Stacy felt like a true Drakethorn. She had her mother's form, hair, and face, as well as her father's eyes and determined demeanor. Amy was right. She didn't need the jewels to be the most looked-at person in the room.

Amy whistled. "You're smoking, Stacy. You and Ethan are definitely going to do it after dinner tonight. I mean, you have to, right? Ethan won't be able to keep his hands off you after seeing you in this!"

Stacy slid on elbow-length black gloves and fitted silver bracelets on each wrist. "Ethan has to be at his shop tonight, so he isn't coming with me." She glanced at Amy through the mirror. "I still have an open plus-one. I want you to come."

Amy gaped. "Me? But isn't this event open to magicals only?"

Stacy lifted her chin. "I'm Anastasia Drakethorn and the guest of honor. I'll bring who I want. Besides, I think you'll have a hard time saying no when you see the dress I bought for you."

Rowan drove Stacy's car to the front of the hotel, got out, and opened the door for her and Amy. The women stepped onto the sidewalk, drinking in the sight of the illustrious hotel. "The finest in the city," Amy chortled. "I can't wait to write about this night."

Stacy looped her arm through Amy's. "As long as there's a lengthy description of my beautiful best friend."

Amy blushed.

She really was beautiful. The deep navy dress Stacy had bought glittered under the streetlamps, and the silver jewelry and white gloves were perfect. Amy's golden curls fell over the open back of her dress. It would be difficult for many to keep their eyes off Stacy tonight, but she felt some would have a hard time not gawking at Amy, too.

"Good luck, ladies," Rowan told them. "I'll be nearby, ready to go whenever you are."

Stacy thanked him, then tugged Amy toward the entrance. Inside, they found a wide open foyer filled with people dressed in attire similar to theirs. Heads turned, and whispers passed between groups. Stacy held her head high. Those who did not know her soon would. She noted the number of people. A few hundred, at least. She'd known the city's paranormal factions were plentiful, but she had not imagined so many leaders would be present tonight.

She bristled inside. Where had all these people been during Victor's oppressive reign? Why hadn't they done anything?

Tonight, we make friends, she reminded herself. *Allies. We can confront them after we've all gotten to know one another.*

Under glittering chandeliers, Stacy and Amy roamed the room, holding glasses of champagne as they peered at art and acknowledged people Rowan knew. Stacy soon found herself flooded with new acquaintances.

"You're no longer a mere lawyer," one druid leader remarked. "You're a leader in your own right. We heard what you did for the Shinnecock nation and the werewolves. I suppose it will be good to have one of our own on hand when legal misfortunes arise."

Stacy pressed a smile to her lips. "I am here to be of service to anyone I can, as long as the ventures yield proper justice to those who deserve it." A firm reminder that she wasn't interested in being anyone's puppet.

The druid gave a curt nod and moved off. Amy chuckled.

"What?" Stacy demanded.

"You have them wrapped around your finger."

"I'm not sure I like that," Stacy grumbled, then spotted an elderly, stately-looking woman weaving through the crowd toward them. Her air of prestige and determination rooted Stacy to the spot.

The woman approached with a smile. "Anastasia Drakethorn, it is an honor to finally meet you. Your reputation precedes you."

Earlier that day, Rowan had run them through a list of leaders they could expect to meet at this dinner, but Stacy did not know who this woman was.

The woman extended a gloved hand. "My name is Ms. Eleanor Ravenscroft. I am the host of tonight's event."

Stacy shook her hand. "It's a beautiful event, Ms. Ravenscroft. Thank you for inviting me. I would like to introduce you to my friend, Amy Greentree."

Amy dipped her head in greeting.

"Pleasure to meet you both, and please, call me Eleanor." A tinkling laugh followed. "If we become familiar enough, in time, you can call me Ellie like all my friends do." She shifted closer, lowering her voice. "I've wanted to meet with you for some time. Now that you come highly recommended by the elven queen herself, I had to arrange a way for us to meet. You see, my coven is looking for new members, and we think you will make an excellent addition."

Stacy arched her brows. This woman was a witch.

"I didn't know there were covens in the city," she stated. "I was under the impression that all covens had left long ago, taking to more elusive places to practice their magic in natural surroundings."

"We have mostly been operating outside the city, it is true," Eleanor admitted. "After we received word that the Thorn heir was making waves in the city, we decided to come here and see for ourselves. You do not disappoint, Ms. Drakethorn."

Stacy was wary about working with a coven, knowing they could be staunch about rules she didn't necessarily follow. Besides, she had a growing coven with Ethan. *I need allies, though,* she thought. *I shouldn't shut the door on this woman anytime soon.*

Stacy smiled. "I would love to talk about this more another time, Eleanor. You are welcome at my estate any time."

Eleanor beamed. "Thank you! I would love to see the place where the great Catherine Thorn lived and worked."

Warmth surged through Stacy, and the locket around her neck hummed with magic. At the back of the room, she spotted Elentya and the Graytails' alpha standing together against the wall. "I see two of my friends, Eleanor. Please excuse me."

The older witch nodded, smiling as if all she'd hoped for tonight had come true. As Stacy and Amy wove through the crowd, Amy leaned close to Stacy's ear. "Do you believe it? A few months ago, we were two newly acquainted women trying to figure out what Leonard Dolos did in his free time. Now, we are conquering the greedy and bringing justice to every corner of the city. We're like superheroes."

Stacy smiled. "We're better than superheroes. We're a couple of badass women."

THE STORY CONTINUES

The story continues with book six, *When Justice Has Claws*, coming soon to Amazon and Kindle Unlimited.

Claim Your Copy Here

ISABEL'S AUTHOR'S NOTES

19 SEPTEMBER, 2024

Thank you for reading book five! And here you are in the back.

New tack: LMBPN invited me to participate in a new universe they have developed in the urban fantasy arena, and I accepted! I'm so excited. It's an urban fantasy series called *Claudia Richelieu: The Chimera Agent*, and it's in the Spiderking Universe, full of vampires and other supernatural beings. The first book is *Shadows of Prejudice*, and it will be out on October 15. You can preorder it Shadows of Prejudice

The first book in the wide Spiderking universe is Secret Inheritance

That series is my first endeavor in this new world, and if that goes well, I will write a bounty hunter series in the same universe. Aside from that...

It's almost autumn, my favorite time of year

And may I say, I am so very glad that the UK does not follow the silly American custom of pumpkin spice everything appearing in August. I read Renée Jagger's author notes on the topic, and it sounds awful. Of course, that called for me to write a haiku:

Pumpkin Spice, you are

A plague on America

I hope you stay there

As always, it's quiet here. No big trips planned or anything, just writing. Emma likes the colder weather, so we have been taking lots of walkies with Nat and Tara, then down to the coffee shop for a fresh-baked whatever deliciousness Ayleen has whipped up and a coffee. It's a wonderful life. And maybe I'll see the Aurora Borealis for the next few months on evening walkies, so how could it get better?

The usual business

I always have to thank LMBPN's staff for making my journey to publication as painless as they could. From the beta team who suggests improvements to the series to Kelly O, who does *everything,* to the editor who smooths my prose to the just-in-time team who catches last-minute errors, it is a joy working with you!

Thank you for taking a chance on my series! If you enjoy it and you have a moment, leaving a review would be very helpful for me (as it is for any writer).

I look forward to catching up with you in the next book.

I look forward to catching up with you in the next book.

Izzie Campbell

BOOKS FROM ISABEL

The Chronicles of the WitchBorn
(with Michael Anderle)
The First Witch-Mage (Book 1)
The Witch-Mage Awakens (Book 2)
Witch-Mage Liberation (Book 3)
Witch-Mage Uprising (Book 4)
Witch-Mage Breaking (Book 5)
Witch-Mage Ascending (Book 6)
Witch-Mage Convergence (Book 7)
Witch-Mage Legacy (Book 8)

The Magic Academy of Paris
(with Michael Anderle)
The Forbidden Incantations (Book 1)
The Treacherous Alchemy (Book 2)
The Cursed Enchantments (Book 3)
The Perilous Secrets (Book 4)
The Sinister Onslaught (Book 5)
A Resilient Requiem (Book 6)

CONNECT WITH THE AUTHORS

Connect with Isabel Campbell

Facebook: https://www.facebook.com/IsabelCampbell.author

Website: http://isabelcampbellauthor.com/

Connect with Michael Anderle

Website: http://lmbpn.com

Email List: https://michael.beehiiv.com/

https://www.facebook.com/LMBPNPublishing

https://twitter.com/MichaelAnderle

https://www.instagram.com/lmbpn_publishing/

https://www.bookbub.com/authors/michael-anderle

OTHER LMBPN PUBLISHING BOOKS

To be notified of new releases and special promotions from LMBPN publishing, please join our email list:

http://lmbpn.com/email/

For a complete list of books published by LMBPN please visit the following pages:

https://lmbpn.com/books-by-lmbpn-publishing/

BOOKS BY MICHAEL ANDERLE

Sign up for the LMBPN email list to be notified of new releases and special deals!

https://lmbpn.com/email/

For a complete list of books by Michael Anderle, please visit:

www.lmbpn.com/ma-books/

Made in United States
Troutdale, OR
01/23/2025